Squeeze Play in Beantown

A Will Beaman Baseball Mystery

G. S. Rowe

Pocol Press
Clifton, VA

POCOL PRESS

Published in the United States of America
by Pocol Press
6023 Pocol Drive
Clifton, VA 20124
www.pocolpress.com

Publisher's Cataloguing-in-Publication

Rowe, G. S. (Gail Stuart), 1936-
   Squeeze play in beantown / by G.S. Rowe. – 1st ed. – Clifton, Va. :
Pocol Press, 2004.
   (A Will Beaman mystery)
   p.cm.
   ISBN 1-929763-05-0

   1. Baseball–United States–Fiction. 2. Boston (Mass.)–History–
Fiction. 3. Historical Fiction. 4. Mystery fiction. I. Title. II. Series.

PS3618.O94 S684 2004
813.6–dc22   0404

Cover art © 2004 by Todd Mueller. Adapted from a photograph of Jimmy
Collins from the McGreevey Collection at the Boston Public Library.

Disclaimers

While many of the events and personalities in this story are taken from history, this is a work of fiction. Names, characters, places, incidents, and dialogue either are the product of the author's imagination, or are used fictitiously. License has also been taken with chronology, some game accounts, and with conversations by historical figures for purposes of plot. Base ball is spelled here as it was in the late 19th century.

Acknowledgments

I have accumulated many obligations in the process of writing this book and its predecessor. I owe thanks to members of Alpha Group; including Margaret Bailey, Jim Cole, Karen Duvall, Shannon Dyer, Vicki Kaufman, Janet Lane, Michael Phillips, and Bonnie Smith, who read early drafts and offered helpful advice and inspiration. I owe special thanks to Ken McConnellogue and Mike Peters who have gone out of their way to be helpful. Mary Borg's insightful criticisms and counsel have substantially enhanced the work and her unfailing enthusiasm has provided much-needed encouragement. Thanks, too, to my wife, Mary, who has graciously endured my obsessions with baseball and earlier times—and has provided suggestions to improve my work. I have also learned much from individual members of the Society for American Baseball Research (SABR) and from a long list of SABR publications. I alone am responsible for any failings.

1

I never walk into Arthur H. Soden's office at Boston's South End Grounds, home of the National League's Boston Beaneaters, without thinking of a counting house in a Dickens novel. It's not so much its physical resemblance that triggers the image, as its similarity in emotional and spiritual deprivation. Naked avarice pervades the place and threatens to seep into the very vitals of all that enter. Soden himself, despite having accumulated an eye-bulging fortune in the roofing business besides his interest in the Beaneaters, moves about with the pinched-face of a Scottish paymaster. It's not easy to stroll into that office each day without succumbing to his sour mood.

What helped me fight off the corrosive gloom on this late August Saturday was my improving financial condition. Earlier in the season, as a favor to my father, Soden had hired me to boost attendance. My father was unhappy with the drift of my life and pressured Soden, an old army chum, into giving me employment. At any rate, having gotten the job, I was free of debt for the first time in two years. What's more, after clearing my financial obligations, I still had enough for one week's rent, and I would be paid again in two weeks. Mine wasn't exactly a scintillating success story, I'll admit, but compared to the past months my current pecuniary circumstances were cause for celebration. I nodded to Soden and plopped down at my desk.

He paid me no heed. He sat slumped at his desk, frowning at an open ledger. His *sotto voce* grumbling told me he was in an even fouler mood than usual. Soden was the principal owner of one of the National League's most successful teams, champions in 1891, 1892, and 1893, and contenders again here in 1897. At heart, however, he was an accountant, a collector and counter of fifty-cent admissions. And at the moment, though his Boston nine had defeated the Cleveland Spiders this afternoon, the gate clearly bewildered and outraged him.

Ignoring his grousing, which I'd become accustomed to by now, I began once more to review the notebook that served as my own account ledger. My intention to ignore my boss's nasty mood was frustrated almost immediately, however, as Soden's fist slammed down on his ledger with a smack that sounded like a gunshot. "Judas Priest!" he bellowed, his face flushing in anger. "We're drowning in red ink!" He fumbled in his jacket pocket for one of his ubiquitous cigars. At that moment, he became conscious of my presence. He fished out a fat stogie and beckoned me with it.

I slipped my account book inside my coat and strolled to his desk. Not in a mood to be his whipping boy, I deliberately moved close to him to emphasize my 6' 2" height and my two hundred-pound frame. And I purposely stood between him and the wall lamp to cast him in shadow.

If he was aware of my maneuver—or impressed by it—he gave no hint of it. He let a long moment crawl by, ignoring me, staring balefully at the ledger. His left hand nervously tapped the desk with his cigar. His right hand clutched his head, fingers worrying his thinning hair. His mouth, nothing more than a twitching thin line, looked like a worm crossing a hot sidewalk. After what seemed like an eternity he pounded the ledger again and looked up at me. "I've no choice, Mr. Beaman. None."

He quickly won the battle of intimidation. At his words, my bowels cramped as if they'd just discovered last night's steamed prunes. I knew instinctively that Soden's current financial lamentation was not his usual fare. He was going to fire me. After only three months. Fire me. I knew it as surely as I was standing there. My bold stance melted faster than a sailor's reserve in a dockside brothel.

"No choice in what?" I croaked, as much to delay the inevitable as anything.

He pointed his cigar at me. "I've got to let you go."

"Sir!" I huffed, "Only weeks ago you promised me a raise." And it was true. I'd done pretty well, I'd thought. In a burst of euphoria after I'd helped him discover who had assaulted his star shortstop, Germany Long, a month before, Soden had promised me both raise and promotion. Though neither the change in status nor the increase in salary had materialized, my debt was now behind me. Until just moments ago, the security of the job left me confident that my rewards would surely come.

Soden swept aside my reference to a raise. He jabbed a thick finger at the ledger. "It's impossible to please the damned cranks in this city," he seethed. "First, they complain we're playing shoddy ball and refuse to pay to watch us. Then, when we win, they moan that there's no competition, and they stay away." He scratched a match into flame on his shoe and lit his cigar. He sucked deeply, then blew a ribbon of blue smoke toward the ceiling. "There's no pleasin' the bastards. We're in a virtual tie with the Orioles for the League lead and yet our attendance is miserable. We'll have to put fractions on the damned turnstiles if it continues."

Unamused by his exaggeration, I held my ground. "Boston is doing better than most teams now," I told him, my voice rising. "And the pennant race'll bring even more fans in. September will be a dog-fight between us and Baltimore."

"It's not that simple, Mr. Beaman," he growled. "We have to turn revenues of $33,000 a year. That's as clear as Eastman's celluloid. That sum covers sixteen ball players, grounds crew, office personnel, payments on the ball park and its upkeep, and the team's expenses." He spat a particle of tobacco carelessly onto the rug. "Profit comes after $33,000. And we're not even *close* to that." He shoved the cigar into the side of his mouth and puffed on it like a runaway steam engine.

"What with your monopoly over the printing of tickets, concessions, and fence advertising, you have more revenue possibilities than most teams," I argued. "I've worked up promotions in past weeks that have spun the turnstiles. I can organize others. You've got to give me a square chance."

Soden continued to drum his fingers noisily on the ledger, as if he hadn't heard me. "$33,000," he grunted, "it might as well be a bloody million." He riveted me with his eyes. His shoulders were slightly hunched which widened his already-thick neck. He looked like Buddha himself. "This business is cutthroat, son. When a player loses a step, or a second on his swing, or the spin on his curve, he's gone. Ancient history. If a manager doesn't win, he's down the road. If teams don't make money, owners fail and teams disappear. Same with leagues. Who remembers the Union Association, eh?" He unclasped his hands and drew deeply on his cigar, exhaling a thin stream of smoke. "When profits dwindle, salaries suffer and staff gets trimmed. That's how economics operate, Mr. Beaman. It's as true in 1897 as it's been in the past thousand years. You've read Darwin, Spencer, Sumner, those boys?"

I had, and I tried to stave off his drift. "Sir, you're painting a gloomier picture of conditions than is warranted. In the next weeks fans will swarm—"

He waved me off. "The red ink says we can't afford you, son."

"Surely not, Mr. Soden, sir," a deep voice said.

Together Soden and I swiveled toward the sound. There stood John Haggerty, groundskeeper at the Grounds, and despite the differences in our ages and the brevity of our acquaintance, a boon companion of mine. "You can't do that, Mr. Soden," he said.

Soden held up a hand like a conductor signaling a trolley to halt. "John," he said, "this is a matter between Mr. Beaman and myself."

Haggerty stepped into the room, holding his sweat-stained hat before him in huge, battered hands. "Sir, Will here 'as done a terrific job. He's done ever'thing you've asked of him, he has. He's a fast learner. You've seen that."

Soden leaned forward, hands splayed in front of him, flat on the desk.

"Mr. Haggerty," he said, his voice steely. "Your duties are confined to the upkeep of the Grounds. Matters of personnel—"

Haggerty was not to be put off. He clutched his fedora tighter, wadding it up like a clump of waste paper in his sausage-like fingers. "Mr. Soden, sir, Will here, given a chance, will boom attendance. He's a quick lad, a Harvard boy 'n all. He's got grand ideas." He edged closer to Soden. "The lads licked Cleveland today, 14-5, they did, and pounded Cy Young. You shouldn't make changes when the lads win. It's bad luck. We'll need all the luck we can muster in the coming days to hang with Baltimore."

Soden shook his head. "Mr. Haggerty. John. The matter is . . . closed."

"That's givin' the lad and the team awfully thin soup," Haggerty muttered.

I slumped in my chair. My solvency had lasted less than a day! Tomorrow I'd owe another week's room rent and had just enough cash to cover it. After that, who knew? With my purse empty and my employment with the Bostons terminated, any hope of marrying Claire Denihur seemed as likely as Bryan Democrats urging high tariffs. I glanced at the door that was about to close on me for the last time. That is, if I went quietly. But when had I ever done anything quietly and conventionally?

I motioned Haggerty quiet, and stood. "Mr. Soden, if you terminate my services, you'll be making a grievous mistake. You'll be—"

A loud jangling cut me short. Then a second and third. We all shot glances at the brass bell on the small wooden box on the wall behind Soden. Soden stared stupidly at the box, his jaw working up and down as if he were trying to talk and couldn't conjure up any sound. One minute the man was ranting like a hard-shell Baptist preacher, the next he was a vaudeville mime.

"It's the telephone," I said.

"Of course," he mumbled. He stood and moved cautiously toward the box. When it rang again he retreated a step.

I pointed to the receiver. "Just pick it up."

He knew what to do, but was intimidated by Bell's new-fangled telephones, and despised using them. I was the one who'd convinced his partners to take advantage of Boston's recent renovation of its telephone exchange to add the Boston National League club to its list of clients. Boston had had telephones for twenty years, since an enterprising businessman hooked up property owners as part of his burglar-alarm service. Still, many in the city, including Soden, continued to dismiss its potential. Fortunately, others in the organization had agreed with me that the telephone would facilitate communications with league teams and advertisers. Now he was staring at the jangling box as if it were the featured attraction in P. T. Barnum's freak show.

Again I motioned toward the receiver. "Sir, just pick it up."

He lifted the receiver, peering at it as if it were rotten fruit, then held it hesitantly to his ear. After a moment, he shouted into the mouthpiece, "Hello!" He listened intently gaping at the mouthpiece as if he might see the person he was hearing.

Haggerty cocked his head toward Soden and raised his eyebrows in question.

I shrugged. I didn't know who Soden might be talking to. Whoever it was, was delivering bad news. Soden's face darkened and his frown deepened. "Who?" he shouted.

I sat down and motioned Haggerty to join me. He complied, sinking his burly form into a chair next to me, clasping the chair's arms with powerful hands. His large knuckles and knobby fingers testified to his years as a ball player before gloves commonly were worn. Shaking hands with him was like thrusting one's hand into a barrel of walnuts. He leaned his leathery, mustachioed face close to mine. "Why's Soden sacking you, Will?"

I shot a glance at Soden who was still preoccupied on the phone, the muscles in his jaw now jumping like spit on a hot iron. "Red ink," I told Haggerty.

"That bastard," he mumbled, glaring at Soden. "It's *always* red ink with him. He has the heart of a turnkey. We had eight thousand at the game today. Boston is making more money than any team in the league. He'd sure as hell lay off a player or worker before he'd cut into any of *his* profits." Haggerty's litany was familiar, one that I'd heard my first day on the job, and which had been repeated dozens of times since. Haggerty was known around the National League for his skill in putting fields into playing shape. Soden named him chief groundskeeper and even talked of making him a director. Even so, Haggerty saw his interests resting with the 'working stiffs', as he liked to call himself. He invariably sided with unions against management and talked with enthusiasm of Mother Jones and Eugene Debs. He viewed McKinley and his Republican cronies as usurers and money-lenders in labor's temple. To him, Soden was in league with J. Pierpont Morgan and Commodore Vanderbilt as oppressors of working men, although so far as I knew he'd never shared his opinions with his boss.

"Murdered you say?" Soden shouted into the mouthpiece. "We'll be there as soon as we can." He slammed the receiver onto its cradle. "That was Detective O'Dwyer, John," he said. "We're going to Battery Wharf. Get a carriage. It's urgent."

Haggerty's face crinkled. "What's up, sir? *Who* was murdered?"

"For the love of Christ, John! Just get the bloody carriage," Soden snapped, reaching for his greatcoat.

I knew that once he stepped out the door my career with the Beaneaters was over. "Sir, I can help," I told him, trying not to plead. I didn't know if I could help or not, but I had nothing to lose.

Soden's eyes turned hard as flint as they probed mine. I could sense his ledger-like mind computing the debits and credits, carefully weighing the sums. After what seemed an eternity, he clapped my arm. "Maybe you can at that, son. Come with me."

2

I didn't have to be told twice. I knew that Detective Dennis O'Dwyer handled homicides. And if Soden knew the victim, perhaps I did too. I don't mean to be crass or unfeeling, but a homicide is enough to intrigue anyone and, in my case, I knew it just might save my job. If accompanying Soden meant I remained employed and drawing a salary, I was happy to oblige him. Even one more day's pay would be welcomed.

Haggerty had a hansom cab waiting for us when we emerged from the Grounds. Soden and I settled into its soft leather seat. Haggerty sat up with the driver. As we started off, Soden told us it was Jimmy Collins and Amos "Shady" Porch that Detective O'Dwyer had called about. Collins was Boston's third baseman, the quickest third sacker in the National League. He'd nearly ended bunting by teams against the Beaneaters with his ability to pounce on the ball and throw runners out. Amos Porch, an aging catcher, recently had been purchased from Fall River in the New England League as a change for the often-injured and often-absent Marty Bergen. O'Dwyer reported that Collins and Porch had been mugged and tossed into the water near the North End docks.

"Good God! And O'Dwyer thinks they were murdered?" I asked.

"A ragamuffin witnessed the attack and fetched a copper," he said. "So far as O'Dwyer knows the bodies are still missing, but he has yet to go to the wharf to see for himself. He'll meet us there."

I leaned forward as if by doing so I might urge the horses more swiftly as they clattered from the broad, well-lit thoroughfares around the Grounds to the crazy quilt of narrow alleys, dark lanes, and sudden corners that passed for streets in the North End. Soden, too, sat forward, fists doubled on his knees, muttering "Judas Priest" over and over. Haggerty said nothing, but his jaws pulsed as he clamped a cold pipe in his teeth.

By the time we rolled up to the wharf at the end of Battery, a large Saturday night crowd of drunken stevedores, sailors, and carousers were milling around in the pale glow from the street lamps. Several blue-coated coppers, conspicuous by their bullet-shaped hats, were urging the crowd back from a police wagon parked some hundred feet out on the pier. Its horses snorted and lunged against their harnesses, their hooves thundering on the planks.

Class deference still surfaces on occasion in Boston. In this case it permitted Soden to step down and ease through the crowd. Even the most hard-bitten, inebriated fellows gave way without protest before such an impeccably dressed gent. Haggerty and I followed in his wake, like two badly rumpled manservants behind their Squire. Soden maneuvered us past the still hard-blowing and agitated horses and circled the police wagon. There we came up against a copper whose height and breadth blocked our view of all but Detective Dennis O'Dwyer who was studying something at his feet.

Recognizing Soden, or perhaps just deferring to his expensive clothes and impressively-carved cane, the policeman nodded and turned aside. A corpse, pale in death, stretched out before Detective O'Dwyer. Even with his lank hair plastered over his face, his burly body and lumpy hands left no doubt that the stiff was Amos Porch. Sitting at the edge of the wharf, huddled in a blanket, his black hair wet and slick against his skull, very much alive, was Jimmy Collins. I barely knew Porch who'd joined the team only recently. I talked with Collins daily. Seeing Collins hunched there, safe, I expelled breath I didn't know I'd been holding.

Soden spotted Collins at the same time I did. He stepped up to the pencil-thin O'Dwyer to announce our presence, resting his hand lightly on the detective's shoulder. For the moment, however, he spoke to Collins, his voice full of wonder. "Jimmy? What'n tarnation?"

Still clutching the blanket around him, Collins struggled to his feet. He was a half-foot shorter than I am, and perhaps fifty pounds lighter. His shoes and stockings were gone and his face was as bleached as his feet. "I'm all right, Mr. Soden, just wet and cold—and plenty miffed." He glanced around as if aware for the first time of the crowd and his location. Stretching up on his tiptoes, he looked back toward Battery Street. "They caught the three of us when we came out of the pub, smacked us around, then dragged us down here, robbed us, and pitched us into the drink." He glanced at the lifeless body of Amos Porch. "Poor ol' Shady," he groaned.

O'Dwyer, the shadows on his face making him seem even more cadaver-like than usual, nodded at Collins, then turned to Soden whose hand was still on his shoulder. "One of the lads hawking newspapers saw the whole thing, recognized Mr. Collins, and ran to get a policeman. He thought Collins was dead. He didn't tell us there were *three* victims."

Soden seemed not to pick up on Collins' or O'Dwyer's reference to three victims. His eyes flew to Porch's inert body, but refused to rest there. "Have you contacted Jimmy's wife?" he asked O'Dwyer.

"She's been notified he's safe. Porch had no immediate family." The detective looked me in the face for the first time and acknowledged my presence with a mock scowl. "Hello, Will. You going to be poking your nose in this, are you?"

"Well, sir, I—"

"I don't think they were professionals," Jimmy Collins broke in. "They didn't waste much time with me. Bopped me, hauled me to the end of the wharf, wrestled my gold watch from me, and tossed me in." He held up his wet wallet and shrugged. "Didn't even bother with my billfold."

O'Dwyer pointed at Collins' bare feet. "They took the time to boost your shoes 'n stockings," he observed matter-of-factly.

Collins dropped his gaze and stared stupidly at his feet, as if suddenly comprehending that he was barefooted. He twisted to gaze at Porch who, though he'd now been partially covered by a gray blanket, exhibited bare, fish-white feet. "What the hell—?" he muttered.

Soden took his hand from O'Dwyer's shoulder and touched Collins lightly on the arm. "We need to get you home, son," he said.

I edged closer. My father always said I could smell opportunity while dicing onions in a slaughterhouse. "I could look into this, Mr. Soden. Help the police a bit. I did pretty well finding out who assaulted Germany Long." A month before, knowing I'd had some experience in my father's Minneapolis detective agency, Soden had pressed me to discover who had brained Germany Long, his star shortstop, in the team's dressing room before a game. I had done so. With the help of Lieutenant O'Dwyer, and others.

Soden ignored me and turned back to Collins. "You're fine? Truly?"

Looking pale and dazed, Jimmy Collins spread his hands. "I'm okay."

I edged closer to Soden and spoke under my breath. "I could help investigate the attacks upon Porch and Collins, sir."

Soden looked at me as if I was a bad case of shingles. "Not now, Mr. Beaman."

He, Haggerty, and O'Dwyer moved off, ushering Collins toward the police wagon. Two stretcher-bearers, accompanied by a dark-suited man with a medical bag, bore Porch's body toward an ambulance that was being backed through the crowd.

For the first time I saw beyond the clump of officials. A good sixty feet up the pier was a second blanket-draped figure. He or she was sitting on the edge of the dock, legs dangling over the side. This had to be the other victim Collins and O'Dwyer had mentioned. I strolled to the figure. The blanket pulled up over the head like a hood was darkly blotched, dampness from the victim having soaked through it. There wasn't a policeman in twenty yards of the poor soul. "You all right?" I asked.

The blanket-draped head slowly twisted toward me.

I gasped. "Sean?" There slouched Sean Dennison, sketch artist for the *Boston Globe,* and my best chum. At the moment, he didn't look much like

15

an artist for the city's largest circulating newspaper or the high-gear cyclist he also was. He looked like the proverbial kitten in the cistern. I knelt beside him. "Jesus, you all right, Sean?"

"Hey, Will," he said so quietly that I could barely hear him. "Why're you here?"

I canted my head toward the police wagon. "O'Dwyer called Mr. Soden, told him Collins and Porch had been mugged, perhaps killed. He didn't mention you."

Sean shrugged. "I can see why Mr. Soden might be worried about Jimmy."

I glanced to where Soden hovered over his third baseman like a family member celebrating a returned heirloom. "Well, of course he is," I told Sean. "He cares about Shady Porch and you, too."

Sean's expression told me he didn't believe me. Hell, both of us knew it wasn't true. Soden wasn't the type of man to give a hoot about anyone or anything not related to his team or his profits or himself. Anything or anyone outside Soden's primary circle of interests he treated like a hard bout of inflamed hemorrhoids.

"What happened?" I asked, as much to change the subject as anything.

Sean pushed to his feet, clutching the blanket tightly about himself. He's an inch taller than Collins and twenty pounds heavier. Has the thick thighs and muscular calves of the professional biker he is. Where Collins is dark-haired, Sean is carrot-topped and freckled. "We—me 'n Jimmy 'n Porch—had a coupla beers up on Hanover," he said. "I was doing a few sketches of Collins for Sunday's *Globe*. Shady was just taggin' along. When we came out we walked toward Battery. Five men grabbed us and pummeled us good." He patted his pockets through the blanket. "Jaysus, Mary, and Joseph. They took everything." He pulled the blanket tighter around him. "Get me outta here, Will," he growled, "I'm wet and cold and I stink." He pulled something green and stringy from his hair and stared balefully at it. "By the blessed skirts of Mary, if flotsam were flowers you'd think this was an alderman's funeral."

"Have you told your story to O'Dwyer?" I asked.

"Twice—and to the big copper once. Come on, get me outta here."

I told him to stay put. I checked with O'Dwyer and got permission to take Sean home. And I took one last shot with Soden. "I could look into this business," I told him.

Even as I said it, I knew that Soden had already weighed the sums and calculated the odds. He could easily find a replacement for Porch. And with Jimmy Collins safe, he had no further need for me.

"That won't be necessary, Will," he said. "Good night."

"I'll see that Sean gets home, then."

Soden didn't even glance at me when I mentioned Sean. He continued to pat Collins as if he still couldn't believe his cherry infielder was alive.

I gave it one more try, still hopeful that he'd give me an assignment to keep me on the payroll. I'm not too bright, but I am persistent. "Would you like me to talk to Sean? See if there's anything I can find out?"

He didn't rise to the bait. "No, you go on," he said. "We have things under control here. The newspaper lad saw everything that Sean did. Collins' father is a police captain in Buffalo. O'Dwyer'll do everything in his power to find who assaulted his son. You go on now. Good luck."

Good luck. There was something terribly final about his hollow wish.

As I started to leave, Soden seized my wrist. "Stop by the office Monday."

By God, a reprieve. My luck held.

"You can pick up your severance pay," he said.

3

Forty minutes later I had Sean at the boardinghouse on Magnolia in Dorchester where we let rooms. We used the rear entrance and tiptoed up the back stairs so as not to awake Claire or Cait Denihur, our landladies and love interests. Sean was sweet on Cait; in fact they were unofficially engaged. I was sparking Claire. We thought it best to enter unobtrusively tonight. We were a fine pair of swains: Sean was wet and bedraggled, stank of the harbor, and was poorer than yesterday. I was flat-strapped and unemployed.

Sean took a steaming bath before joining me in my room with our convivial companion, John Barleycorn. Though a permanent guest of ours, our bottle of John Barleycorn was never mentioned to the Denihur sisters who believed that even the smallest nip of the devil's brew was a moral lapse of Bunyanesque proportions. I gave Sean the easy chair and poured him a generous portion. Sitting on my narrow bed with my back against the wall I saluted him with my drink. "Want to talk about it?"

Sean took a noisy gulp, grimacing as he swallowed. "Nothing much to it," he croaked. "They slugged me 'n told Collins and Porch to take a hike. When Jimmy and Shady didn't move fast enough they thumped them and dragged all of us down to the water and rolled us in." He shrugged. "They figure'd we'd drown, I suppose, and that would be that. Apparently, Shady did."

"They thumped *you* first?"

"Uh huh."

"And told *Jimmy* and *Shady* to scram?"

He stared at the floor as if looking into the murky depths of the bay. "Yeah."

"You told this to Detective O'Dwyer?"

He suddenly looked up at me. "Of course. What're you going on about?"

"Seems strange, is all. Jimmy and Shady were expensively dressed. Still, they grabbed *you* and told *Jimmy* and *Shady* to scram?"

Sean sucked in his cheeks and looked like he was passing a kidney stone.

I slumped further down the wall. "Well, the police will get to the why of it."

Sean lurched forward. "Look into it, Will. Help out this wee bogtrotter."

Whoa. I showed him my palms. "I suggested that to Soden. He made it very clear he didn't want me to bother with the Collins and Porch thing— or your problem either."

"You ask better questions than the police. Like just now. Why *did* those mugs try to chase Collins and Shady off? Why *would* they pay more attention to me? And why kill Shady?" He looked at me for answers, but I had none to give him. He held his empty glass toward me and gestured with his head toward the bottle.

I refilled his glass. "You *sure* they clobbered you first?"

He sipped his drink then nodded slowly, his face sullen. "Like I told you."

"Where were Collins and Porch?"

"Ten feet or so in front of me. When I stopped to look in a store window they strolled on. The bastards came up behind me and conked me." He rubbed the back of his head and grimaced, as if reliving the attack. "Caught me right behind the ear."

"Then what?"

"I was knocked silly, landed on my hands and knees wondering what the hell was going on. I heard someone yell, 'Get your bloody arses outta here. *Now.*'"

"Yelling at Jimmy and Porch?"

Sean sipped his drink. "Yeah. Both, I guess."

"What then?"

Another sip from his drink. "Not sure. I was on my hands and knees with my sketchbook under me. One of the thugs picked it up. The guy holding me ripped at my watch and fumbled for my billfold." He shook his head in confusion. "I was still trying to get my arms and legs to work, and my head to clear."

"You weren't unconscious at any time, then?"

"Not then, maybe later. I remember being dragged toward the pier. I could hear the ships against the pilings. You know, that sound they make. I don't know where Jimmy or Shady were." He took a large swallow of his drink and shuddered. "Then I was in the water thinkin' I was gonna drown."

I scooted to the edge of the bed and leaned toward him. "You'll be okay," I told him. "Apparently, nothing's broken, including that thick Irish cranium of yours. You remember anything else?"

He grinned sheepishly. "I remember thinking I'd like to be 6' 2" and two hundred pounds, like you. I woulda raised some hell with them thugs."

I tried to comfort him. "Size doesn't matter when you're outnumbered from the jump, and waylaid to boot."

"Well, boyo, it would've helped. One was a real big 'un."

"Oh? You got a good look at him?"

"No. But he was huge. And strong. Tossed me around like a doll, he did."

"Could you draw him?"

He thought about it. "Nah, first he was behind me, then on top of me. I did see his hand, though. Huge paw, big and hard as a concrete slab."

I stood. "Well, you've done all you can. You've told O'Dwyer what happened. And so, apparently, has the newspaper hawker. O'Dwyer'll work on it. All you can do is get some sleep."

He fingered his lower lip but said nothing. He stood and set his empty glass on the dresser before pausing at the door. "I do need some shuteye. Thanks for the bracer, Will. Sure you won't consider looking into this? As a favor to me, 'n all?"

I should have told him about my being fired. I just couldn't do it. He had problems of his own at the moment and didn't need to add mine to them. I shook my head. "It's being taken care of, Sean. Whether or not the thugs meant to kill Shady, they did. Dennis O'Dwyer will pursue them to the ends of the earth. And when he finds out who killed Shady, we'll know who mugged you and Collins, and stole your stuff."

"I'm not so sure," Sean muttered. "Now that you mentioned it, that business about shooing Collins and Porch away seems cockeyed. I think they wanted me." He opened the door. "I have a little money. I'll pay you to get to the bottom of this."

I waved off that idea as he stepped into the hall. "No. The police can do everything I could—and they will, with Shady dead. I won't take money you're putting away to marry Cait. Besides, I won't have the time."

He gave me a sharp look. "Things hectic at the South End Grounds, are they?"

I put my glass down. I gave him an answer that closed off the conversation rather than opening it up. "Well, they're getting hectic with me," I told him, again letting the opportunity pass to tell him I'd been canned. "I'm going to turn in and dream of Claire. You dream of cabals and conspiracies, if it suits you."

He smiled wanly and shut the door behind him.

I sank down on the bed and pressed my hands over my eyes, thinking I should take my own advice, get a good night's sleep and get on with my life. Sean's mugging was but a flyspeck on the wall of my life. As much as I was loath to admit it, so was Shady Porch's death. I didn't really know the man. If I didn't find work soon, I would be nothing but a flyspeck on Claire Denihur's wall.

4

I slept in Sunday morning. Everyone was gone by the time I descended the stairs. Claire and Cait were probably at the Catholic Church they attended faithfully. Sean was also a regular at Catholic services and apparently last night's assault hadn't caused him to miss this morning's Mass.

My parents had dragged me to the Lutheran Church in Minneapolis during my youth. But Lutherans were too dour and preoccupied with sin and retribution for me. I abandoned the church as soon as I had the freedom to do so, much to the chagrin of my father who believed a liberal dose of trepidation prepared a man for life's inevitable failures and disappointments.

Sunday was no day to look for employment and the Boston nine did not play on the Sabbath. So, following breakfast in my room, I joined hundreds of other bicyclists in Franklin Park where I spent the day exercising and enjoying the sun. Despite Arthur Soden's lamentations about the lack of interest among citizens for the Beaneaters, the Sunday crowd buzzed with excitement over the upcoming September race between their Boston stalwarts and the hated Orioles of Mugsy McGraw and Hughie Jennings. Still, as the parsimonious Mr. Soden would be quick to point out, citizens in a public park celebrating his team's upcoming chances put no silver in his coffers.

I returned to the boarding house late in the afternoon. Instead of going into the house that I knew from experience still radiated from the heat of the day, I plumped down in a lawn chair in the backyard to thumb through the *Herald* and the *Globe*. By then, the sun was low in the sky. I dozed off. Perhaps it was only a dream, but I had the distinct sense that Claire Denihur was singing while I slept. The echo of her lilting voice flitted about in my consciousness like frames from an Edison kinescope.

I awakened fully with a start, opening my eyes to see Claire brushing dust and splinters from her sleeves, staring down at a bound roll of lath at her feet. She was a tall, slender, full-bodied woman with raven hair and porcelain skin. I'd met her several months ago when Sean encouraged me to take a room at the boardinghouse she ran with her sister, Cait. I became infatuated with her almost instantly. Whether she harbored truly strong feelings for me continued to elude me. The roll of lath she was staring at rested next to a can and a hammer.

"Going to build something?" I asked her. I wanted to comment on her singing but I was unsure whether it was part of my imagination—or a dream.

She spun toward me, eyes wide, face flushed. "Mr. Beaman. Will," she gasped. "You startled me; I didn't see you back there."

"I started out catching up on my reading. I ended up catching up on my sleep."

"You and Sean came in late last night." If her words were meant to be critical, the criticism was blunted by the lilt in her voice. "You were working?"

I nodded. "Two of the Boston nine were assaulted in the North End last night. One drowned. I was there with Mr. Soden."

Her face blanched. "That's horrible," she sighed. "There's so much violence on the waterfront."

"Yes, there is," I agreed. "It took awhile for the police to finish their investigation and let me go." If I wasn't going to share news of my firing with Sean, I certainly wasn't going to let Claire in on it. Not yet, anyway. And I would let Sean tell her about the assault on him, if he cared to. I wasn't going to tell her before Sean could tell Cait. I pointed again to the roll of lath. "What is it that you are going to build?"

"I'm going to add to the trellis. I've thought of hiring a handyman to do it, but perhaps I can do it myself."

I sprang from the lawn chair. "I'll help you. I'm not too bad with a hammer."

She beamed and stooped to retrieve the hammer for me. "That would be wonderful, Will. I'm awkward in these matters, I'm afraid."

I took the hammer. "What is it you want to do?"

It was warm now, warmer it seemed than at mid-day. The orange afterglow of sundown had turned the yard into a bathhouse, hot, moist, humming with insects. Claire unbuttoned two buttons at her throat and rolled up the sleeves of her white blouse. With her arm she wiped away the sheen of perspiration from her brow. Pointing and gesturing, she explained what she had in mind to extend the trellis.

I broke open the roll of lath with the hammer and inspected the can of nails. "We'll need some larger boards for bracing," I told her.

"There's some in the shed," she said, pointing to a small building in the rear corner of the yard.

Once I'd returned with two-by-fours and a saw we worked steadily. She measured the boards for the bracing and I cut them. Later, she handed me the laths one at a time, and I nailed them to the two-by-fours. We placed the lath in a cross-hatched pattern which supplied the needed bracing while permitting light to penetrate. It would provide additional shade in the sprawling yard.

We touched often. Our hands brushed as she handed me the boards. We shooed mosquitos and flies from each other's face. We leaned into each other as we carefully gauged the placement of individual laths. When Claire pinched a finger, I playfully kissed away its pain. While I was hammering a piece of lath into place, she used her handkerchief to dab sweat from my eyes. Despite the disappearance of the sun, we were both perspiring freely. I rolled my shirt sleeves to my biceps and doffed my lid. She took off her wide-brimmed hat, sweeping up and repinning curls that had tumbled down. Her eyes glowed with humor and intelligence. While doing close work she squinted in concentration and stuck the tip of her pink tongue between her teeth. After a half-hour or so, she excused herself, left, then returned with two glasses of lemonade. We sipped the cool, tart liquid, chips of ice clacking as we drank.

She turned to me. "You said two players from the Boston nine were assaulted last night," she said. "Which two?" Claire had become quite a fan of the Beaneaters in the past month. I had taken her to the Park Theater to see one of the electric recreations of an away game and she was so taken with it that she pressed me to take her to an actual game. She became an avid crank after watching a Boston-Baltimore game at the Grounds. She now follows the team's progress in the *Globe* with the fervor of Billy Sunday on the Chautauqua circuit. I told her about Jimmy Collins and Amos Porch.

"What a tragedy about poor Mr. Porch," she sighed. "But, and it's a terrible thing to say, Boston can better withstand the loss of him than they could Mr. Collins. I see where Baltimore defeated Cincinnati again yesterday. Boston will need Mr. Collins." She tilted her head and looked at me out of the corners of her eyes. "When are you going to take me to another game?" she asked with a teasing smile. "The pennant chase is exciting."

I matched her smile with one of my own. "Whenever you're free, Miss Denihur."

"Good," she replied, very perky like, "That's settled." She turned more serious then. "Almost as interesting as the pennant race is the Massachusetts Civic League's efforts to permit young men to play base ball on Sundays. Have you read about the League? The newspapers are full of its proposals. Do you think your Mr. Soden will ever schedule his team on the Sabbath? "

I hefted the hammer several times as I thought about the Civic League's advocacy of opening the city's playgrounds on Sunday, and encouraging base ball on the Sabbath to reduce juvenile crime. "I've read about the League and its hopes," I told her. "But most people think that St.

Louis will win the Natioal League pennant before the Beaneaters ever play a game on Sundays."

She giggled and returned her attention to the trellis and studied it for a long while before observing, "My mother always said that work we did ourselves had more value than that which we paid for."

"Your mother was a wise woman."

"Ummm. She was. I miss her. Mother was full of wonderful advice, and always willing to listen to our problems. Following her death, father didn't know how to take care of his business—or his daughters. Mother was the glue. When she was no longer here to hold us together, father let his business go, and eventually left me and Cait this house and not much else."

"Your mother would have been proud of her daughters," I assured her. "Your father, too. You and Cait have done wonders with the house."

She smiled in appreciation. "Well, mother always said hard work solves most problems. We're working hard and making progress." She emitted a long sigh. "Of course, there's always the temptation to walk away and begin afresh."

I winced. Despite my hopes for our relationship, she wouldn't be walking away *with me* any time soon. I was financially strapped, unemployed, and without prospects. A great catch I was for this remarkable woman. "What stops you?" I asked.

She suddenly stirred herself, as if shucking aside all thoughts of her future for the moment, smiled ruefully, and moved toward the trellis. "I want to see Cait and Sean settled first, then I'll decide what I'm going to do. Sean is doing well at the *Globe* and with his racing, and he knows Cait wants more in life than overseeing a boardinghouse."

"And you want more than that, too." I made it a statement rather than a question.

"I think so, yes. I just don't know what. I've been too busy being a mother to Cait and trying to make a success of the roominghouse."

"You're doing a cracking good job with both tasks. Cait is a fine young lady. And I haven't heard a single complaint from boarders."

She weighed my comments. "Yes, well. Mother always said progress cannot be hurried." She glanced at the sky. "But you and I had better make some quick progress. It'll be dark soon."

A half-hour later, we completed the job and stood back to view the results. Our shirts were now gray with perspiration, our hair damp, our faces flushed. We'd worked efficiently, rapidly. We'd talked and laughed at our efforts, keeping up a stream of mock disparaging remarks about our skills and awkwardness. Claire laughed easily, her smile bright enough to light a city and sear my heart.

"More lemonade?" she asked.

"Please."

When she returned with our glasses refilled, she handed me mine and brushed a mosquito from my cheek with her finger. "Thank you, Will," she said, turning again to appraise the new construction. "I'm so very proud of my new trellis."

I watched the movements in her throat as she sipped her lemonade. The urge to kiss her glistening neck triggered a groan deep in my chest.

Claire brushed another mosquito from my face. "They *are* annoying, aren't they?"

The moment had passed. I let her misunderstanding of my groan stand. "We work well together," I told her. "And we've built something good here this afternoon." I could only hope that was true.

5

Sean wasn't at the breakfast table Monday morning. Two salesmen with rooms on the first floor were there, as were two gents who shared the second floor with Sean and me. The young female who rented the attic room, as usual, had eaten and departed. I pulled out a chair and sat, leaving two vacant chairs between a bespectacled curtain salesman and me. "Morning, gentlemen," I said. "As usual, everything looks delicious."

They responded with an assortment of grunts, mutterings, and vague gestures, all without missing a forkful. This was not a gathering of Boston's literary or oratorical giants. But, then, Monday conversations generally are as thin as workhouse porridge. This morning it mostly consisted of two salesmen grousing about Boston's dropping two of the first three games to Cleveland. Boston's victory over Cleveland on Saturday apparently didn't slake their thirst for Beaneater domination.

Claire Denihur came in and set fresh plates of steaming potatoes and eggs before us. Her tresses, piled high and pinned, seemed as black and shinny as a crow's wing. Picking up a large blue enamel coffeepot, she began to fill up cups. She rested a hand on my shoulder. "Coffee?"

I held up my coffee cup for her. "Please. Sean been down yet?"

She shook her head. "Not yet." She left the coffeepot on the table, scooped up several empty platters, and headed toward the kitchen.

I called after her. "Are you and Cait free this afternoon? I thought the four of us might go to the new North End swimming beach. It's going to be another scorcher."

She drifted back toward the table. "That'd be fun. However, we're going to attend the new exhibit of Frederic Remington paintings at the Hart and Watson Gallery. Cait said Sean also wants to see it and he'll have some time today."

An art exhibit? By some unknown western dauber? On what promised to be a blazer of a day? I'd rather sit on nails. "Claire," I pleaded, "think about that cool water. It'll be a lot more comfortable there than in some stuffy gallery."

She swept my arguments aside. "Cait's excited about seeing the Remington exhibit, Will. And, frankly, so am I. His *Colliers'* covers are marvelous."

My chance of spending the day at the beach with the comely Denihurs was clearly fading. "Ask Cait about the beaches, Claire. Please?"

She stepped back and gave me one of her wonderful smiles. "All right, Mr. Beaman. You talk to Sean about it." She moved off toward the kitchen, leaving me to chow down with the others.

I was working on a porkchop when Sean slid into the chair next to me. He seemed no worse for wear from Saturday's assault. "Good Morning," he yawned.

"Morning to you, Mr. Dennison. Survived your ordeal, have you?"

Sean's the kind of guy who can smile with a bum full of boils. He shot his boyish grin at me. "We sons of Eire are a resilient lot. Dumber than a barrel of hair, but resilient." He reached out for the platter of porkchops and pulled one onto his plate. He pointed at the plate of eggs. It was only after he'd heaped his plate that he turned to me. "Still think I was making a mountain out of a molehill?"

I paused in my attack on the porkchop. "Probably."

He shrugged his concession of my point. "But, as you pointed out, boyo, I seemed to be the object of their attack. Jimmy, with his fancy duds and gold watch, should have been. Even poor ol' Amos Porch presented a more lucrative target than I did."

Could someone be unhappy with your recent efforts at the bike races?" I asked. "Perhaps some gambler angry at your not winning?"

"I've *been* winning," he huffed.

"Then, maybe, someone doesn't *want* you to win."

He cupped his face in his hands and thought about what I'd said.

I waggled my fork at him. "Ahh, nuts. You three were victims of being in the wrong place at the wrong time. That's all. And Porch drowned while unconscious."

He seized my wrist. "Join me in some amateur detective work, Will. We did a crackerjack job trackin' down Billy Ewing after he conked Germany Long, didn't we? Mr. Soden thought we were some pumpkins then. So did Detective O'Dwyer."

I laid my hand on his arm to stop him. "Sean, I don't have the time to investigate your mugging. Really, I don't."

He frowned his concern. "Soden is keeping you hopping?"

Once again I let the opportunity to tell him of my firing pass. "Yeah. That, and you're saving money to marry Cait. You shouldn't be so eager to give it away."

He studied me for a long moment. "By Jaysus, you're in a fine mood today."

I leapt at that cue. "Want to change my mood?" I asked. "Get the women to go swimming with us." I pointed out the window with my knife. "It's gonna be brutal today."

"You don't have to remind me of the heat," he growled, tugging his collar away from his neck.

"Talk to the women, then. The Remington exhibition will still be open tomorrow, won't it?"

He pursed his lips. "I promised Cait and Claire that I'd go with them today. They want to see what all the hullabaloo is all about, and so do I. In fact, I'm giving up a day of practice at the bike track to see the exhibit."

I've been told on more than one occasion that I could sell Paine's Celery Compound to a week-old corpse, and I turned my salesmanship on Sean. I extolled the virtues of the new beach facilities, the fun of a day in the water, the opportunity to cavort with the scantily-clad Denihur sisters, blazes, to observe swarms of young women in swimming wear, and the chance to show off our athletic skills.

But Sean responded to my eloquence with a dismissive grunt. "I thought you were a university man," he sneered, "Shouldn't you be the one arguing to visit the art gallery?"

A low blow, that. "I love art, "I assured him. "I'd go anywhere to see a John Singer Sergeant exhibit or the works of Thomas Eakins. But I'm not interested in some amateur who paints horses."

Sean made a sound in his throat. "Look, boyo, Cait, Claire and I'm going to take in the exhibit. You gonna come with us, or not?"

It didn't take Thomas Edison to figure that out that I could accompany Claire and pretend to be interested in Remington's work, or I could—what? Lose perhaps a last chance to spend time with Claire? I laid my knife and fork on my plate. "What time?" I asked in resignation.

"One o'clock. And I expect you to be as prompt as a landlord after his rents."

I laughed, pushed my chair back, and stood. "One o'clock it is."

That would give me time to get to the South End Grounds, pick up my severance pay, and get back in time to go see Remington's art works. My severance pay would take care of one week's rent payment and leave just enough for trolley fare to the gallery.

6

I'm often more optimistic than practical. My father says I'm more visionary than sensible. His brother, my uncle, says I don't know shit from shingleberries. In any case, I entered the South End Grounds hoping to find Soden absent and one of his partners there. His partners at least would cushion my fall with a bit of blarney and hollow best wishes. Soden would dispatch me with frosty precision. He had the sensitivity of a Hun. On the other hand, if Soden were there, I was also hoping he might have had second thoughts about firing me, or about me investigating Saturday's assaults.

It was going to be an early game today so Patsy Tebeau's Cleveland Spiders could catch a train west. The Boston players and a few of the Spiders were already on the field, loosening up, their uniforms baggy and filthy. The fiery Tebeau wasn't in sight, but I watched briefly as infielders Ed McKean and Bobby Wallace lazily flipped ground balls to each other. Spiders' pitchers Nig Cuppy and Cy Young sat next to the grandstand, chatting and laughing with a reporter from the *Herald*. I'd met both before. I gave them a wave and headed for Soden's office.

Soden was the only one there. He sat at his desk glowering at a newspaper. "Good morning, sir," I said cheerfully, standing over him. He paid me no heed. In a haze of blue cigar smoke he glared at the newspaper as if it told him he must undergo an enema. Suddenly he slammed it down and pounded it with the flat of his hand. "First, it's the shoemakers, then it's the damned glaziers and gas fitters."

"Sir?"

He glared up at me. "The shoemakers are on strike again. Glaziers and gas fitters, too. And the brewers'll be next, you watch. Damned anarchists."

I didn't want to offend him unnecessarily, but I was determined not to go out wearing his collar. "They want a decent wage, sir," I said.

"Wages are set by the market, son. Pure and simple."

I thought of my own unemployment. "The market hasn't much compassion for a man and his troubles," I told him.

"Poppycock," he grunted. "Labor is a commodity, just like, ah, ah,"—he waved his hands as if batting at flies—"oil and gas. Herbert Spencer and Adam Smith laid it out as neat and plain as a Hausfrau's doily, son."

I glared at him. A commodity, was I? "Working men deserve a living wage," I told him. "Besides, the glaziers and gas fitters want shorter hours, not higher wages."

John Haggerty would have been proud of me.

Soden wasn't. "Drivel," he snapped. "It's the same nonsense that that rascal Debs spouts. We all sell our skills, our intelligence, our labor, son. If you don't have a buyer, you go where there is one. Yes, sir. Supply and demand."

I was angry now. "Bull feathers. The strikers are the same people who buy tickets, or want to buy tickets, to watch your Beaneaters. That urchin hawking newspapers who reported the mugging Saturday night recognized Jimmy Collins. He is probably a fan of the team. His father probably is, too."

Soden snorted and skipped past my point. "They're calling for the end of capitalism. They're madmen and revolutionaries." He suddenly sagged back in his chair as if exhausted, shook his head and drummed his fingers on his desk for a long moment. "We've gotten away from business, Mr. Beaman. Your, ah, situation?"

Situation, my Aunt Agnes! My termination.

He made no attempt to sweeten his message. "We've got to let you go. Of course, we'll give you severance pay and good letters."

My brief career with the Boston Beaneaters was over. "Thank you, sir," I replied, my bitterness clearly echoing in my words. For a parting shot, I added, "Permit me a bit of advice. Offer workers inexpensive games at convenient times and see how many of them show up. Play on Sundays. You let John Haggerty and the Royal Rooters hold special games for orphaned children. Why not do the same for workingmen and their families? The strikers are no more anxious to destroy capitalism than you are."

He rocked back in his chair, frowning and continuing to drum his fingers. After a long moment he waved toward the large window. "See all those new hotels and museums and symphony halls and libraries? Your friend the working man might lay the bricks and pour the concrete for them, but its men with education, money, and vision who are the true builders." He leaned forward, elbows on his desk, hands clasped in front of him. "Herbert Spencer got it right, son. Men with talent, skill, brains, and ambition, naturally end up with the resources. And men with the resources in this city care about its people—and build the facilities to distract, exercise, and amuse them. And the buildings to house and educate them." He was getting excited now. "And they're the ones behind this week's commemoration of the return of the Bradford manuscript. Not the workers, Mr. Beaman. Businessmen like myself, and the gentry, and the city's Brahmins."

I didn't agree with his assessment, but at least I understood it. Everything, that is, except his reference to the manuscript. "Bradford manuscript?" I asked. "What's the Bradford manuscript?"

He indicated with a wave of his hand that the details weren't fresh in his mind. "It's a manuscript history of early Plymouth, I think. It's being returned to Boston after being in England for two hundred years, or something like that. There's a celebration scheduled with the mayor, governor, representatives, senators, and the ambassador. I've been invited as a representative of business."

"Well," I snapped facetiously, "I'm sure the working classes will be well represented." I continued to gather up the few items from my desk, telling him over my shoulder, "They're every bit as concerned about the soul of the city, its libraries, museums, galleries, and history as the wealthy and influential are. And they're as interested in sporting events as the classes you think so highly of. Probably more."

He sneered. "Well, none of them has come forward to help us discover who killed our reserve catcher and mugged our third baseman."

I matched him sneer for sneer. "You've thrown away your best bet for finding those responsible."

He looked startled. "How's that?"

"You fired me," I snapped. "I solved the assault on Germany Long and I could get to the bottom of this mess." Even as I said it, I realized how impulsive and foolish it was. I had discovered Long's attacker as much by luck as by guile.

My impertinence raised his dander. "Wager on that, would you?" he asked.

My dander was up, too. "I would."

He glared at me a long time, his face flushed. "Sit down, son," he said finally, pointing to a chair. I seized the chair and swung it in an arc as I returned to Soden. I placed it close enough that when I sat my knees almost touched his. Our eyes locked.

He tapped my knee with his fist. "Here's my bet. I don't expect you to unearth those who attacked Collins and Porch. You don't have the resources. The police will look into that. But a month or so ago a contingent from Buffalo, Jimmy Collins' hometown and where he played his first professional ball, came to Boston to present him with a gold watch. Hometown lad makes good, 'n all that."

"Yes?"

Soden stubbed out his cigar in a large glass ashtray and groped in his highly-polished humidor for another. "Collins loves that watch. The thieves will doubtless pawn it, or try to fence it. Tracing that business may be within your ability. Get Collins' watch back and I'll give you, uh, one hundred dollars."

I gave him a withering look. "That's a damned puny reward," I grumbled. "If I can find the watch, I can probably learn who pilfered it. And if I do that, I'll know who killed Porch and mugged Collins. That information should be worth more to you than one hundred dollars."

He meticulously snipped off the end of the cigar with small cutters that hung on his watch chain. "One hundred dollars is a princely sum for someone unemployed."

I sighed, and stood. "I'll take your bet."

He brushed the tip of the cigar that had fallen in his lap onto the floor. "You'll be doing this on your own," he said. "You no longer work here."

My voice rose in spite of myself. "I said I'll take it."

A look of suspicion crossed his face. He held up a finger. "One moment," he said. "You're a confident young man, Mr. Beaman. But what if you fail? The penalty should be commensurate with the reward." He cocked his head toward me. "No severance pay. No letters," he said, gracing me with one of his icy smiles, clearly impressed with his cunning. "We'll hold back your severance money to await the outcome. Still game?"

I knew I should take my week's pay and walk away. Get on with my life. Do what I'd advised Sean to do. I needed to search out new employment. And God knows I needed the severance money. But I didn't cave in. I couldn't. Not in the face of Soden's smugness. "I'm game," I told him.

He held up his hands, palms toward me. "There must be a time limit, of course." The man was going to squeeze until I squealed like a rat under a wagon's wheel. I took a deep breath and exhaled noisily. "Thirty days. That seems fair."

He puckered his lips and looked at me through squinted eyes. "Let's say two weeks," he said, after the briefest pause, and extended his hand. "Still game?"

What the hell. I wasn't sure the extra two weeks would make any difference. Emotion had been the basis for my agreeing to the hairbrain wager in the first place. Why let intelligence interfere at this late stage? "Still game," I sighed, and clasped his hand.

I headed back to the boardinghouse and my rendezvous with the cowboy's daubings.

7

Uninterested in what I presumed was a hack painter, I was nonetheless intent on demonstrating to Claire that I was eager for her company, and cared enough to defer to her preferences. I put on my best face, determined to be enthusiastic about our visit to the gallery whatever the shortcomings of Remington's work. Putting the upcoming game with the Spiders at the Grounds out of my mind, along with the excursion to the seashore, I smiled broadly at Claire and reached for the Hart and Watson gallery door.

The substantial double doors which comprised the entrance led into a small lobby. Two additional doors stood in front of us, an elevator to our right. Painted in gilded letters on the door to the left was "Rare Books, Almanacs, Manuscripts, Historic Maps and Relics." Beneath this, more gilded letters assured customers that the books were first editions and the relics authentic. The door to the right was virtually a twin. Similar gilded letters announced "Paintings—Original and Copies—Landscapes, Still Life Paintings, Portraits, and Prints." "Hart and Watson" was emblazened on both doors in bold black letters. We entered the door on the right, into the gallery. The cloying aroma of flowers engulfed us. It was like stepping into the city's botanical gardens. Running along two walls, spaced evenly, were highly polished tables, topped by colorful vases filled with equally colorful floral arrangements marking off the Remington works.

"There's enough flowers for a dozen aldermen's funerals," Sean groaned.

Even among the vivid flowers, the four dozen or so paintings and sketches that adorned the two walls seized our attention. Claire sucked in her breath and reached for Cait's arm. Both women were dressed in identical but different colored full skirts and long-sleeved, high-necked blouses that billowed at the shoulders. Their flower-adorned hats were wide-brimmed. With their black hair, onyx eyes, and ivory skin, they looked very much like the women painted so captivatingly by John Singer Sergeant. I understood why Claire had gasped. I found my own gaze sweeping the room, my jaw slack in amazement.

A voice said, "Please, feel free to enjoy the paintings at your leisure."

Standing just inside the door was a man in a three-piece black serge suit and high, starched collar. Clean-shaven, his dark curly hair was parted in the middle. He stepped forward and handed each of us a printed program. "If I can be of any help, please let me know," he said. He faced us while delivering his little speech, but his eyes never left Claire's, and his words seemed for her alone. She reddened and broke eye contact.

Sean chewed on his lower lip, nodded at the man, frowned at me with clouded eyes, but said nothing. He urged Cait to the nearest Remington painting with a firm hand in the small of her back. Taking my cue from him, I ignored the man's forwardness and Claire's obvious pleasure in it. I touched her back and she and I followed Sean and her sister.

"This is the first time there's been a comprehensive showing of Remington's works," Claire told me eagerly, as if trying to reassure me of her attention.

I again took in the large room with its hardwood floor gleaming like a bald man's pate. Only three other visitors, two women and a fireplug of a man, shared the gallery with us. The women were wearing summer dusters and dark wrap-around hats. The older and slightly frumpy-looking woman seemed familiar to me. Her moon face and shell-rimmed eyeglasses gave her the intense look of a scientist. The younger woman was more slender and fairer-skinned. Wisps of reddish-blond hair peeked from beneath her hat. Her eyeglasses were round and gold-rimmed. I guessed her to be five or six years younger than her companion. The male, who could have been their father, stood off from the women, examining from afar the same painting they were discussing. The sound of their shuffling feet and muted voices echoed in the exhibit hall.

Unable to pinpoint where I'd seen the older woman, I turned back to Remington's artwork. There were surprisingly few easel oil paintings. Most were pen sketches, wash drawings, or water colors. I paused first to appraise a large oil of three cavalry men on a treeless plain under siege from Indians. I have to admit that Remington conveyed action with what my former Harvard art history professor called "deft handling of line." Unfortunately, that's about the extent of my memory of that class. I'd paid more attention to paintings of plump nudes than to what the old codger was prattling about. I'd certainly never seen anything like these works in the readings and assignments for his course.

I continued to stare at the embattled cavalrymen, huddling among their dead and dying horses, firing at hostiles circling them. I could feel the heat and smell the dust of the parched ground. It was as if I stood among them in the hot, yellow powdery dirt, part of the horsemen's desperate struggle. Claire, Cait, and Sean had moved on and were studying a large oil called "A Dash for the Timber," where a half dozen colorfully-dressed cowboys and vaqueros spurred their mounts away from pursuing Indians.

The handsome fellow who'd met us at the door had sidled up beside Claire and was pointing out something in the painting to her, using a rolled program in his hand as a pointer. He leaned close to her and spoke softly. I noticed for the first time that he was sporting western style high-heeled boots. Jealousy stabbed at me. The man was young and attractive, and much too possessive of Claire. The fingers on his left hand rested lightly at the small of her back as he gestured at the painting. Claire listened intently, mouth slightly open, cheeks flushed, eyes glued on the painting.

Despite the continuing pull of Remington's battle scene, I moved swiftly to them and spoke before I'd thought about it. "Remington's not the only artist to paint the American Indian," I offered, pointing at the large oil. I knew I'd made a gaffe almost before the words left my mouth. I understood as much about western art as Joseph Pulitzer knew about fair news reporting.

The gent did not let me off the hook. He stopped mid-word and turned to me, a mixture of surprise and amusement on his face. "You're familiar with artists of the American Indian?" he asked, cocking an eyebrow.

Jeez, I'd stepped on a dog turd, and I knew it. "Well, not exactly—" I retreated a step and looked at Claire to gauge her reactions to my *faux pas*. She was staring at me with wide, unreadable eyes. Defensively, I glanced around to see who was in hearing distance. Luckily, the three visitors were now across the room from us. The more studious-looking woman was leaning close to her male companion motioning emphatically at a pencil sketch. Somewhere I'd seen those gestures, that energy, the manner in which she bobbed her head while speaking. The younger, prettier woman was looking my way. I turned back to find Claire also staring at me, an expectant look on her face.

A hint of a sneer curled our guide's lips and his brows rose higher. "Are you familiar with the work of Alfred Jacob Miller? George Catlin?" he asked, condescension dripping from his question.

"N-No," I stammered.

He dismissed me then, turning back to Claire, putting more pressure on her back with his left hand, leaning in still closer to her. "Notice the movement Remington conveys, not just with line but with color. See how he employs an economy of—"

Obviously aware of my embarrassed silence, and perhaps now unnerved by the man's forwardness with her sister, Cait touched his right arm. "The *Evening Transcript's* art critic claims Remington is indifferent to color," she said. She waved the column that she'd cut from the previous evening's newspaper.

The man faced Cait. "Miss, the *Evening Transcript's* reviewer is so intellectually and emotionally tied to traditional standards that he—"

But Cait was not to be put off. "He calls it a formidable handicap for an artist," she insisted, looking at the column in her hand, as if for confirmation.

The man was unflustered. He smiled down at her in amusement. "You are—?"

"Caitlin Denihur."

He took her hand. "Winthrop Hart." He cast his perfect smile at Claire. "And you are?"

"Claire Denihur." She hesitated, then swept an arm toward Sean and me. "Mr. Hart, this is Mr. Will Beaman and Mr. Sean Dennison."

Winthrop Hart took his eyes off Claire only briefly as he clasped, in turn, Sean's hand and mine. He quickly dismissed us, turning back to Cait. "You see, Miss Denihur, most reviewers still cling to the standards of classical art. Their minds and eyes are shut to true originality. Mr. Remington's talent is fresh, his paintings burst with authenticity and western *novelty*."

Her initial motive for interrupting obviously now forgotten, and caught up in Hart's intensity, Cait blurted, "You've been out west?"

He beamed. "Oh, yes. And I'll be returning shortly."

Winthrop Hart was starting to get on my nerves. The women seemed to think Hart was the main exhibit here. My suggestion that we all go swimming now seemed even more intelligent to me. Sean and I could be frolicking in the sea with Claire and Cait, and without the pushy Winthrop Hart.

My pique didn't slow down the loquacious Mr. Hart. He continued to tell Cait and Claire his plans. It seems that he had just come from Montana where, among other things, he'd scouted local artists. He believed that Americans were ready to embrace western art and he was determined to supply it. By now I'd already seen enough of him to last me a lifetime. The only thing that really interested me was his statement that he was returning to Montana shortly. But the girls obviously did not share my opinion. They continued to stare at Hart with wide, bright eyes, absorbing his every word.

I glanced at the canvas to my left, an oil titled, "The Fall of the Cowboy." It was a haunting winter scene depicting two cowboys and their mounts braving the winter chill. I was so taken by the bleakness of the land and the fate of the men captured so compellingly by Remington that it was minutes before I realized I was alone. Mr. Hart and the women had drifted to the far wall and were peering closely at a small watercolor. Apparently in a snit over Mr. Hart's impact on the women, Sean had wandered back toward the entrance where a half-dozen pen and pencil sketches hung. The older woman who looked so familiar to me and the man were still deeply engrossed in discussion, this time over a large oil. Seemingly, the younger woman had lost interest in the exhibit. She stood where she'd been when I last noticed her, arms crossed. She was a fetching young woman. She was gazing toward me; whether she was looking *at* me was not clear.

I ambled over to Sean who was watching Cait and Claire with unfeigned funk. There we took silent inventory of our new rival, the cowboy. The man *was* handsome in a rugged way, every illustrator's ideal of Frank Merriwell. He had dark eyes, a thin nose and high cheekbones. He was deeply tanned and his hands were the hands of a man who'd worked outside. I stood two inches over six feet and he was taller than I. His arms were also longer and his hands larger. They reminded me of the hands on Remington's cowboys. I found myself wondering if, with my Harvard boxing background, I could box his ears.

Sean and I probably looked like ragamuffins who'd lost their candy. "Hart's like a postage stamp," Sean mumbled. "He sticks to something until he gets there." We lapsed into silence.

It was Claire rushing over to us leading Winthrop Hart that finally shook me out of my reverie. "Mr. Hart has never seen a professional base ball game," she gushed. "I think we should take Mr. Hart to a game before he returns to Montana. He tells me that all he's heard on the streets and in the restaurants is talk of the pennant race."

Before I could respond, Mr. Hart, who had followed Claire, broke in. "Please, Miss Denihur, call me Win."

Win, was it? Win Hart? I hoped that his name didn't portend any success with Claire. I glanced toward Sean. His expression told me he was thinking the same thing about Hart and Cait. There wasn't much I could say without disappointing Claire. So, feeling a bit like the Pope at a Baptist dunking, I reluctantly agreed to arrange for all of us to attend tomorrow's game. Pop Anson's Chicago Colts would be in town. Rumors are that Anson will quit at the end of the season after almost three decades as a professional player, but he still puts on quite a show. Boston fans love to jeer him as he rages at umpires' calls in his booming voice, and as he unmercifully rags Chicago's opponents and fans alike. I had to admit it would be a good game for introducing a newcomer like Win Hart to professional base ball.

The day had not been a blazing success. I'd hoped to spend it at the shore in the company of Miss Denihur whose attention would be focused upon me. At the seashore Claire would witness my wit and charm, as well as my athletic physique. Seemingly, the charm and good looks that fascinated Claire today were Mr. Hart's, not mine. Coupled with that, now with no income coming in, I had to dig up money for five game tickets.

When we departed the gallery, having arranged a get-together at the South End Grounds, I tugged the door closed behind us. As I did so, I looked back into the gallery. Hart's eyes were following Claire. The older woman and the fireplug of a man were studying a minature oil sketch. The young lady with the gold rimmed glasses remained standing apart from her companions, arms across her breasts. She was eyeing me.

8

A blazing sun beat down on the South End Grounds, wilting men's collars and searing the outfield grass. Muttering and cursing, cranks shrugged out of their coats and fanned themselves with their straw skimmers. Women glistened with perspiration despite their efforts to produce a breeze with their scorecards. Dogs, no longer with energy to yap, moved like molasses or found shelter to crawl under. Outside the gate horses stood dozing, their weight on three legs. Smoke from trains drifted over the left field fence, smelling of oil and shimmering in the heat.

I saved five seats behind home base. Sean had offered to pay for the tickets, but I declined his offer, still without telling him of my firing. Instead, I went to John Haggerty for a loan. By then, Haggerty knew my firing was final and, bless his big Irish heart, he slipped me five free passes.

I had gotten to the Grounds early, having spent a frustrating morning canvassing the docks and surrounding neighborhoods. I hit every pawnshop within two miles of The Battery. And I visited every grogshop in the dank and inhospitable alleys near the piers. I got the same answer at each place: no one had turned in Collins' gold watch or any item belonging to Sean— and the police had already inquired about them. Nor, according to them, were they familiar with the giant Sean described as one of his attackers. Dispirited, I gave up and headed for the ballpark.

I wanted to confer with Tim Murnane before the others arrived. Tim was a friend and sports reporter for the *Boston Globe*. He was among the first to introduce himself to me when I went to work for Soden, and it was he who introduced me to Sean. The three of us had worked closely to solve the mystery of who had badly beaten Boston's shortstop Germany Long a month before. Murnane was a one-time professional ball player known for having good hands and surprising speed. He stole the first base in the history of the National League. Following his playing days he'd turned to scouting and managing and, recently, to overseeing a minor league. At present a bit portly and his shock of hair and mustache showing signs of graying, he was one of the more talented base ball writers, producing columns for *The Sporting News* as well as the *Globe*. It was said he knew every base ball player and fan in New England. He was standing near the press area when I spotted him and approached. I skipped the usual preliminaries. "I need your help," I told him.

"How's that, darlin'?"

"You've got contacts on the waterfront. All over Boston, in fact. I need suggestions on where to look for stolen items, and who fences them."

He gnawed at his bottom lip. "This have anything to do with Shady's death and the muggin' of Collins and Sean?"

"How'd you know?"

He pushed his mustache away from his mouth with his thumb and finger. "Soden told me about Collins' mugging and Porch's death this morning. A terrible thing, that. And poor Sean."

"Sean says one of the muggers was a giant. He shouldn't be too difficult to find."

Tim's nod indicated he agreed. "But why do you want to look into that? O'Dwyer and his detectives are on it."

"I've got a wager with Soden," I said.

His eyebrows shot up a notch.

"Just a gentleman's bet," I added, "I'm not looking into the killing or the assaults. I'm just trying to get Collins' gold watch back."

He rubbed his forehead. "Well, perhaps I can help you, but—" He paused and his eyes went past me to where Winthrop Hart, Cait, Claire and Sean were pushing through the gate. "There's the women and Sean," he said. "Who's the big gent with them?"

I'm sure my irritation showed. "Winthrop Hart. He's with the Hart and Watson Gallery and Rare Bookstore. We're going to show him our Beaneaters."

Tim stuck a clay pipe into his mouth and chewed on it as he stared at Hart. "Well, me darlin'," he said. "You might be showing off more than the Beaneaters, I'm thinking."

That was the last thing I wanted to hear. Tim punched me playfully on the arm and gestured toward the cramped section that served as a press box. "I've got to get back to me perch. Talk later?"

I nodded and hustled toward my guests.

Hart shook my hand in his large paw. "This is wonderful," he told me. "We play base ball in Montana, but we're rank amateurs. I've never seen professionals play." He glanced at the Beaneaters who were practicing in the infield. "Their uniforms are a wonder." The Bostons were sporting white pants and blouses and caps. They wore crimson stockings and a crimson Old English B on their breasts and caps. Today their white uniforms were freshly laundered and seemed incredibly bright in the sun. "Who's the enemy today?" Hart asked, surveying the field.

"Pop Anson's Chicago Colts," I told him. "They're in town for four games." The Colts had already taken batting practice and were lounging around their bench or warming up in front of it, waiting for the bell to start the game. They wore gray uniforms and caps, with black letters spelling out Chicago on their chests.

"Who're their best players?" Hart wanted to know as he craned his neck to take in the field.

"Watch Bill Lange in center field. He can run like a deer. And Billy Dahlen at shortstop. Anson at first base is still a wonder to watch, but he's getting long in the tooth. At the moment the Chicagos are in sixth place."

"And how are the Bostons doing?" he pressed.

"They're neck-in-neck with the leaders," I told him. "Nichols beat Cleveland yesterday, 6-2 to keep Boston in a virtual tie with Baltimore, ahead of New York and Cincinnati."

"Please," Claire urged. "Let's sit down."

There were already four or five thousand cranks in the Grounds by this time. Our seats were in the pavilion shade, a dozen rows up from the field. It was blistering even in the shade. Claire sat next to me, Hart next to her, then Cait and Sean.

The game started slowly for fans that like fireworks. Buttons Briggs for the Colts and Fred Klobedanz for the Beaneaters mowed down batters in the early innings. The five of us were content to watch the game, occasionally commenting on a play. In the fifth inning, Claire, dabbing at her brow with her hankie, asked Hart if Montana had heat like Boston's. Apparently, she'd forgotten that we'd discussed weather at the gallery.

Hart flapped his hat in front of his face. "Oh, yes. Even in the mountains around Missoula it gets hot. We have summers where you'd think the land is going to burn up. It's not this wet heat, though," he said, tugging at his collar. "Thank goodness for that."

Sean leaned forward and half-shouted across to me. "Klobedanz's curves are breaking a mile today." By now, however, the women had lost interest in the succession of strikeouts, groundouts, and fly balls. Before I could respond to Sean's opening, the subject had switched again to Montana.

"Are your winters mild, then?" Cait asked.

"Hardly mild, Ma'am," Hart told her. "We have lots of snow and when the wind blows, as it usually does, the drifts pile high. Why, one time I saw a hat lying on the snow. When I picked it up I discovered a man's head beneath it. 'We'll have you out of the drift in no time atall, podnah,' I told the buried man. 'And will you get the horse I'm riding out, too?' the man asked."

The girls giggled. Sean rolled his eyes and blew an imaginary smoke ring.

"Are you a rancher, then, Mr. Hart?" Claire inquired.

Hart cupped her hand with his own. "Please. Call me Win. But, yes, I'm a rancher of sorts."

"I thought you were an art collector," piped up Cait.

41

"Actually, I'm both," Hart told her. "I have a small gallery in Missoula and acreage north of there, near Ronan."

"A large ranch?" Sean asked, his tone indicating that he hoped it wasn't.

"Nah," Hart said, waving his hand as if to brush away the idea. "Less than seven thousand acres."

"Oh," Sean said weakly.

The women were looking at each other, eyes bright.

Hart offered a dismissive shrug. "That's not large out our way. Lots of cattlemen have plenty more. You need land if you're going to run cattle in Montana."

"And you're returning soon?" I asked hopefully.

"As soon as I conclude my business here. I have to settle my father's estate. My long-term interest is enlarging both my gallery and my spread. I'm also trying to convince friends that business opportunities abound in Montana." He turned to Claire. "With your experience running a boardinghouse you and Cait could make a fortune there. Lots of young people are casting their lot in the west."

That's all I needed to hear. I quickly tried to change the subject. "Do you also run the rare bookstore attached to the gallery?" I asked.

"A partner oversees that part of the business," he said, without enthusiasm.

Cait wasn't interested in books. "Are all men in Montana cowboys?" she asked.

Sean grimaced and turned his attention to the game. I pretended to concentrate on the game, too. The score was 4-3, Boston, in the seventh inning. Hart began regaling the women with stories of cowboys and Indians and bears and majestic mountains. He told his stories in a deep and warm voice, lacing them with humor and derring-do. He was in the middle of still another tale when Colt Billy Dahlen hit a home run with a runner on. Umpire Thomas Lynch ruled it fair. Shortstop Germany Long and leftfielder Hugh Duffy screamed their displeasure, stomping their feet and flapping their arms. The crowd joined in the jeering.

A large florid-faced fan sitting in front of us, with hands the size of shovel blades, became particularly incensed. "You're blind as a bat, 'n crookeder than a politician!" he screamed. "Ya couldn't see shit on your shoe!"

I leaned forward to tap the man on the shoulder to remind him to watch his language, that there were women present, but Hart beat me to it. He grasped the man's shoulder. "Easy, podnah. Tone down yore words," he growled.

The man spun toward Hart and shucked off his grip. "Bugger off," he snarled. His hands weren't the only part of him broad and coarse. His neck seemed as thick as my waist, his forehead wide and flat as a bull's. I've seen more refined gents flailing away in bareknuckled brawls in North End dives.

Hart seemed unintimidated by the man's size or bluster. "You'll watch your mouth, mister," he spat.

"And you'll shit ballbearings," the man growled. His companions snorted in amusement at his wit.

Hart reestablished his grip on the man and snapped him around. I eased in front of Claire. I could see Hart's knuckles were white from effort.

The man looked into Hart's eyes, then shot a glance at me. He was impressed with one of us and broke eye contact. "The ball was foul," he muttered.

"I thought it was fair, old fellow. Clearly fair," Hart responded amiably, clapping the man's shoulder like a long-time chum. The man turned back to the game, hunched and silent, his coat stretched to the breaking point across his broad shoulders. Claire and Cait exchange glances that I couldn't read.

Boston scored in the ninth and at the end of nine innings the game was deadlocked at seven. Both teams scored in the tenth inning and the tie still held at the end of the eleventh inning when umpire Thomas Lynch called the game because of darkness. At that point, Hart was in the midst of a yarn about two Indians and a grizzly cub. Claire and Cait seemed to resent the umpire's efforts to interrupt his story.

As we watched the players scoop up their equipment and trudge off the darkened field, Hart stood and stretched. "Well, you win some and you lose some, and some you tie," he said.

Hart's comments made me think of Arthur Soden. Maybe Soden was right that life was a ledger. Debits, credits, and sums. Black ink and red ink. My debits for the past few days were obvious: I'd lost my job and my niche in base ball. In addition, I'd met a handsome Montanan who'd shown great interest in Claire, and she in him. Credits? I'd come to see more clearly how much Claire meant to me. I wasn't sure in which column to record my introduction to Remington's genius, my wager with Soden, or my running across the young lady at the gallery who couldn't take her eyes off me.

Most of these last developments, like my decision to keep my friends in the dark about my unemployment, couldn't be ciphered yet. Whether Soden was right or wrong, to me the whole equation seemed less an account book than the Rosetta Stone. That is, it was notations, characters, and numbers as yet a mystery.

9

By the time we departed the Grounds the sun had dropped below the skyline. The streets were a maze of purple shadows creeping across the pavement like kelp in the sea. In high dudgeon at the women's seeming preoccupation with Hart, Sean and I made craven excuses and turned the responsibility for accompanying the women to the boardinghouse over to him. Our actions were childish and our excuses were spurious. At the moment, however, I didn't give a fig. As an irascible uncle once told me, knowing you shouldn't break wind in public isn't always enough to diminish the relief and satisfaction of doing it.

After we'd strolled a block, Sean groused, "This wee bogtrotter is going over to McGreevey's for some serious drinking. Coming, laddybuck?"

"I'll join you shortly," I told him. "I've got to see Mr. Soden."

His brow furrowed. "Why'n earth for, this time of night?"

I suppose I could have confessed that Soden had canned me. It was as good a time as any. For reasons not clear to me, I didn't want to. Not yet. Perhaps when I had a better idea of my future. Instead, I told him about how, as a favor to Soden, I was going to look into the attack upon him, Jimmy Collins, and Amos Porch.

Sean bristled. "Oh, by jaysus, you'll do it for that skinflint, but not for me?"

Stepping back involuntarily, I said, "Actually, Soden bet me I couldn't solve it," I confessed. "That changed my mind. Sean, I—"

He cut me off. "What makes you think you can find out who killed Shady 'n beat the crap outta Jimmy and me?" he spat. "Lieutenant O'Dwyer and his finest don't seem to be making much progress."

I conceded his point with a nod. "I'm not really looking for who attacked you as much as I've agreed to try to find out where they fenced what they stole. In particular, Jimmy's gold watch, the one his Buffalo fans gave him."

Disappointment washed across this face. "How about *my* sketchbook and watch?" he whined. "You going to look for them? My watch ain't as fancy as Jimmy's, but me da' gave it to me. And my sketches are worth money to the *Globe*."

I held up my hands to calm him. "I'll reclaim as many of the items as I can."

He waved me off in disgust and, spewing profanities, headed for McGreevey's.

I was still in a foul mood when I reached Soden's office. I paused at his doorway and peered in. I wasn't the only unhappy chap it seems. Unaware of me, Soden sat at his desk glumly fingering piles of coin stacked before him. A formidable gray ledger with green leather corners lay open to his left. He'd removed his coat and unbuttoned his vest. He idly fluttered his fingers on the ledger and chewed nervously on an unlit stogie. I was tempted to ask him if he was a dime short, but thought better of it.

When I stepped into the room he looked up and glowered. "Forget something?"

I nodded. "I forgot to discuss a park pass with you. If I'm to have any chance of running down whoever took Collins' watch, I need access to Collins."

His eyes narrowed to slits. "You want me to let you take up a paying customer's seat? And make it easy for you to win the bet?"

"It's only fair that I be able to talk to Collins when I need to."

Soden spun quickly in his chair. For just a moment I glimpsed the young, quick Soden who'd been a fleet amateur centerfielder with skills good enough to occasionally play against professionals, and who'd been invited to accompany the Boston league team to England in 1874. "Well, Mr. Beaman," he said. "A bet's a bet. It's a test of wits and intelligence, as well as luck." He hunched forward. "No free access, either before or after games. See Collins outside the Grounds, if you must." He held his hands out to the sides, palms up, and canted his head. End of discussion.

"This hasn't been one of my better days," I muttered.

He snorted. "Well, if it's any consolation, it hasn't been one of my better ones either."

I wasn't sure what he meant by that. I doubted it was a reference to his having fired me or having denied me free access to the Grounds. I assumed he was alluding to the fact that Baltimore had licked St. Louis today and his nine had not beaten Anson's Colts. "A tie isn't fatal," I told him, letting my annoyance show. "I expected to find you cheering that you're still just a few percentage points from first."

He chewed more vigorously on his unlit and now soggy cigar. "I *am* generally pleased with the team's play. The team hasn't let Porch's death derail it. Nor has Collins let the incident hurt his play. We're hitting well and we're playing good defense."

"Well, then?"

"It has nothing to do with the game today," he growled. He scratched a match on the sole of his shoe and lit his cigar, puffing heavily and belching a cloud of blue smoke above the desk. He pointed at a chair, motioning for me to sit down. "Someone filched the Bradford Manuscript."

"Sir?"

He looked at me, made a face, and shrugged. "Someone at the ceremony lifted the damn thing. After all the hoopla and speeches, the manuscript wasn't there." He made a gesture with his hands, as if turning a bird loose into the air. "Gone. Poof."

"Oh, come now," I groaned, my moodiness over Hart's presence and Soden's niggardly behavior easing. "Just how valuable was this old book?"

Soden scooted up to the table and folded his hands in front of him. He made a steeple with his fingers. "I didn't know how valuable until today. Apparently, it's one of the Commonwealth's real treasures." He cocked his head toward me. "Know anything about it?"

I confessed I knew almost nothing, although I vaguely remembered a Harvard history professor alluding to it in a class where I found it possible to doze only fitfully.

Soden meticulously gathered the bags of coin, tied them tight, and began stuffing them into a canvas bag. "As I understand it," he said, "William Bradford, the governor of the Plymouth Colony in the seventeenth century, wrote a history of the Pilgrims' first years, calling it "Of Plymouth Plantation." It was never published, but it circulated among learned men, and one writer used it to publish his own history of New England."

I couldn't hide my surprise. "They just passed it around?" I said.

He shrugged. "Seems so. For more than a hundred years it circulated among scholars until it finally disappeared during the American Revolution. It stayed *lost* until fifty years ago or so, when an English bishop quoted from it."

I was struggling to follow his story. "The manuscript ended up in England?"

He took another drag of his cigar and blew a smoke ring.

"Mmm. Experts think that a British officer stole it during the American Revolution and took it to England. After the bishop revealed that the manuscript was there, the Massachusetts Historical Society made an appeal during our Civil War to have it returned."

"That was nearly forty years ago! Why wasn't it returned then?"

He chewed on his cigar. "Don't know. But it wasn't until the politicos got involved that anything happened. Our senator got interested and so did the governor. They put pressure on the United States Secretary of State who in turn pressured the American Ambassador to the court of St. James." Soden took a deep inhalation of cigar smoke and blew a perfect smoke ring. He watched his handiwork as it floated toward the ceiling before proceeding. "Under the ambassador's prodding, the British Prime Minister agreed to the return. The ambassador himself delivered the document to state officials today."

"Wasn't it under guard?" I asked.

His face contorted. "Judas Priest! Yes, of course, there were policemen there. Following the public ceremony the document was to be taken under guard to a joint convention of both Houses of the General Court where the mayor, governor, state and national senators, and a covey of other big wigs were to formally accept it."

I was stumped. Frankly, the theft didn't make a lot of sense to me. What possible motive could there be for taking it? Some disgruntled English scholar wanting to keep it in English hands? A perverse collector looking to add to his treasure? Someone hoping to ransom it back to our city fathers? "Who'd want it?" I asked.

"No one seems to have the faintest idea why it was taken," Soden told me. He put the bag of coins and receipts in the office safe and returned to stand by the table.

"I can see why you might be disturbed," I told him, conversationally, "but the truth is this theft is just a pebble in the city's shoe. Boston faces more pressing problems than the theft of an obscure manuscript."

Soden raised his eyebrows a notch and idly thrust his cigar in and out of his mouth, looking at me over his glasses. "Meaning what?"

I shrugged. "The city and the Commonwealth have bigger problems than the loss of a few pages of its history, that's what I mean."

Soden continued to stare at me over the tops of his eyeglasses. "Like what?"

"Well, for heaven's sake," I said, my voice rising, "You said it yourself: Boston is plagued by labor unrest. Working and living conditions for most laborers are abominable. More important things are stolen than old manuscripts."

"For the love of Christ, it's not the manuscript," he fumed, slamming his fist on the desk. "I don't know a damned thing about history or historians. Don't want to. It's pinching the document that boils me. Crime is everywhere. And mounting every day. A man can't walk the damned streets without being robbed—or murdered." His face was livid now. "It's moral decay, is what it is. It's the constant assault upon laws and the lawful by derelicts, anarchists and Socialists. And the damned strikers're in their bloody pockets." He plunged the stub of his cigar into the ashtray and ground away at it, as if gouging the eye of some nefarious Marxist.

I didn't recognize it at the time; in fact, I was amused by his fears, but Soden's outburst was not as far-fetched as one might think. Without my pass, I headed for McGreevey's and a beer with Sean. But my thoughts were on the work I had ahead of me. Damned quick I needed to find employment—or Collins' watch. I hoped my carrot-topped friend could offer help in the latter task. The burdens of finding the Bradford manuscript and saving Boston and the Commonwealth from strikers, anarchists, and the unwashed would have to be shouldered by others.

10

Sean had already quaffed down several beers by the time I arrived at McGreevey's. He was surrounded by fans replaying today's game. Their red faces and shouted exchanges made clear they had imbibed a good deal more than Sean had. You'd have thought the Beaneaters had lost to Anson's men rather than tied them. Each fan had his own explanation for Boston's inability to put away the Colts, and vied among themselves to see who could bellow his opinion more forcefully and profanely. Proprietor McGreevey took a back seat to no one in these manic exchanges, railing about Klobedanz.'s persistent wildness. You'd never know that their beloved Boston nine was a mere seven percentage points behind the hard-charging Orioles.

Sean disengaged from the fans when I entered, and found a table at the back of the room for us. He wasn't able to suggest additional places that I should check for stolen items. He was still sulking and preferred to grouse about Hart as a threat to our relationship with the Denihur sisters. We had several more beers and went home. The heat among the drinking fans had abated not one iota when we departed. By the time we got to the boardinghouse, Hart was gone and the women had retired for the evening.

The following day Sean and I joined Arthur Soden, John Haggerty, and Beaneater players at funeral services for Amos Porch. It was a pathetically small gathering. Beyond the players there were maybe a half dozen men gathered around the grave, including Tim Murnane. No family members were present, so far as I could tell. The ceremony was brief and perfunctory. The bareness of the service made the loss of the man even bleaker.

Already dressed in my best suit, I excused myself following the ceremony and headed to the North End to continue my search for Collins' and Sean's stolen items. To be truthful, I combined two goals, contacting every bank and loan office on Washington in search of employment, and pestering any merchant or shop owner who might act as a conduit for "used" or "found" items. Being circumspect and careful not to impugn the motives or exchange habits of any of the merchants or storekeepers did not help me find Collins' watch. Three hours of canvassing brought me neither job offer nor lead on who might have stolen from Jimmy Collins and Sean. More than a little peeved, I headed for the South End Grounds and Jimmy Collins. I had my coin in my hand as I approached the gate. Luckily, John Haggerty spotted me and motioned me to duck under the turnstile bar while Soden was busy arguing with a fan. I still had friends at the Grounds.

Despite perfect weather, the crowd was late arriving. There wasn't a hint of the breeze that most days kept stadium flags flapping and popping. Great belches of white steam from the trains beyond the left field fence rose straight into the cloudless sky; soft, tall pillars supporting no roof. Players from both teams milled about in the sun, warming up for the second game of a four-game series.

Tim Murnane spotted me and moved in my direction. By the time he'd chatted with a dozen friends on his way to me, Beaneater righthander Ted "Parson" Lewis had coaxed two ground balls from Chicago hitters and the game was two outs old. As the Colts' strapping Bill Lange stepped in to hit, his sun-darkened face scowling, Boston's rightfielder made a tent with his hands to shade his eyes. The players on the right side of the infield pulled their caps low against the bright sun and high sky.

"What's up, darlin'?" Tim asked. "I assume you haven't yet won your bet with Soden."

I rolled my eyes heavenward. "Hardly."

"How much is it?"

"A hundred dollars."

"Oh, good luck with that," Tim barked. "Soden'd give up his firstborn before he'd hand over one hundred dollars."

"Well, I'm determined to win. Can you help? You've got connections."

At that point, Sean, who had been over near the Chicago bench sketching some of the Colt players, joined us. Tim greeted him by patting him on the shoulder but continued to look at me. "That was yesterday, darlin'," he told me. "I've been assigned to write a special column. It's going to take all my time. Someone stole the Bradford manuscript during the festivities to celebrate its return to Massachusetts."

Before either Sean or I could respond, the crowd let out a roar and we all looked up. Everett had popped one of Lewis' pitches to Tenny who made a sprawling grab.

"What theft?" asked Sean, getting back to our conversation. "Sure 'n I never read about no theft."

"It wasn't in the comic strips," Tim snorted good-naturedly.

"I don't just read the comics," Sean protested, his voice rising.

Sean had changed clothes since the funeral. I reached out and fingered his green plaid trousers, and winced. "It's clear you read the clothing advertisements, too."

Tim eyed Sean's trousers and matching jacket critically, then scowled at Sean.

"Apparently you don't read the right ones. You look like an opening act at the Bijou."

"By all the saints in the *Ould Saud*, if you two aren't kettles calling the pot black!" Sean growled in mock fury. "You're real fashion plates yourselves, you are. You dress like sidemen for Scott Joplin. All you need is a trombone."

The sparse crowd groaned as Colt pitcher Danny Friend fanned Lowe on a pitch in the dirt.

Tim held up his hands in surrender. "Enough," he said. "Let's watch the game. Friend looks like he's on his game today."

Sean wasn't interested in Boston's futility against Friend's slow curves. He tapped Tim on the knee with a balled fist. "First, Mr. Murnane, what about the theft?"

"Someone stole an important manuscript history of early Plymouth," Tim explained. "One that the British were returning to Massachusetts."

"And how did this prize end up in England?" Sean wanted to know.

Tim exhaled loudly in exasperation. "It's a long, weary story, Sean darlin'."

"The manuscript is pretty valuable, is it?" Sean asked.

"Quite valuable; one of a kind—and important to the city and to the state."

Sean's brow furrowed. "And what would a thief do with this fine book?"

It was the question I'd posed to Soden without getting a convincing response. "I don't know," I confessed. "Keep it. Sell it to a collector maybe. Perhaps ransom it." At that moment, I noticed Collins picking up a bat and moving toward home plate. I pointed at the third baseman. "Got any suggestions for where I should start in looking for Collins' watch?" I asked Tim.

Tim glanced toward Collins and wrinkled his nose as if he smelled something unpleasant. "This whole business with Sean and Jimmy and Shady Porch doesn't make sense to me. I'm not sure I can help you even if I could find the time. I've already spent hours around the piers trying to get a lead on who attacked them. No one seems to know anyone who matches the descriptions our friend here and the newspaper lad gave the police. I spent a fortune on drinks, I did, and got nowhere."

People around us cheered derisively as Collins managed to put his bat on a tantalyzing Friend curve, bouncing the ball weakly back to Friend who snatched the ball and threw Collins out. One fan beat a funeral lament on his drum.

"Maybe it's the labor agitators in town," Sean offered, ignoring the game. "Lots of 'em are in Boston at the moment, helping the strikers 'n all."

Following Sean's thought process was sometimes like tracking a rabid dog. "Why would the labor types roust the three of you?" I asked. "Working men look upon ball players as their own. Why should they kill Shady and beat up Collins, not to mention you, another working stiff?"

With more force than usual, Sean jabbed me with his finger. "Well, why did they roust the photographers at the rally? Some of 'em are nasty sunuvabitches, that's why."

Had I missed something? "What rally? And what were you doing at a rally?"

"The front page editor asked me to substitute for a sketch artist who was ill."

"And sketch *what*?"

"The labor rally. Emma Goldman and others."

I felt my heart pounding. Emma Goldman! Now it was my turn to stab Sean with a stiff finger. "That's the woman at the gallery! I *knew* that I recognized her. Didn't you see her, with the young woman and the older fellow at the Remington exhibit?"

Sean growled, "I didn't pay any attention. Kept my eyes on Cait and that masher, Hart, sniffing about her like a mutt in heat."

Tim made an unpleasant sound to indicate his disinterest in what happened at the gallery. He eyed Sean skeptically. "You're telling us that the mugs roughed up photographers taking pictures of Emma Goldman? *Why,* for heaven's sake? Everyone knows she's in Boston—and right in the middle of things. She doesn't hide that. And there are lots of photos of her taken in Europe and the states both, darlin'."

"No, no," Sean protested. "They didn't care about Miss Goldman. They beat up photographers when they tried to take pictures of her cronies and advisors."

This was getting curiouser and curiouser. "Did you know those hanging around Miss Goldman?" I asked.

At that moment, the Colts' Jimmy Ryan singled through the infield. The crowd stirred restlessly, urging Lewis to bear down. The Boston nine couldn't afford to drop further behind the Orioles in the tight National League race. The crowd's frantic imploring made no impression on Sean. "Nope. I didn't know any of them," he said.

"No one?" I pressed.

"There was a bunch of 'em, heads together, whispering. I sketched the whole lot of 'em as background material. Caught details on a few of 'em."

My heart thumped in my chest. "You sketched the *same* people photographers got mauled trying to snap?"

Sean looked at us, his smile slowly widening and his eyebrows sliding up his forehead. "Yeah, I did. Holy Mother! How about that? You thinking what I'm thinking?"

Interesting speculation: that people in Goldman's entourage had assaulted Sean in order to get his sketchbook because he had drawn individuals craving anonymity. And that the death of Shady Porch and the beating of Jimmy Collins resulted from the thugs' desperation to prevent Sean's drawings from appearing in the *Globe*. Unlikely, I thought, but perhaps worth a look. Maybe they were planning more violent union tactics. But one had to wonder, too, if there was a connection between men who wanted their anonymity guaranteed and the theft of the Bradford manuscript. A lot had transpired this week.

The crowd around us exploded as Mal Kittridge ripped a shot to Collins' left and almost past him. Collins stabbed the ball, pivoted completely and threw a dart to Bobby Lowe at second. Lowe caught it and, like a ballerina, twisted to dodge Jimmy Ryan coming in, and flipped a throw to Tenney at first for the double play to end the inning. No other third sacker in the league could have made that play. Fans threw coins onto the field, screaming their appreciation of the Beaneaters' defense. Two of them down the third base line danced a jig.

Shaking his head in amazement at Collins' grand play, Tim sat and pulled a small appointment book from his coat. He rifled through its pages, theatrically and repeatedly wetting his finger to do so. He finally found what he was looking for. "Ah, here it is, lads," he said. "Miss Goldman is speaking at the Workingmen's Hall tomorrow night."

I smiled at Sean, "I'm thinking you and I ought to attend her lecture," I told him. "And you ought to take a sketchpad. You just might meet some old friends. And I just might be able to dip my hand into Soden's pocket."

"Well, darlin's," mused Tim, "Though I can ill afford the time, I'm going with you. Emma Goldman always puts on a show. And maybe her friends will, too."

11

We agreed to meet at the Workingmen's Hall on Massachusetts the following night. In the meantime, I had to talk to Collins, get my money's worth, even if I hadn't coughed up the fifty cents for the game. Then, speaking of coin, I had to find work. After all, it had been three days since Soden canned me. My first chance to meet with Collins came in the eighth inning. Boston was up 7-4 and Kid Nichols had come in as a change pitcher for Lewis. I motioned Collins over to the railing.

"Heard any news from the police?" I asked him.

He wedged his glove into his back pocket. "Nothing. Why?"

"I'm looking into the incident. Mind answering a few questions?"

Puzzlement clouded his handsome face. "The word is Soden tossed you."

"He did. I'm doing this on my own."

"Why?"

I could have told him the whole story. About my bet with Soden. About my need for money. About my desire to end Soden's smugness. About my determination to make Soden see the stupidity of his decision to terminate me. About my desperation to remain with the Beaneater organization. Instead, I merely said, "It's a personal thing, Jimmy. How about those questions?"

His eyes swung to the grandstand where Soden sat. "I dunno. Mr. Soden told me to let the police do their work, not to drag others into this."

"He mention my name?"

A sheepish grin crept across his face. "He might have."

That ended my cupidity. "Come on, Jimmy, what Soden didn't tell you is that he has a bet with me that I can't find your watch. He's a lot more interested in winning the bet than helping you find your timepiece. You know Soden. And you know it was me, not Soden, responsible for finding out who messed up Germany Long last month."

Collins glanced up as Chick Stahl punched one over third into left field. "I've got to get ready. I follow Duffy who's up now." He selected a bat and took a few practice swings as Duffy stepped in to face Friend. Duffy grounded out on the first pitch, moving Stahl to second, and Collins moved to the plate.

I couldn't resume my conversation with him until after the inning. He didn't come to me; I had to wave him over. "You know I was the bird dog that flushed out Long's assailant," I reminded him.

His eyes again flicked toward Soden. "Look, Will, you know all us players appreciated you finding the guy who roughed up Germany but, hey, I'm in my first full year with this club. I can't afford to rile Mr. Soden. Make this quick. What do you want?"

I didn't bother to take out my notebook. "Okay. What did you do before you met Sean at the restaurant the night you were mugged?"

He leaned against the wall separating the field from the seats, closing the distance between us so he could speak more quietly. "Nothing, really. After the game, my wife and I spent the early evening on Washington, in the department stores. We met Shady. She took a hack home when I went to meet Sean. Sean needed to make some sketches of me for Tim's Sunday column. Shady was alone, so I asked him to come along."

"Who chose the restaurant?"

"Sean. He had another assignment on Hanover. It worked out for both of us."

"Notice anyone paying particular attention to you, either in the restaurant or before you got there?"

"No."

"What about a big bloke? Huge hands. Has the look of a pugilist."

He shook his head slowly, while peering toward Soden. "Look, I've got to go."

I followed his gaze. Soden had left his seat and was moving toward us. "Just a few more questions, Jimmy. No incidents in the restaurant? Or in the pub later?"

He edged away. "The usual. People came up to talk, shake hands, buy us drinks. All very congenial, like I told Detective O'Dwyer."

"No one seemed overly interested in the money you were carrying?"

"Hell, no one saw my cash. Everyone was trying to buy our dinner and drinks."

"Trying to get you drunk?"

"Nah. Nothing like that."

"You and Shady were dressed more expensively than Sean was. Clearly you two had more money than he did. Hell, Sean's a working stiff; one glance tells you that—and yet Sean seemed to be the primary target."

A frown creased his face. "I know that. I've got to go."

Soden was now level with us and approaching fast. "Did any of the attackers say anything that might suggest their motives?" I asked Collins.

Collins rolled his eyes. "I've gone over and over this. With O'Dwyer. With a half dozen detectives. I haven't a clue why they killed Shady or took Sean's sketchbook or copped my watch." He glanced toward the field. "I've got to go."

I held him. "Got any ideas why they took Shady's shoes and socks, and yours?"

He gave me a pained expression. "I'm sorry. I told the police and you all I know. I just want the police to find out who killed Shady, and get my watch back." He stepped back. "I'm in the middle of a pennant race. I've got to concentrate on playing ball and helping my teamates, not on a lost watch." He jogged away.

It wasn't fifty cents worth. But, then, I hadn't paid fifty cents, had I? Not wanting to verbally fence with Soden who was now about sixty feet away and closing, I turned and started up the aisle. And ran smack into Winthrop Hart.

12

Hart grabbed me, his strong hands squeezing my biceps. "Whoa there, Podnah! Don't stampede us now."

"Sorry," I said. "I wasn't watching where I was going." I glanced toward Soden who had abruptly reversed his course and was returning to his seat, glaring at me over his shoulder the whole time. I turned back to Hart. "Becoming a fan, are you?"

He beamed and spread his arms to take in the ballpark. "Yes, sir. I am." His eyes twinkled. "Did you see that double play Collins started? The man's as quick as a cat."

I couldn't help but nod my agreement. But the Montanan was the last man I wanted to talk to at the moment. He was like a boil on your ass. You know it's there. You understand you have to deal with it at some point. Later is better. I started to mumble some banality and leave Hart to the game when I noticed a striking female behind him making no attempt to pass us or to proceed to her seat. In fact, she was resting a hand on Hart's shoulder. She had the longest, whitest, most graceful neck I'd ever seen on a woman. My eyebrows soared in spite of myself.

Hart noticed my reaction. "Ah, excuse me," he said, turning to the woman and sliding his hand familiarly down her arm. "Will, this is Ella, my . . .uh, cousin. Ella, this is Will Beaman. He works for the Bostons." His hand remained on her arm. Very proprietary, I thought.

Now it was her eyebrows that shot up, and her cheeks colored. I couldn't tell whether her reaction stemmed from her pleasure in meeting me, or in response to Hart's designation of her as his cousin. Whichever, her expression seemed a mix of pleasure and amusement. I reached out to grasp her hand, not bothering to correct Hart about my status with the Beaneaters. Or admit this was my fourth day of unemployment. When I released my grip, she clung to my hand a second or two longer.

"Are you a fan of our Beaneaters?" I inquired.

She smiled enigmatically. "Not really. But the players are truly skilled."

I picked up on her remark about the players. "You have a favorite player, do you?" It was an obviously banal question, designed merely to keep the conversation going until I could come up with something more worthy. Still, she weighed my question as if I'd ask her the meaning of life. On the other hand, my question clearly amused Hart as he stood by, patiently awaiting her answer.

Finally, she clasped her hands under her chin, eyes bright. Then she pointed to Chick Stahl in right field. "Well, that player out there is awfully handsome."

Hart joined me in laughing at her yardstick for rating ball players. I chuckled despite my suspicion that she was having us on, my rising sense that, just maybe, the amusement and diversion at the moment was not limited to the base ball diamond. But, unable to put my finger on just what stirred my suspicions, I tried to keep the conversation polite and superficial. For the life of me, however, I couldn't think of any intelligent observations or questions to facilitate the conversation. In addition to her cryptic remark and the undercurrent of tongue-in-cheek kidding, her neck mesmerized me. It was absolutely stunning, long, soft, blemish-free, almost translucent. When she surveyed the stands her neck moved with the grace of a swan. As the sun crept under the brim of her wide hat and shown directly on her throat, it stirred memories of the first time I'd seen a woman's naked breast. A quick early glance told me she also was endowed with a tiny waist, but to confirm that my eyes would have to pass over her impressive bosom. To do that while contemplating *bon mots* was beyond my abilities at the moment.

I was curious about this beautiful woman, but this wasn't time to indulge my curiosity. I decided to excuse myself. Standing around talking to Winthrop Hart and his, uh, cousin didn't pay my bills. "Enjoy the game," I said, "It was great seeing you again, Mr. Hart. And a pleasure meeting you, Miss—?

She told me her name but fans around us groaned so loudly when Bobby Lowe lost a high infield pop fly in the sun and let it fall safely that I didn't hear it. Before I could ask her to repeat it, Hart clasped my hand enthusiastically. "Please. Call me Win."

I nodded lamely, and decided to let the issue of Ella's name pass. "Fine, Win it is." I said, and moved toward the gate.

"Will."

Hart had followed me. He quickly closed the distance between us and laid a hand on my shoulder. "Sorry. I know this isn't the time or place, but I need to talk to you. Our meeting here was not completely unpremeditated."

I shot a look at Cousin Ella who was now sitting in the first row and watching Boston catcher Marty Bergen throw a runner out at second on an attempted steal to at least temporarily preserve Boston's 7-4 lead. I would have preferred to study her, but Hart was standing directly in front of me. "What is it?" I asked.

"Claire tells me you're a detective. That you found out who assaulted Boston's shortstop last month."

"With all due respect to Claire, I wouldn't call myself a detective," I told him. "I guess I'm an amateur sleuth. I do enjoy puzzling out human activities. Why do you ask?"

He glanced around, then pulled me into an empty seat and slumped beside me. "For a week or so the gallery has been visited by suspicious patrons."

"Suspicious?"

"Patrons who know nothing about art. People who act like they've never been in a gallery before. People who clearly aren't buyers."

This was getting close to home. It sounded as if he were describing me that day at the gallery. "Could it be that Remington attracts a different audience than you're accustomed to?" I asked. "That those drawn to his art aren't the patrons of more conventional art or artists? Perhaps a less polished audience? Like *me*?"

He winced and dropped his eyes. "No. No. I didn't mean you. I'm worried the gallery is being cased. That someone is scheming to steal some of Remington's works. I don't know. It's just a feeling I have. I know art and I know art patrons." He clenched his fists. "We've had an increase in interest in our rare book store as well. And then there was last night's incident." He chewed on the inside of his cheek. "A prowler was reported in the alley behind the gallery and bookstore. When he was confronted by a patrolman he fled."

"Is your business the only one to back up to the alley? Maybe the prowler was interested in another store. Or was simply a drunk."

Hart idly pinched his upper lip. "Perhaps, but this business about the Bradford manuscript has me edgy. If a manuscript is a target, so might be a Remington painting or a rare book."

His suspicions seemed pretty vague and I told him so.

He bobbed his head at my comment. "Maybe. But I'd like you to look into it. I'd pay whatever you think fair."

It was a tempting offer. God knows, I needed the money. But Hart's worries seemed far-fetched. I couldn't imagine someone scheming to steal an essentially unknown artist's work. And what did the work of Remington have to do with the theft of the Bradford manuscript? Would a person interested in one also be interested in the other? I didn't think so. "Win, you'd be better off contacting a licensed investigator," I told him. "Someone with more experience than I have. There are several in the city. I don't know a thing about art or who purchases it. And even less about rare books."

He stood up, his disappointment obvious. "You're positive?"

"Yes. I know nothing of the world of book and art collectors. I know even less about fencing such items."

He shrugged in resignation and shook my hand. "If that's your preference. Give my best to Sean."

I assured him I would, stood, stepped into the aisle, and started up the steps.

"Will?" It was Hart again.

I whirled peevishly to face him. He was looking sheepish and holding his arms wide, palms up. "Are you engaged to Claire?" He hunched his shoulders, his arms still wide, as if to say, 'I had to ask.'

I instinctively spread my feet, balanced myself. "No."

"You haven't discussed marriage with her?"

I moved down the aisle toward him, uncomfortable with this conversation. "No."

"I suppose I have no right to ask, but are you considering it?"

My relationship with Claire was not going to be the subject of public discourse. It was not going to be the topic of conversation between Hart and me before it was between Claire and me. "You're correct, Mr. Hart, it is not your right."

"Sorry," he said, shuffling his feet. "Westerners tend to be blunt, I'm afraid."

I headed for the gate, leaving him standing there. I didn't know what about the past half hour troubled me more: Soden's order to Collins not to aid me, Collins' inability or unwillingness to shed light on his mugging, Winthrop Hart's "cousin," Hart's impertinence, or the fact that I'd wasted half a day. All I know is my mood was fouler than a one-armed sailor in a rowboat.

13

Thursday morning I returned to the docks, this time with Sean. Despite its proximity to the sea, the pier area sweltered. The air hung thick and heavy. With no breeze to soften the heat or reduce the humidity, workers moved as if in molasses, their shirts dark with sweat, their flesh glistening. Their cursing could be heard above the creaking of hoists, the thump of crates dumped onto wharves, and the squeal and rumbling of wagon wheels on planking.

Sean had skipped a day of bicycle practice to join me in the further hunt for his attackers, arguing that he had greater familiarity with the waterfront than I had. He arrived dressed more like a roughneck than a professional bike racer and illustrator for the *Globe*. And he'd urged me to wear work trousers and suspenders and to leave my good collar, tie, and coat at the boardinghouse. He insisted that our casual attire would make talking with stevedores and teamsters easier. Before we began to mingle with the drayman and longshoremen he scuffed my shoes. "Keep those lily-white hands in your pockets, boyo," he growled, "and, jaysus, forget all them long Harvard words."

We sauntered among the workers and piles of cargo for ten minutes before Sean stopped. "Whoa, we may have lucked out," he whispered to me. He tugged me toward a short, well-muscled man in a sopping gray undershirt and bowler hat. Though he looked to be sixty years old, he was effortlessly hefting sacks of rice that would have made men half his age groan. He hadn't shaved for several days.

"Tony," Sean greeted him enthusiastically, "How are ya?"

Having just hoisted an eighty-pound bag of rice onto his shoulder, the man squinted at Sean for a long moment. "Well, hell, it's been a long while, Red," he finally said, offering a nearly toothless smile.

Sean nodded. "Been spending most of my time at the Grounds or at the tracks."

The old man hunched his shoulders and shifted the weight of the rice. "I see your name in the papers ever' onct inna while in the racing stories. Yore doon all right, Red. Winning all those race like you done. And so are those Beaneaters of yores. You watch, they're gonna whip them Baltimores, sure. McGraw and them arrogant Baltimore bastards are gonna scream like stuck pigs. I see w'ar Collins made a cherry double play yestiddy." He suddenly stopped. "What're ya doin' down here?" he asked.

Sean gazed around. "Business, Tony."

Tony bent his knees, straightened up suddenly and lifted the bag of rice from one shoulder to the other. "Wha' kinda business, Red?"

Sean reached out and touched Tony's arm. "You know most of the blokes who load and unload the ships and move the stuff outta here, don't you?"

The man stood there in the heat with the bag of rice on his shoulder as if it was nothing more than a pillow, his sweat plopping on the planks at his feet. "Sure," he said.

Sean leaned in toward Tony. "Know anyone who does *business* after hours?"

The man wiped at the sweat in his eyes with a thumb and squinted at Sean for a long while. "Like helping a gent put a wager or two down? That kin' o' business?" he asked.

Sean seemed to think about that for awhile. "Nah, Tony. I'm thinking of someone who might facilitate the, uh, *exchange* of goods."

A blocky man with a cigar stuffed in his face, pushing two workers before him, strode by us, glancing our way. "Move your ass, Tony, this ain't high tea," he snarled.

"Inna minnit," Tony said conversationally, no hint of anger in his voice at being prodded by his boss. He turned back to Sean, squinting even more furiously. "Someone who might help get rid of things you don't want, like?"

Sean nodded. "Yeah, or someone who knows someone who collects or buys items others have, say, *found*."

Tony mimicked Sean's nod. Then, for the first time, he swung to me and stared hard, as if he'd only then noticed me. He gaped at my shoes, inventoried my clothes and my size, and studied my hat. He could have been a coroner casually satisfying his curiosity about a cadaver before plunging in his scalpel. He finally shook his head. "Nah, I don't know no one like that," he said as he began to inch away from us.

Sean's face crinkled like an old boot. "He noticed your haircut, Will," he whispered. "Probably thinks you're a city detective." He sighed and bit his lip, then yelled after Tony. "Know a big guy? A giant? Hangs around with the union guys?"

Tony's eyes now frantically panned the pier. "Nope," he shouted back.

Sean arched his eyebrows. "Ah, come on, Tony. Hard to miss a guy like that."

Tony shuffled back toward us. "You're a good kid, Red. Me 'n your da' were chums. But answering questions like you're asking has gotten a couple o' stevedores beaten up purty good." His head was still on a swivel, his eyes nervous.

"By a big guy?" Sean pressed.

Tony waggled his head. "Sure looked like it from the results. No one's talking. I love ya, Red, but you stay the hell away from me." He glanced at me. "Your big friend, too."

Our exchange with Tony, with a few inconsequential variations but the same sad results, was repeated a dozen times in the next two hours. We visited nearby pubs and downed a succession of pints while fishing for contacts. The air in the saloons was even hotter and thicker than outside, and it seemed that we sweated out our beers as fast as we drank them. One burly drayman stood leaning back, a battered growler of beer held above his head, the suds pouring down his throat and over his chin. He listened patiently to our description of the huge, hairy, and ham-fisted assailant, then asked what two strangers like us wanted with his wife's mother.

Dispirited, we headed for the boardinghouse for grub and a soak. And to get ready for Emma Goldman's lecture at The Workingmen's Education Club.

14

The Workingmen's Education Club was packed—and sweltering. Sean, Tim, and I had to take spots against the wall with perhaps fifty others. Sean wore his old bicycling sweater under his coat. Tim and I left our collars and cravats at home and wore open vests and rumpled, unboiled shirts. The three of us had also donned golf-style caps favored by workingmen. It proved to be a wise move. This was not a meeting of the city's Brahmins. Most were working class, sad-eyed and sunken-mouthed women with stooped shoulders and reddened hands, men with threadbare trousers and scuffed shoes. They squinted as if in a perpetual state of disbelief, mouths grim. German, Yiddish, Italian, and the brogue of the Irish competed in the crowded hall in a low babble.

University students, by contrast fresh-skinned and clear-eyed, mixed in the audience. They were young women eager to hear Goldman's radical views on birth control and free love. Goldman had caused a sensation in New York with her lectures. I'd seen photographs of her in New York newspapers. Reporters and photographers there had covered her lecture series with the intensity of a presidential election.

I had no doubt tonight's audience also held its share of incognito policemen and Pinkertons. They had swarmed to Goldman's Gotham lectures. There were some rough looking blokes scattered about the Workingmen's Education Hall, flattened noses and scarred faces testifying to their familiarity with violence.

Sean also must have been evaluating the gathering. He tilted his head toward me. "Sure 'n I'm a Yankee Doodle cock-a-doo if there ain't going to be trouble tonight."

I nodded in agreement. "Some people hate Miss Goldman. Her support of sexual liberation and social revolution has convinced many she's an enemy of America. She also ridicules conventional marriages."

Tim, who'd been listening in silence, pressed closer. "In New York they treated her as if she were the devil himself." He grinned. "She's like an old train chugging through the countryside; everywhere she goes sparks and fires follow."

Sean pointed to the front door. "Here she comes."

Goldman stepped into the room and scanned the crowd briefly before striding briskly down the center aisle to a table that served as the speaker's dais. A small retinue of spear-holders followed. Two of them, rough-looking chaps with flattened noses, scarred faces, and hands the size of shovel blades joined her at the table. She waited for the others to be seated before she pulled back her own chair and took a seat.

I studied her. Short and soft-looking, she had wavy dark hair parted in the middle and pulled back into a bun. She wore the same shell-rimmed glasses I'd noticed at the Remington exhibit. Her black skirt had a high waist, her white blouse long sleeves and a high-buttoned neck. With her intense eyes and severe mouth she looked like everyone's least favorite school marm.

"Oh, oh, here we go," muttered Tim, and gestured at a photographer setting up a tripod slightly behind Goldman in order to capture her and her audience.

Here we go was right. The photographer was pounced upon and ushered out of the hall faster than an eight-legged dog, kicking and protesting, amid a roar of approval from the crowd, and a smattering of boos. His photographic equipment spilled in the aisle behind him, clattering and thumping in his wake. Without so much as a glance toward the departing photographer and his burly ushers, the mustachioed fellow to Goldman's left rose and shushed the crowd with hand gestures. Much of the audience paid him no heed, but he ignored them, talking over their chatter, introducing himself as a leader of the striking boot and shoe workers. I didn't catch his name. In a sonorous baritone, he read a series of announcements relating to union activities. He presented several local labor organizers.

In anticipation of Goldman's presentation, the crowd finally quieted. The mustachioed gent introduced her without frills, announcing simply, but with a smile, "Here's that New York celebrity anarchist!" It drew a rousing roar of approval and laughter from the audience, easily overwhelming a rippling of hisses and boos.

Goldman wasted no time on niceties, plunging into a high voltage attack upon everyday conditions for working men and women. "There has been a criminal patience by management throughout the country in the face of inadequate wages for workers and dangerous working sites," she cried. "Greed and callousness have marked the path of management. Their cruel and systematic exploitation of those who build the country with the sweat of their brows is worthy of every honest person's contempt."

Her eyes flared, her finger stabbed the air. "There must be solidarity among working people. The strikes of our brothers and sisters protesting the unchristian and unconscionable abuse of their working conditions must become our cause." She pounded on the table. "We must support them with our hearts, our spirits, our minds, and our bodies. And"—she paused dramatically—"we must meet violence with violence."

"Anarchist!" someone shouted. "Revolutionary!"

"Guttersnipe!" stormed another.

"Marxist cow!" shrieked still another.

Hoots of derision cascaded toward Goldman's critics. Scuffles broke out. You could feel the pulse increase in the hall. Instinctively, I widened my stance, planted my feet, pressed my back against the wall, and balled my fists.

Goldman ignored the commotion. "We must free ourselves from the shackles of church and societal repression, then break the chains that bind us in the working place—and in our homes. Like men, working women must have the freedom to—"

"Whore!" blurted someone.

"Freedom to fornicate, you mean!" boomed another, sitting only a few feet from us. "We know all about your *freedom*."

An obese woman lunged to her feet and struck this last heckler with her parasol, swinging it in a long two-handed arc, much like a ball player hitting a ball. He roared an obscenity, then roughly shoved her away and hurled another epithet at Goldman. In a blink, pools of furious activity boiled up, sucking in those of us along the walls. The man who'd hollered the last obscenities at Goldman rocked the man next to him with his fist and flung another spectator aside. The spectator's elbow caught me high on the forehead.

I shouldered him aside, knowing he hadn't meant to strike me, only to find myself struck on the cheek by a fellow in a ragged sailor's jacket. I rolled with the punch and put him on his knees with what my old Harvard mentor would have considered a perfect right cross. A burly pal of the sailor, also in a salt's jacket, lunged at me. Sean intercepted him and shoved him into the man who'd started it all with his catcalls. Before you could say Phineas Taylor Barnum, the whole room was in an uproar.

As if on cue, John Law poured into the hall, truncheons flailing. Aided by beefy associates, probably plainclothes dicks, they went about quelling the rowdiness by beating into submission perpetrators and innocent onlookers alike.

With the wall to my back and wedged at the sides by dozens of coppers and scrappers who crammed the aisle, I had no choice but to defend myself against those intent on clobbering anyone in their vicinity. I landed a pretty good punch to the temple of the taller of the sailors. I was cocking for another punch when I was grabbed and flung against the wall. While a muscular copper pinned me there another thickset officer put his face inches from mine. "Move 'n we'll break your skull," he snarled.

I'm a reasonable man—at times. I decided that this would be one of those times. I was here to locate those who might have assaulted Sean, Shady, and Jimmy. I couldn't do that if I were in the hoosegow.

15

It was the prudent choice, although it took a few minutes for me to fully appreciate it. The policeman who pinned me eased off, then turned to a companion and jerked a thumb at the sailors. "Get them jackie bastards outta here," he snarled. He jabbed a thumb at Sean and me. "Them, too."

At that moment, tousled and sweating, Tim Murnane bulled toward us. He spoke to the cop. "They're okay," he panted. "Just trying to protect themselves."

The copper holding me glanced at Tim, then bobbed his head almost imperceptibly. "Leave 'em be," he growled. We were released immediately. The dozen or so protesters were escorted from the hall. It all took maybe ten minutes. From what I could tell, Goldman had observed the scuffling and fisticuffs more curious than frightened, like someone watching the feeding frenzy of pond fish. Clearly she was a veteran of such pandemonium.

Once order was restored, the audience was smaller. Nonetheless, even after many who'd begun the evening against the wall took the vacant seats, there still were no seats available for the three of us. Sean, Tim, and I resumed our posts against the wall. Goldman continued her speech with the same passion she'd shown prior to the chaos. She was a woman on a mission, unmindful of those impeding her progress. The passionate rhythms of her speech and her deeply-felt anguish at the plight of America's working men and women mesmerized the audience. If Goldman had enemies among her listeners now, they kept silent, probably mindful of the fate of earlier dissenters.

Several times I told myself we were not there to admire Goldman, but I nonetheless found myself sucked into her concerns. As I listened to her, I fingered the swelling on my cheek and tried to ignore the burning lump on my forehead. It was minutes before I pulled my eyes away from her to concentrate on her surrounding cast. After all, they were the ones we suspected of assaulting Sean and Collins—and killing Shady. At that instant, a beefy man with a full beard sitting at the end of the second row leaned forward and gave me an unimpeded view of the young lady next to him.

My pulse quickened. It was the young lady in the gallery with Goldman! I was sure of it! The one who seemed to be looking at me each time I glanced her way. I nudged Sean and indicated the young woman, lifting my eyebrows in question. Sean was testing a tooth with his finger to see how loose it was. He'd been tagged during the fisticuffs. Now, he squinted and stared for a long while at the young woman I'd pointed out. Then shrugged to tell me he didn't know who she was.

Tim's attention was pulled away from Goldman by our antics, and he too studied the young lady. He withdrew from his coat pocket the notebook he always carried, and thumbed through it. He studied his notes before leaning past Sean and showing me a name he'd written: Eve Seilor.

He might just as well have written the name of the princess of Timbuktu. But if Emma Goldman and Eve Seilor were there, I wondered if their companion at the galley also was. I scanned those seated next to Seilor, methodically working my way down the row. That finished, I started on the third row. There, seated directly behind Miss Seilor, sat a gent who looked very much like the fire-plug of a man in the gallery, short, muscular, and mustachioed. Sitting on each side of him, like herculean bookends, were the two mean-looking gents that had led the charge against the photographer. But the man between them who'd caught my attention seemed much older than the gent I'd seen in the gallery. He also wore his hair short, and it was white like his mustache. He wore no glasses. Still, something about the silhouette of his nose and jawline troubled me. I went through my inquiry routine with Sean once more.

Again, he shrugged.

Impersonating a vaudeville mime, I asked Tim who the man was and got the same response as Sean's.

Meanwhile, Goldman ended with a flourish and the audience bounded to its feet to stamp, whistle, shout, and clap its approval. Women waved ribbons and swirled handkerchiefs above their heads. A few began to make their way slowly out of the hall. Most surged forward to speak with Goldman.

I pointed toward the elderly man who'd been sitting behind Eve Seilor and motioned for Sean and Tim to follow me. I wanted a closer look at a man who needed two bodyguards.

16

It took ten minutes before we edged our way through the throng to the white-haired gent who, with his two bodyguards, was trying to ease out the back door. In the shuffle, the three of us had changed places; Tim was now in the lead and Sean pressed up against him. I had fallen back. Tim finally managed to reach out to get the man's attention. He had his notebook out and leaned close to to say something to the man whose demeanor made it clear to me that he did not want to talk to anyone.

I was perhaps fifteen feet behind him, separated by four ladies whose youth and high-pitched excitability identified them as students. Eager to get in on the exchange between Tim and the mysterious man, even to ask him a question or two, I slid between two of the students to get closer. As I did so, someone behind me seized my arm and halted me. Puzzled, I turned back to see who restrained me.

I found myself staring into the wide, saucy eyes of Eve Seilor. She stood before me like some Bohemian princess clutching to her breast several pamphlets I took to be radical handouts. Her tresses were spun gold, her skin pale and free of blemishes. Behind gold-rimmed eyeglasses, her eyes were alive with intelligence and as blue as a Minnesota summer sky. The lamps behind her cast her in a soft corona of orange-yellow light.

"You're an admirer of Remington?" she asked, in a wonderful non-sequitur.

I glanced toward Tim who was still trying to engage the white-haired man. I didn't see Sean. "Yes," I managed to stammer.

"You sound unsure."

I shrugged. "Well, I certainly wasn't an admirer of his talents when I arrived at the gallery. Hardly knew a thing about him or his work. By the way, my name is—"

"But you changed your mind about Remington?"

What was it about me that encouraged people to interrupt what I was saying? "I did," I admitted. "What do *you* think of Mr. Remington?"

Her eyes bore into mine. "A genius unfettered by tradition or convention."

The intensity of her gaze made it difficult for me to concentrate on her answer. "Ah." I groped for more to say. Fortunately, two gents muttering apologies pushed between us, elbowing their way toward the rear exit. I let them pass and followed them with my eyes. Tim was no longer in sight. Goldman stood in the doorway, engulfed by a large cluster of admirers. I turned back to Eve Seilor. "And Remington's art? What do you think of it?"

"Portraits of men and women unencumbered by conventional restraints, not yet exploited by the forces of industrial capitalism," she said.

That might well be, but I wasn't eager to discuss cowboys and Indians and their relationship to industrial capitalism. I'd exhausted my thoughts on Remington and was eager to turn the conversation to her. Although I knew the answer, I asked anyway. "And you're an admirer of Miss Goldman?"

Her eyes shone. "She's everything I want to be."

"And that is?"

"A liberated woman. Emma pursues causes that attract her. She ignores laws that repress her. Denounces those who sicken her. Takes lovers who excite her."

This *was* a bold young woman. Obviously intense, articulate. But I couldn't tell how much of her speech was designed to shock and how much of it represented deeply-held views, or just rhetoric culled from radical literature. Trying not to smile, I tested her. "You see Boston plagued by exploitation and repression, do you?"

"I do. The commonwealth seethes with injustice and man's inhumanity to man." She said this crisply, enunciating each word as a self-conscious professor might.

"You're a Socialist, then?"

A janitor trimmed the lamps in the front of the hall. "Closing up," he shouted.

Eve Seilor paid him no heed. "I am a socialist, yes." She smiled, arched her eyebrows daring me to comment, I thought.

"And an anarchist?"

"Yes," she answered hotly.

I pressed on. "And a *sexual* revolutionary?"

If she caught the teasing tone of my question, she didn't respond to it. "Of course, I am." She frowned, her mouth a small pout. "How could an intelligent person not be?" She looked me up and down. "I doubt seriously if you are either a Socialist or a revolutionary. Your clothes betray you, for one thing."

Conversation with Miss Seilor was as tough to follow as a dog with his tail on fire. I looked down at my clothes. "These aren't the clothes of a rich man," I protested.

She gave me a withering look. "They aren't the clothes of a worker either. Nor were those you wore at the gallery." She pointed a slim finger at me. "There you looked very much like a banker."

I again probed for a sense of humor. "I wear my only good suit and you take me for a capitalist oppressor who forecloses on unemployed workers and drives destitute widows into the snowy night?"

She let my effort at humor pass. Her eyes shot up and locked into mine. "Perhaps you're a Pinkerton," she said, drawing it out, "spying on Emma and her allies."

I leered theatrically. "Now I'm an evil capitalist intent on turning you over to those who will torture and corrupt you?"

The janitor was now trimming the lamps toward the back half of the hall. "Closing up," he bellowed again.

Goldman and her followers stepped through the doorway into the alley. I finally spotted Sean who was lingering by the exit.

"Closing up," the lamp-trimmer called again, irritation rising in his voice.

Eve ignored him, keeping her eyes riveted on me. She let the facetiousness in my last comment pass without comment. If she had a sense of humor, she'd given no indication of it. "I think you're a Pinkerton, yes," she said, "though at the moment a bruised one."

I fingered my swollen cheek. "Pinkertons are a unpopular lot, it appears."

She took my hand, sending a warm buzz through me. She canted her head toward my knuckles, red and scrapped, crusted with blood. "It appears Pinkertons mete out more violence than they receive." At that instant, a portly man deep in conversation with another and hurrying toward the exit, jostled me, pushing me up against Eve, our faces mere inches apart, her hand still clutching mine. I could smell her sweet breath and feel it soft against my face. She didn't blink or step back. We stared at each other for a long moment in the dim room, saying nothing. I was the one who finally pulled back, not her. "Pardon me," I mumbled.

She reminded me of Emma Goldman when confronted by protesters: she simply ignored the interruption. She didn't even glance at the men whose haste had thrown us up against each other. She canted her head and appeared to think about something. "On the other hand," she said slowly, "if you were a Pinkerton you would not have let the young man at the gallery so easily hang horns on you."

Now I *was* flabbergasted, not only by her comment regarding my being cuckolded, but by the fact she continued to clasp my hand. Even a dog ablaze ran a more recognizable course than Miss Seilor did. "Hang horns on me? What in the world are—"

Interrupting me, she removed her hand from mine. "The tall, dark-haired woman in the gallery. She's your wife?"

No one would ever criticize this young lady for reticence. For her impertinence, definitely, but not for her reticence. "No, she is not," I replied with some heat.

She shrugged as if the relationship were unimportant. "Still, she was in your company and the cowboy courted her in front of you, without regard to your feelings."

"You saw all that did you?"

She lifted her chin. "I saw it all."

I was tired of being on the defensive with this blue-eyed beauty. And I still wasn't sure yet whether she was ribbing me or not. But suddenly realizing that we still had not formally introduced ourselves, I put *her* on the defensive. "You're Eve Seilor," I said.

Her eyes widened in surprise. "You know who I am?"

I played a hunch. "You're a close confederate of the gentleman who was sitting behind you." I made it a statement of fact rather than a question.

Her eyes panned the room, lingering on the exit. "Of Mr. Krael?" Almost before the words tumbled from her mouth, her eyes widened and she shook her head furiously, then tried to look puzzled. "Oh, no. You meant the man behind me? I don't know him." She shook her head again for emphasis.

Her efforts to cover up her indiscretion in providing Krael's name were comical. I pushed harder. "He was at the Remington exhibit with you."

She chewed on the inside of her cheek. "No."

I wagged my head in mock confusion. "Mmmm. Looks like him. Is he the man's father?" I cocked my head and gave her an exaggerated puzzled look.

She giggled. "No."

I decided to let go of the bone. Glancing at the audience now rapidly disappearing through the exits, I observed, "Well, all in all tonight was fairly uneventful considering the room was full of terrorists."

She wrinkled her nose. "Hardly terrorists. Reformers and revolutionaries, perhaps."

"Ah," I said, as if her distinction made absolute sense to me. "And, you, Miss Seilor, what revolutionary act can I expect from you?"

The corners of her mouth moved slightly and her eyebrows rose "You are—?"

Finally. "Will Beaman."

She arched her eyebrows. "Ah, Will Beaman. You do *what?*"

"That's a complicated question, Miss Seilor. At the moment, I'm trying to find out who killed one of the players on the Boston nine and mugged another and stole his gold watch. Not very glamorous, but that's what I'm doing." So, I exaggerated a bit.

"You *are* a policeman!" she exclaimed, her eyes widening.

I held out my hands, palms toward her. "No, I'm not. I'm merely looking into the matter as a favor for friends. And helping the owner of the Boston nine. "

A shadow passed in front of her eyes. "The players in the newspapers? Everyone at the workers hall was talking about them. Collins is a grand player, they say."

The janitor scooped up a bucket and mop and moved toward us. "Please," he said, sounding plaintive. I glanced toward the rear exit. Only Sean stood there. Except for him and the disgruntled janitor, Eve Seilor and I were now the only ones in the dim hall. Since Eve paid no attention to the janitor's pleas to leave, I stood my ground, too. "The newspapers reported on Amos Porch's death and Jimmy Collins' misfortune, yes."

She pursed her lips, all the while seeming to reassess me. She looked me up and down. "I knew you weren't a policeman—or a reporter," she finally said. "If I thought you were either I wouldn't have been so candid with you. But I like to be candid."

I gave her another theatrical leer. "Is that so?"

She edged closer, her uplifted face mere inches from mine. She rested a hand on my arm. It was the third time this evening this bold young woman had touched me. "Oh, yes. It is so. And you want to know what rebellious behavior I am up to?" she asked. She saucily lifted her eyebrows a notch. "Well, Mr. Will Beaman, I'm going to follow my heart and take you as my lover."

She swept toward the exit, leaving me open-mouthed over who had been pulling whose leg.

17

Tim and Sean were waiting when I left the hall, coats buttoned tight against the thickening fog, hands crammed deep in their pockets. Sean chuckled as I approached, sending clouds of white breath into the night. "You made a bold new friend," he said.

I buttoned my coat and pulled up the collar. "You noticed, did you?"

He snorted and cuffed me playfully on the arm. "She was nose-to-nose with you, Will. By all that's holy, I'm thinking that to separate the two of you me an' Tim was going to have to use a crowbar."

Before I could respond, Tim grabbed each of us by the arm. "Come on, darlin's. This isn't the place to be this time of night. Let's find us a trolley, fast." He hustled us down the dimly lit street, past clusters of rough-looking, shabbily-dressed men and slatternly women warming their hands over barrels of burning trash. The smell of rotting food and waste was heavy in the air. Our passage through the bleak neighborhood reminded me there were many Bostons, some a good deal worse off than others. The unknown factor for me was whether the condition of those we hurried past was the result of financial or moral poverty. With Emma Goldman's angry protests echoing in my head, I suspected that she and Eve were more familiar with the Boston we were walking through than my chums and I were. Though the men eyed us sullenly, no one moved. Perhaps theirs *was* a poverty of the cupboard rather of conscience. I have to admit, though, it was with considerable relief that we boarded a trolley on Prince. It was late so we agreed to share what we'd learned at tonight's meeting when we met for lunch at McGreevey's the following day.

I spent Friday morning job hunting, trying to get interviews or leave my resumé with every bank, loan office, counting house, and department store on Boynston. I generated not one spark of interest. By the time I reached McGreevey's, the fog had burned off and the sun blazed bright in a cloudless sky. It was perfect weather for base ball—and for cold beer. Unsettled as I was from the previous evening, and by my luckless quest for employment, this promised to be a three-brew lunch. Assuming that I had sufficient coin.

Tim, Sean, John Haggerty, and I had gotten into the habit of eating lunch at McGreevey's Third Base Saloon on game days, before heading to the Grounds. A sign beside the door proclaimed, "The Last Stop Before You Steal Home." Most patrons stood at the long oaken bar, drinking and helping themselves to the free pickles, peanuts, cold cuts, cheese, and boiled eggs. Base ball posters and photographs of ball players and politicos lined the walls. Beaneater souvenir balls, bats, gloves, and caps vied with hundreds of bottles, glasses and steins for space on the tavern's shelves behind the bar. The place smelled of stale beer, human sweat, eggs, and cleaning solvents. It was the favorite hangout for the city's Royal Rooters, rabid fans of the Beaneaters.

Tim, Sean, and Haggerty were already there when I arrived. The tables behind us were empty. The long bar was deserted except for a half-dozen gents at the far end. McGreevey was nowhere in sight. "For a Friday this place is deserted," Sean groused.

Happy to have something to do, a waiter scurried over and took our orders. When he left, Sean glanced around. "Where's the base ball crowd?" he groused. "Where's the arguments? The betting? Wagering's usually as common in here as soiled doves on Battery." He stretched to look behind him. "By all the saints, how's a man like me to make any money with the *Globe* if there's no celebrities to sketch? Where's Honey Fitz Fitzgerald an' his chums, anyway?" Unlike me, he was full of ginger today. Had the energy and exuberance of a sheet music salesman.

"You must have sold some sketches," I suggested.

"Half a dozen of 'em," he crowed. He drummed his fingers enthusiastically on the oaken table. "Who knows?" he said, turning to Haggerty, but jerking a thumb at me. "Maybe this place is empty because everyone had the good taste to let us discuss in privacy the behavior of our wayward friend, here."

Haggerty's head shot up. "Wayward friend?"

"Actually, John, it wasn't Will here who was misbehaving. He was just standing there with his mouth open, like some rube watching a stallion cover a mare. The indecent proposals was coming from his saucy companion, they was."

The waiter plunked down our pints.

Haggerty eyed me suspiciously. "What's Sean babblin' about?"

"I'm talking about Will's radical miss offering to haul his ashes," Sean replied, punching me lightly on the shoulder.

Haggerty looked incredulous. "No woman said that!" he sputtered.

Slamming his freckled hand down on the table, Sean leered at me. "I swear it. I heard the whole thing. In a public hall 'n all, she said it. By God, John, Eve Seilor just looked Will here in the eye—"

Haggerty's head snapped up. "Seilor? Ain't she one of them free-love lasses?"

That caught my attention. "What do you know about Eve Seilor?" I asked.

He held up his hands, palms toward me. "Nothin', really. She's smack in the middle of the union movement, I know that. Working people see her as somethin' o' a Joan of Arc. Says some wild things, she does."

I snorted. "She wasn't being serious with me. Trying to shock me. Or, maybe, just trying to convince herself that she really is a radical."

Haggerty pushed back his chair and stood. "Well, I don't know whether she believes what she says, or not, Will, but you stay away from her. You have enough problems without adding her. Claire is the proper woman for you." He dropped some coins on the table. "I've got to go. Got to get the Grounds ready."

"What happened with our boys yesterday?" I asked.

"Kloby beat Anson's lads, 6-3. And we still couldn't make up ground on the Orioles who whupped up on St. Louis. We need to best the Chicagos today."

"Why're you leaving so early?" piped in Sean.

"Me boys are coming today." His 'boys' were over a hundred kids from the Guardian Angels Orphanage. Several times a season he hosted orphans at a game, providing each with a bag of peanuts and two lemonades. Today, Haggerty's kids would see the final game of the Chicago series before Cincinnati came to town. Haggerty poked my shoulder. "You need help, you know where to come." He moved toward the door.

Sean watched him leave. "The man's a saint," he said. Sean had spent almost ten years in the orphanage. He'd attended many a game complements of Haggerty, and it was Haggerty who'd spotted Sean's ability to draw, and introduced him to Tim, laying the foundation for his career at the *Globe*.

Tim had been silent to this point, but now he beamed and shook his head in admiration. "He is that," he sighed. "He is that, indeed."

Entering McGreevey's as Haggerty departed, were two bare-footed ragamuffins. The spindly-legged girl went up on tiptoes to ask the barkeep something. He pointed to our table with a towel he was using to wipe glasses. The kids giggled and ran up to us. "Mr. Beaman, sir?" the girl asked, her big eyes looking at each of us in turn. I identified myself and she thrust a folded paper into my hand. I reached for a couple of pennies, but the kids didn't wait for payment. They scampered away, shrieking with laughter and leaving the door swinging wildly in their wake. I held the note below table level, unfolded it, and read: *Mr. Will Beaman. Old Howard Theater? Tonight? At Eight? Eve.*

Sean canted his head toward the note. "Good news?"

I refolded the note and tucked it into my vest pocket. "Nothing important." The looks on their faces told me they didn't believe me, but neither pursued it. Even before the urchins' arrival, my ability to concentrate on winning my wager with Soden over Collins' watch had been seriously compromised by Eve Seilor's brassy suggestion of taking me as her lover. She entered my life like a Scott Joplin tune: jarring, troubling, unforgettable. She buzzed around in my mind. The thought of her as an eager and uninhibited lover wouldn't leave me. In God's truth, I'd initially been amused by her statement about taking me as her lover. At least I'd been amused after getting over the initial shock of it. But, let's face it. She was a beautiful young woman. Reason enough to suffer a distressing mixture of fascination and guilt.

Even with my occasional moral lapses, I understood enough to know my fascination with Eve undercut the moral high ground I wished to hold. How could I be angry with Claire for her being impressed with Hart, when I was attracted to Eve and the prospects of bedding her? The note suggested Eve was more literal in her proposition than I'd conceded. Still, I loved Claire and I wanted her to love me.

Sean interrupted my rumination. "What did John mean about you having troubles? Other than Hart's interest in Claire, what do you have to worry about?"

"Soden canned me." I just blurted out the news. Well, why not? Sean had recovered from being assaulted. He could handle it.

Sean paled. "When? *Why*?"

"Last Saturday. I thought he might keep me on when he heard about Porch and Collins, but he didn't."

He glared at Tim. "You knew about this?"

Tim nodded. "Soden told me."

"Haggerty know?" Sean pressed.

"He was there," I told him.

Sean continued to glare at Tim. "Why didn't you tell me?"

Tim cradled his glass in his hands and moved it around in circles. "The same reason John didn't. It's Will's business. And Will's choice whether or not to tell you. And when to tell you."

Sean's scowl shifted from Tim to me. "Soden give a reason?" he asked.

I shrugged. "Low attendance. Low revenue. 'Bout what you'd expect."

"Cheap bastard," Sean spat.

"It's a familiar litany in the church of Soden," Tim added. "Despite the fact that Boston is drawing well, probably averaging over three thousand a game. Soden'll make more money this year than virtually every other owner in the league. He insatiable."

Sean wasn't interested in Tim's philosophizing. "By jaysus, We've got to get you work. Can you make your rent?" I knew he was calculating the implications of my predicament for his own relationship with Cait. If unemployment undermined my chances with Claire, or if Claire went to Montana with Hart, Cait would go as well. Without waiting for my answer, he spun around to look behind him. "Where'n hell is Honey Fitz when you need him?"

I gave them a confident pose. "Relax. I'll find work."

But Sean was not appeased. "Dammit, I told you. I'll hire you. Find out who mugged me and get my stuff back. I have money."

I shook my head. "We've been through this. I'm not taking your money. I'll get on somewhere. In the meantime, I'm going to try to find out who mugged you and what they did with the items they stole 'cause I want to win that bet with Soden."

"Have you come up with *anything*?" Tim wanted to know.

I shook my head no. That was just one of many reasons behind my funk today. I had only ten days left to win the bet. And I still had no prospect for employment.

"Me neither," Tim muttered. "I just came from a chat with Dennis O'Dwyer. Almost a week after the robbery, he doesn't know a damn thing about who did it. It's all very strange." The waiter came with more beer and another bowl of boiled eggs. As he departed, Tim leaned toward me, cupping his pint in both hands. "People all over town know me from my playing days and my columns. I've cultivated connections. An' I can't learn a damn thing. This town's suddenly as silent as a chippie at a Methodist picnic."

"The police have turned their attention to the Bradford theft," said Sean.

"I can't find out a ding-damn thing about that, either," Tim groaned.

I assumed a confident pose, clasping my hands behind my head and leaning back to address Tim. "Learn anything from the white-haired guy at the meeting last night?"

He rolled his eyes. "Not even his name. He stonewalled me, then his friends shoved me away and kept me at a distance."

I leaned back farther and pasted on a Cheshire Cat grin. "Well, I know his name. Krael."

Tim couldn't hide his excitement. "Gunther Krael? I've heard of him. Lots of talk about Krael being behind the union movement in the Northeast. The police watch him like a hawk. When they can find him, that is. But the fellow I talked to last night sure didn't look like the man I've heard described as Krael."

I played a hunch. "Dark-haired, wears it long and just runs his fingers through it to comb? Glasses? Short, muscular, sharp-chinned, mustachioed?"

Tim spoke slowly. "That's him. And the fellow I talked to last night was all those things except for the color of his hair and the absence of eyeglasses." He shrugged. "It'd be easy enough to cut and powder his hair 'n leave his specs home. We know he doesn't want the police to find him." Tim seemed to ponder his own observations. "Mmmm. Gunther Krael, is it?"

I pointed out the obvious. "The big thug who roughed up Sean wasn't there last night. The two blokes on each side of Krael, if that's who it was, were big and mean-looking, but they weren't as big as Sean described."

"No," Tim agreed. "But according to Dennis several dock workers have had the bejesus beat outta them in the past few days after being seen with O'Dwyer's detectives. Seems it was a big guy done the beatin'. He's probably lying low, 'n all. Or Krael doesn't want to be seen with him."

Sean crunched noisily on a pickle. Tim sipped at his beer. I continued to eat but my mind drifted again to Eve. Initially, I'd thought her observations were classic socialist jargon and mere rhetoric. After all, for someone obsessed by feelings for workingmen, she'd paid little heed to the janitor's pleas for us to leave the hall. But her insistence about revolutionary acts being necessary, and sometimes pure and honest, kept nagging at me. So did her observations about seemingly 'senseless' acts cutting past hypocrisy and tradition to achieve a larger good. Still more riveting was her example that if two adults were sexually attracted to each other, why shouldn't they be candid about their feelings and act on them? Why let societal conventions deny them their pleasure? Eve had been arguing that society's sexual conventions were silly, even while conceding that society would defend them and label individuals disregarding them as saboteurs of order and morality. What would Claire Denihur say to that? I wondered. Could my relationship with Claire ever be as frank and uninhibited as that suggested by Eve? I wanted to think that Claire was more important to me than anything. I told myself that over and over. I assured myself Eve's appearance in my life was an intoxicating but ultimately insignificant event. I fingered the note from Eve in my pocket.

I was suddenly aware that Tim was grasping my wrist and pulling on my arm. "Dammit, Will darlin', look into it. *I'll* carry you financially while you do it."

His plea caught me in mid-swallow. I laughed in spite of myself and the beer flooded my nose and caused me to choke. I swabbed at my face with a napkin and wiped my eyes as I tried to compose myself. "Look into *what*?" I finally gasped. "In the past six days I've lost my job, seen two friends assaulted and an acquaintance killed, watched a Montana cowboy spark Claire, had him introduce me to his mysterious 'cousin' and try to hire me to protect his art collection. On top of that, I've met Emma Goldman and any number of her questionable associates, been propositioned by a radical feminist who, it seems, likes western art. I've bet my former boss that I could find a stolen trophy watch and risked my severance pay and letters of recommendation doing it. I've since discovered that the police care more about the pilfering of an obscure manuscript than they do a case involving homicide and assault and theft. I ask again: look into *what*?"

Tim nodded his appreciation of the confusion of the past week and my dilemma, then tossed his napkin onto his plate. "Life's a whirl, ain't it, darlin'?" He stood. "I've got to get to the Grounds." He added to the pile of coins. "Coming?" he asked us.

"One more beer for me," Sean told him. He signaled the waiter, then glanced at me. "You, too? The round's on me, pal o' mine." It took me only a second to make up my mind. I held up two fingers.

Tim smoothed his mustache with his knuckle. "Stay in touch, Will, darlin'." He waggled his fingers goodbye and moved toward the door.

18

Sean watched him go, loudly expelling his breath and sinking back in his chair, his arms straight out in front of him. Pensive now. "You've got problems, bucko. I'm especially interested in the one that involves Claire. 'Cause that involves me, too."

The waiter brought our pints. I nodded at Sean's comments, but said nothing, content to watch the waiter set the brimming glasses on the table, pocket the coins, and whisk away the empties.

"What're we going to do about Win Hart?" Sean said it plaintively and looked at me with worried eyes.

"I don't' know, but we need to do it fast. Krael is none of my business, unless he stole Collins' watch. I just hope I can get your stuff back and get a job. However, all that's secondary. I've got to figure out where I stand with Claire."

"What about *Eve*?" Sean asked, his voice rising.

What about her? "She's an attractive woman. It was flattering to have her flirt with me. But, she wasn't serious." I knew this last was a lie; the note in my coat pocket was proof of that. I clasped his shoulder. "Anyway, I can't let her distract me. It's Claire I love. We need to find out what kind of inroads Mr. Hart has made with her and Cait."

His mouth was grim. "Let's do it. At breakfast tomorrow. Let's just straight out ask them." His eyes suddenly widened. "Jayzus, the luck o' the Irish." He waved at someone behind me. "Honey Fitz. Fitzy. Here."

I twisted to look over my shoulder. Coming toward us was a small, clean-shaven man with a ruddy complexion. He wore a dapper three-piece suit with a white flower in his lapel, and a bowler. A handsome man, he walked with a jaunty bounce. He had two companions in tow, both bigger than him. "Good day t'ya, Sean lad," he said.

Sean popped out of his chair and indicated me. "Honey Fitz," he said, "This here's me bonny chum, Will Beaman."

John F. "Honey Fitz" Fitzgerald arched his eyebrows in exaggerated curiosity as he reached for my hand. "A loyal voter, are you?"

"He ain't Irish or Catholic," laughed Sean. "But he's a chum and a good man 'n all." He paused. "And he needs work."

Again, Honey Fitz's eyebrows rose as he studied me. "Do you, now? Well, we can make a voter of you. What kind o' work does a big fella like you do, Mr. Beaman?"

"Well, sir, I—" Suddenly I felt as awkward as a three-fingered man with a five-button fly.

Sean came to my rescue. "He's worked for the Beaneaters doin' virtually everything. Sold advertisements, helped keep the ledgers, arranged promotions." He looked expectantly at Honey Fitz, searching for an encouraging sign. "And he found out who put Germany Long out of the lineup last month."

Honey Fitz, who rooted for the Beaneaters with the same intensity that he watched over his neighborhood's political machine, pumped my hand once more. "You did, did you? Found out who conked Germany, eh? I think maybe Art Soden mentioned that to me. It was a fine thing you did. It permitted the boys to concentrate on the game and not have to keep looking behind them." He suddenly straightened and canted his head. "Why aren't you still working for Soden?"

I kept it simple. "Economics, Mr. Soden tells me."

Sean leaned closer. "He's a clever lad, Honey Fitz. You could use a clever lad."

Honey Fitz whirled and motioned the two men who'd entered with him to the far end of the bar. He seized the chair next to me and pulled it out. "May I, Mr. Beaman?"

I made room for him. "Please."

Once settled, Fitzgerald steepled his fingers. "You've had some experience in investigations, have you?" he asked.

Sean didn't let me answer. "He has, indeed," he blurted. "He's worked at his father's detective agency in Minneapolis. Trained under him 'n all, he did." He was excited now, pointing at me. "I tol' you he's done some detective work for Mr. Soden. And he's helped Lieutenant Dennis O'Dwyer, too."

I motioned for Sean to be silent. "I'm looking for a respectable job with a fair salary," I told Honey Fitz. "I'm not trained as an investigator and I've had limited experience as one."

Honey Fitz cocked his head and contemplated me, seemingly ignoring my disclaimer. "Do you know who I am?" he asked.

I did. I'd seen him often enough at the Grounds with the Royal Rooters. And besides that, the newspapers were full of him, calling him the Napoleon of Ward Six. A congressman, he'd recently been in a heated public debate with fellow Bostonian Henry Cabot Lodge over immigration and the legitimacy of the American Protective Association.

"You're John Fitzgerald. Member of the House of Representatives from the North End," I said.

"That I am," he beamed. "Representing the good people o' ward six." He patted my arm with a surprisingly large hand. "Perhaps you can be of some help to me."

Sean beamed and slapped the table with the flat of his hand. "I knew you'd have a job for a friend, Honey Fitz."

Honey Fitz held up a palm to quiet him while peering around the saloon. He hunched down as if to tell them something confidentially. "I've served in Washington for three years now. And I've served my district well, if I might be permitted some immodesty. Now I have my eyes on bigger fish." He waited, clearly expecting us to demonstrate our comprehension. I had no idea what he was talking about.

Sean did, and blurted, "You want—"

Honey Fitz thrust up a warning hand. Apparently the idea was to acknowledge that we understood but not speak of it. I still didn't know where this was going, or what it had to do with employment for me. I knew nothing about politics and had no experience in political campaigns. Promoting sporting contests might be useful in championing candidates, I suppose. "I see," I murmured but, really, I didn't see anything.

Again, Honey Fitz surveyed the room. Once more he hunched his shoulders and closed the distance between us, speaking in the hushed tones of a confidant. He asked if I could get away from the city for a day or so. I told him for a job I could. He pulled out his wallet and peeled out several bills that he handed to me. He told me he'd see me in Old Orchard Beach late tomorrow afternoon. And that someone would meet me at the station. He added that if I didn't know how to get there, Sean would tell me. Sean was nodding like a man with palsy, repeating, "sure," "sure," "you bet."

Honey Fitz's voice lowered as he strained even closer. "Tomorrow we'll talk about what you might do to help the cause."

"The cause," I repeated stupidly.

He stood. "That's right, Mr. Beaman. The cause. Tomorrow, then? I've got to get to the game and teach old man Anson some humility. And to make sure me Boston nine shows some ginger. Ever since I was a stub of a boy I've hated losing. As Sean knows, I hate to lose at politics or mumbly-peg. I hate my team to lose. But most of all I hate my team to lose to Anson's men. That ol' bastard crows like a demented rooster when he wins." He gripped my hand and then joined his friends at the bar.

So there it was. Fitzgerald's political ambition held the potential for my financial salvation, it seemed. Exactly what the connection was I couldn't fathom. I slipped a finger into my vest pocket and felt the note. My trip to Old Orchard Beach would eliminate any opportunity to meet Eve. That was one temptation taken care of.

Sean and I sat in silence for a long while before I finally spoke. "What the hell's going on? Do you know?"

He frowned. "Besides the fact that you're going to get a job?"

"What's the bigger fish Fitzgerald wants to fry?" I asked.

"He wants to be mayor," Sean whispered, grinning in pleasure over his own astuteness. He began to empty his pint in rapid, noisy swallows.

Now it was my turn to frown. "Mayor?"

He put down his pint and wiped his mouth with his fingers. "Sure. Hibernian politicians like Honey Fitz want more power. Their machines run the neighborhoods, but they want more. And the power is there if they can attract voters besides us Micks. Ward Six has been flooded with Russian Jews and Italians in recent years. They want to be heard, too. Honey Fitz is one of the few politicians to curry favor with these new immigrants. That's why he's opposing the new immigration law supported by Lodge and the American Protective Association. By courting newcomers, he hopes to become a hero beyond the Sixth Ward. That's how he sees himself becoming mayor, doncha see."

For someone who read only the sports columns and the comics Sean knew a lot more about Boston than I did. "What do you imagine Honey Fitz will have me doing?" I asked him.

Sean shook his pencil at me. "I don't know, laddybuck, but for a man whose cupboard was bare a moment ago, you certainly have a full plate."

I let that pass, not sure exactly what would come from my trip to Orchard Beach. Instead, I asked, "Where's Old Orchard Beach?"

Sean's skeptical look told me he couldn't believe I didn't know. "Maine," he said with some exasperation. "Between Kennebunkport and Portland. Boston's lace-curtain Irish go there to swim, boat, shoot skeet, play tennis, sit in the sun. There are all kinds of shops, galleries, cafes, outdoor bazaars. It's a resort. You *know*."

If I had known I wouldn't have asked him, but I let the opportunity to point that out pass. "How do I get there?" I asked.

He stood, tucked his sketchpad under his arm, and flipped several coins on the table. "The Boston and Maine Railroad to Portland goes through Orchard Beach. Board at Haymarket Square station. Come on, let's take in one more game before you go to work for Fitzy. Any game involving Pop Anson is worth seeing. My treat."

I pushed out of my chair and drained my beer. "You don't have to ask twice."

"Gentlemen?"

We looked into the skeletal face of police Lieutenant Dennis O'Dwyer, his ubiquitous pipe screwed firmly into his mouth.

"Well, well. To what do we owe this pleasure?" Sean asked, smart-alecky like.

O'Dwyer didn't smile. "Did you two talk with Tony Onofrio on the docks yesterday?" he asked. No pleasantries. No preliminaries. Just the blunt question. My stomach tightened and my breathing quickened. Sean paled, and said slowly, "Why do you ask?"

O'Dwyer chewed his pipe. "Tony's dead," he said. "Someone beat him to a pulp."

19

By the time we got to the Grounds Boston's slender right-hander, Charles "Kid" Nichols, had completed his preparations. Cloud cover now cooled the day, and the breeze had grown stronger, making the pennants pop and crack like gunshots. It carried with it a mist-like rain. There were less than two thousand fans scattered about the damp bleachers on this Friday afternoon, virtually all male.

Dennis O'Dwyer's conversation with us at McGreevey's had been brief. He was in no mood to share the details of Tony's death with us, only that Tony's body had been discovered this morning. And that dockworkers had remembered us talking with him and had given our descriptions to the police. Our 'disguises' aside, it didn't take Dennis long to recognize that witnesses were describing the two of us. He wanted to know what we were talking to Tony about. And whether we'd seen him after our conversation on the pier. All the while, he made no effort to disguise his interest in our hands. It didn't take Tom Edison to figure out he was checking us for skinned and bruised knuckles. And, unfortunately, both of us had them, courtesy of the Emma Goldman rally.

O'Dwyer's visit left us badly shaken. Sean, especially. We hoped that our explanation about the Goldman rally had satisfied O'Dwyer. But Tony had been like an uncle to Sean. Tony's death was not only a personal shock, but it brought home to us how serious this whole business of the assault on Sean, Collins and Porch truly was. No one kills to cover up a simple mugging, or even an inadvertent death such as Amos Porch's. On the way to the park we went over and over why someone might kill Tony just because he talked to us. Or why he might have been killed if it had nothing to do with his talking with us. We also mulled over the possibility that the killer might now target us. As usual, we were better at identifying the questions than coming up with answers.

As we made our way to our seats, Nichols and the Beaneaters took their positions on the field. Lean and tanned Wild Bill Everett, the Colt's first batter, leaned on his bat at the plate, awaiting the first pitch. I tried to change the subject from O'Dwyer's disturbing news. Taking advantage of Sean's shock and grief over Tony's death, I pleaded to delay our confrontation with the Denihur sisters. "We could talk to the girls about Hart tomorrow," I suggested, settling on the hard plank that constituted seats behind first base. "Lunch might be best. Before I have to catch the train to Old Orchard Beach."

Sean grunted and rolled his eyes, a habit of his whenever I said something to frustrate him. "You sniveling coward," he sneered. "You want a quick escape if things don't go well. We'll do it at breakfast."

Nichols sent a pitch that popped into Marty Bergen's glove. The crowd murmured. Everett flashed a funny look toward the Chicago bench. Nichols had his speed today.

"I don't want to bait them the first thing in the morning," I told Sean. "It'll be awkward to bring up under those circumstances. Too many boarders around."

"Then, by the beards o' the saints, I'll do it myself," he grumbled. "We sit around any longer and there'll be two fewer females in Boston and Mr. Hart'll have a start on a nice Mormon-sized family out there in Remington country."

After that I shut up while Sean began producing dozens of sketches for Tim's column, concentrating primarily on the smooth-working and hard-throwing Nichols who was looking for his twenty-sixth win. The light rain had stopped. Sitting there with my elbows on my knees and my head cupped in my hands, I watched the game unfold, content to put aside my private troubles and just enjoy the contest. Pop Anson's Colts weren't the Chicagos of old, not the Chicago that had dominated the 1880s. Anson himself was at the end of his career and no longer the formidable threat at the plate he once was, or effective around first base. Fast Freddy Pfeffer had lost a step at second base and had pretty much surrendered the position to Jim Connor. Neither of Chicago's catchers provided much offensive punch, and their pitching was mediocre.

On the other hand, the Beaneaters were rock-solid at every position and exceptional on defense. Except for young Chick Stahl in right field, the Boston outfielders were a veteran group. Hugh Duffy and Billy Hamilton, though veterans, could still cover ground with the best of them. Germany Long and Bobby Lowe provided trustworthy play at shortstop and second, and punch at the plate. Fred Tenney at first and Jimmy Collins at third were exceptional defensively, as agile as acrobats. Marty Bergen, for all his bouts of depression and anger, was as skilled a catcher as there was in the league, and a wonderful handler of pitchers. With Nichols as the bell-cow, Boston's pitching staff was strong and deep. Jeez, they had just signed strong-armed Vic Willis from Syracuse, and though they didn't plan on adding him to the staff immediately, he was probably available if needed. This team might falter on a given day, but I was confident that they would be there with the despised Orioles at the finish. What truly drew me to the Beaneaters and fed my desire to return to working for them was their quiet confidence. They had a good number of college men on their roster and were less rowdy than other teams. They were brash and played with moxy but Manager Selee kept them under control. Oh, they spat abuse and kicked when they thought they'd been robbed, but there was none of the roughhouse and naked rowdyism indulged in by McGraw's Orioles and Tebeau's Spiders and, sometimes, even Anson's Colts. The Beaneaters were professionals and acted like it. And I loved them for it.

In the seventh inning, after Sean had completed a sketch of Anson swinging futilely at a rare but wicked Nichols' curve, I tried a last assault. "Let's do it over lunch."

He was having none of it. "No. I've waited too long as it is. So have you."

Chicago's pitching failed them again. With Boston going to bat in the bottom of the seventh, the Beaneaters led 9-0 and Nichols was coasting. I stood, stretched, and flipped what remained of my peanuts to Sean. "I'm going to talk with Collins again."

He rose, stuffed the peanuts in his pocket, and gathered up his materials. "I'm leaving, too. Nichols has this one wrapped up. I've got work at the *Globe* and I need practice time on my bicycle. It'll give me time to think about Tony and what the hell is going on." He pointed a threatening figure at me. "Seven o'clock tomorrow morning, boyo. In the breakfast room. Back me up now."

"You keep your eyes open," I told him. "Don't let strangers get too close to you."

"They'd better look out for themselves," he shouted back, and flexed his muscles.

Despite myself, I smiled at his bravado as I headed for the Boston bench. By the time I reached their bench the Beaneaters were once again in the field. The machine-like Nichols made short work of Chicago in the eighth. When Collins trotted in from his position at third, he went to the bats rather than the bench. I beckoned him. "Can we talk?" I asked.

He selected a bat and moved away, telling me he was up next. The fact is he was the third batter in the inning, not the second, and had time for me had he wanted. I couldn't see any profit in hanging around waiting for someone who obviously did not want to see me. Tim had left his seat in the press box to sit in the weak sun in the bleachers. Wanting to get his take on Honey Fitz, I started in his direction, making my way up the stairs and pushing through the crowd at the top of the pavilion. A ragged little shaver tugged at my sleeve just as I left the pavilion shade.

"Hey, mister," he called. The kid could have been no more than ten or eleven. His hands were dirty and streaks of muddy sweat had run down his face. His straw-colored hair looked like something you'd see on a scarecrow. "Hey mister," he called again.

"What is it, son?"

"Are ye Mr., uh, Beaman?" The kid got it right. Beaman. Hard e.

"I am."

He thrust a wad of brown paper in my hand and turned to leave. I grabbed him, then looked down at the balled up paper in my hand. "Whoa, there. What's this now?" My first thought was this was another note from Eve. But this lad wasn't one of those who'd brought the note to me at McGreevey's. And this was no note; it was a ball of crumpled paper. "What's this, son?" I asked him again.

He stared at me with wide eyes. "Dunno, sir."

"Why give it to me?"

His eyes got larger and he began to swing his head around like he was watching a kite in a tornado. "Dunno."

"Who gave it to you?"

"Dunno."

"Who told you who I was?" I knew his answer by now.

"Dunno."

Still, I persisted. "Someone told you to give this to me."

He stopped his head swiveling and looked at me with defiant eyes. He knew the code of the streets. "Gave me a nickel."

"Uh huh. Man or woman?"

He made a face and tugged at my grip.

"What if I give you another nickel to tell me? How would that suit you?" I released him and fumbled in my pocket with my free hand for a coin. Freed of my grip, he made a dash for it, moving with the swiftness of frightened youth. "Hey," I yelled.

I thought of chasing him but until I knew what he'd given me I didn't know whether or not it was worth it. Slowly I peeled the paper away until I could see what was in it. A watch. Gold and beautifully engraved. I turned it over and read: "To Jimmy Collins from his Buffalo admirers. June 17, 1897."

I looked around wildly for the boy, but he'd vanished.

20

It took me only seconds to make up my mind to take my prize to Arthur Soden rather than to Jimmy Collins. It would be easy to return it to Collins; all I had to do was go down on the field and hand it to him. He'd be grateful and perhaps slip me a few dollars. Maybe more than a few dollars. I could then tell Soden what I'd done. On the other hand, by returning it to Soden personally I would have the added bonus of watching him squirm. The chance to observe Soden having to give back something he'd taken could not be measured solely in dollars. Let him give the watch to Collins.

Perhaps later I could figure out how I'd ended up with the pilfered timepiece. Or who was responsible for seeing that I became its custodian. In the meantime, I waited until Nichols retired the last Colt to preserve a 9-1 win. And I killed time until I was sure Soden would be finished counting the day's take.

Forty-five minutes after the game when most of the Beaneaters had bathed and departed the Grounds, I finally entered Soden's funereal lair. I found him sitting sideways to his desk, one pudgy hand resting on the big gray account ledger, his mind elsewhere. As usual, he appeared to be brooding. Here's a man, I thought, who would complain of the thorns on a prize rose. He took no notice of me until I pulled a chair up to his desk and boldly plunked myself down directly in front of him.

"Mr. Beaman?" he mumbled, clearly puzzled at my sudden appearance.

In an attempt to heighten the drama of my victory, I said nothing. I simply laid the crumpled paper containing the timepiece on his desk.

He stared at the watch for some time, puzzlement creasing his face, before reaching over and picking it up. He held it high and examined it, its chain dangling from his hand. He turned the watch over and slowly read its inscription. "Well, well," he muttered, the furrow in his brow deepening.

I couldn't help but gloat. "Well, well, indeed."

Soden continued to turn the watch over in his hand, as if by doing so, he would spot some sign it was a fake or an illusion. "Where'd you get it?" he said, finally.

Were I more gracious I would have admitted the obvious: that it had fallen into my hands no thanks to anything I'd done. I could have been candid, but I wasn't. Libby's Knickers! Let Soden stew over how I'd come upon Collins' watch. Let him wonder how badly he'd mistaken my talents. Let him rue the day he'd fired me. I shrugged and spread my hands. "I got it. That's what's important. And in less than a week, too, you notice."

He glared at me as a long moment crawled by. "I see," he finally said, defeat hanging in his words. He placed the watch back in its crumpled-paper crib and stood. "It appears that you've won our bet, Mr. Beaman." He walked to the annex and returned with a tin box that he set on the desk and opened. From it he took a pile of bills and began counting them out. He counted aloud, slowly, for my benefit. He reached one hundred, then added several more before handing them to me. "I've included your severance pay," he said. He pulled an envelope from the box and gave it to me. "Your letters of recommendation," he added.

I tucked the bills into my pocket and the envelope into my coat. "Thank you, sir."

I was nearly out the door when he spoke again. "Mr. Beaman?"

I turned to face him. "Sir?"

He stood by his desk, one hand leaning on it, two pudgy fingers seemingly supporting his entire weight. His second hand was rubbing his chin as if he were in deep thought. "Mr. Beaman," he said slowly, "would you consider an, uh, assignment?"

Though my pulse quickened I kept my voice casual. "What kind of assignment?"

His eyebrows inched up a notch and he gave me what for him passed as a half-smile. "You'll find it an intriguing proposition, I think. One suggested by your own comments."

"How much money are we talking about?" I asked, still trying to appear indifferent.

"Quite a bit." He paused, then added, "If you succeed, that is."

"And if I don't."

He gave me a withering look, as if I was a child struggling to grasp adult wisdom. "Success pays, son. Failure doesn't. You know that."

I'd been lucky in the matter of Collins' watch. I wasn't convinced I'd be so fortunate the next time around. Still—

He sensed my hesitation. "It's the kind of challenge you relish," he assured me.

I was reluctant to jump into this, but I was also increasingly curious about what schemes were tumbling about in his mind. Trying to figure out what was brewing in his head was like staring into a dark corner from which a strange smell wafted. You just never knew what you'd find. "What challenge is that, Mr. Soden?" I asked.

He leaned back against his desk, crossing his legs at the ankles, and folding his arms acrosss his chest. "This whole manuscript business. The city's newspapers have been wailing like Banshees over it. You'd think we'd lost the city treasury."

I shrugged. "What's it to do with you or me?"

He straightened up, serious now. "I want you to find the manuscript," he said.

Laughter burst from my mouth before I knew it, and I struggled to stifle it. I managed to abort the laugh, but only at the expense of offering up a series of hoarse coughs. I couldn't believe what I'd heard. I don't know what struck me as the more bizarre, Soden's willingness to fire me, or his apparent conviction that I could locate the stolen manuscript. Either I was a valued asset or I wasn't. "Sir," I said, "I don't have a snowball's chance in hell of finding that manuscript. All the resources of the city and state have been poured into finding it. For almost a week now. I hear they've rousted every known thief and every collector in the state. Anyone interested in historical artifacts. They've failed. If they can't uncover who took it and where it is, I sure can't."

His face showed no indication that he had registered by comments. "Frankly, son," he said, "I didn't think you had a Chinaman's chance of finding Jimmy's watch, either. You've shown yourself to be an enterprising young man—and a very lucky one as well. That's a good combination."

All this was very confusing. "What do *you* want with the manuscript?" I asked.

He scooted farther back on the desk, letting his pudgy legs dangle over the side and clasped his stubby fingers in his lap. "I'm been thinking about your comments regarding increasing our attendance by catering to working men," he said, his voice low and intimate.

I pulled up a chair, flipped it around, and set with my arms folded across its back. "By offering games on Sundays, and scheduling them later on workdays?"

He leaned forward and spoke with some passion. "Yes, that too."

I spread my hands, palms up. "What's that have to do with the manuscript?"

He acknowledged the legitimacy of my question with a bob of his head. "My partners are businessmen like myself, Mr. Beaman. Base ball is only one of our interests. We're in these businesses to make money. I've never made a secret of that. The more the better." He leaned even further toward me, and spoke even more quietly and conspiratorially. "If my partners, Mr. Billings and Mr. Conant, and I could find and return Bradford's manuscript, we would get more good publicity than we could buy in a year. That publicity would translate into profits for my roofing company and for my partners' businesses, as well. And here's the kicker, if I could return the manuscript at one of our games—national treasure returned at national game, 'n all that, you know—with all the city's important people in attendance, all announced well in advance, we could pack the Grounds." He smiled smuggly and pointed a finger at me for emphasis. "They'd be standing ten deep in the outfield." He spread his hands, his eyes wide and bright, like J.P. Morgan fingering his gold. "Everyone wins."

I smiled in spite of myself. "Do it at a *Sunday* game and you'll draw even more. Of course you'll hear from every minister in Boston. And because it's against the law, from every city official, as well, probably. But it would create a sensation." I paused to think about it. "Even though other teams in the league have played on Sunday, it would take some courage to buck those laws here in Boston," I added.

He nodded grimly to concede my point. "It would. I might, in fact, lose more fans that I'd gain by playing on Sunday. Most of the clergy in the state would be after my scalp, pathetic as my scalp is. Many of them and their congregations are still offended by school boys playing ball on the Sabbath. And the law is on the Sabbatarians' side. Oh, Joseph Lee and his Massachusetts Civic League would happily support us, but how many followers does that bunch have? " He paused and grimaced. "Still, courage is needed in any high risk adventure," he said, long and slow, as if to convince himself.

I found myself shifting my feet nervously. "Would Selee and the team play on the Sabbath? A number of the boys are churchmen."

He looked at me with the steely eyes of an English landlord. "Frank and the boys will play when and where I tell them to."

I stared at him, this man who for all his conservative bluster, was on occasion capable of very surprising moves and views. I suppose I should not have been too shocked. After all, he had already earned a reputation for being one of the stingiest owners in the National League when he coughed up ten thousand dollars to buy the great Mike Kelly in 1887, and another ten thousand dollars for the magic right arm of John Clarkson a year later. "And you think the police won't demand the details of how you got the manuscript?" I asked him. "Assuming that we do find it, that is. Or that the city fathers won't resent you orchestrating its return for your own financial benefit?"

He spread his arms dramatically. "Why should the authorities care how a stolen item is recovered or returned? And why shouldn't the man or men responsible for its recovery and return reap the reward? Judas Priest! We give rewards for public service and achievement every day. And the police department pays rewards for help in catching criminals—and gives money to snitches, too, I'm sure."

I'd have to think about this. There were a good many moral and legal questions to consider in Soden's strategem. Not to mention economic ones. And, frankly, it was those last ones that interested me most at the moment. "I should get the reward if I'm successful," I told him. "What would I get out of it?"

He cocked his head and let his eyes pan the room. The walls were bare. No autographed photographs, no base ball paraphernalia, no trophies or loving cups adorned this man's room. His eyes slowly returned to me. "Five hundred dollars," he said.

I demonstrated my unhappiness with a snort. "That's it? Five hundred dollars?"

He shrugged. "Think about it over the weekend. Tell me what you think on Monday." He started to turn away, but paused. "You find employment yet?"

I told him I hadn't.

He pulled a business card from his vest pocket and scribbled on it. Handed it to me. "Go see my son, Charles, on Water Street. He runs my roofing business. You're a big, strong lad. He might be able to help you." He hesitated, then added with a barely suppressed smile, "He won't pay you any five hundred dollars, though."

I left the Grounds unsure of whether I'd bested Soden, or he me. I had money in my pocket and the prospects of work but little opportunity to stay in base ball. That hurt. Wanting to handle and confirm my gains, I fished the bills Soden had given me from my pocket. A piece of paper fluttered to the ground, landing by my shoe. I scooped it up and examined it. Eve Seilor's note. The one I'd tried to put out of my mind. She'd asked me to meet her at eight. Tonight.

No, sir. Not a chance. My Minnesota uncle always told me that even the dumbest pig knew enough not to walk voluntarily into the killing chute. Still, I could ask her about Gunther Krael and inquire about his possible role in robbing Sean and Jimmy Collins. Or in Tony's death. And perhaps find out why Collins' watch had been returned to me.

I consulted my pocket watch. It was eleven minutes after seven.

21

I'm not eager to talk about my personal faults. Who is? Oh, I recognize I have them. I just have no interest in dwelling on them. My father charitably attributes my poor decisions to youthful rashness and to my sense of adventure. He recognizes that I don't feel completely alive unless I'm taking chances. My uncle, on the other hand, is less generous, claiming I can't tell horseshit from mincemeat pie. Whoever's right, I seem to accumulate problems like a seedy hotel draws lint. That, as much as anything, probably explains why, as I strolled out onto Walpole Avenue fingering my newly-acquired cash, my thoughts were on Eve Seilor's note.

What normal male would say no to a tryst with a beautiful and eager young lady? You'll understand, then, why at least I had to *explore* what she had in mind for me, and what she knew about Gunther Krael. I couldn't simply toss her note away and turn my back on her. Curiosity can be a burden equal to debt.

Ten minutes after departing Soden's office, I hopped off the Washington trolley for a quick bite to eat, then flagged down a hack and headed for the Old Howard Theater. It was nearly eight by the time the cab wound its way to the Old Howard through the crooked alleys that passed as streets in the North End. A substantial line was already pressing against the ticket office when my cab clattered to a halt. A pitchman in a too-large Prince Albert coat and silk topper was brandishing his cane at passersby and chanting his spiel in a gravelly voice.

As I paid the driver, I glimpsed Eve in front of a billboard proclaiming the exploits of the Scotti Brothers' trapeze act. She was wearing the conventional garb of female university students, dark blue skirt, white blouse with full shoulders and tight waist, and a wide-brimmed blue hat. Her hair was swept up and piled under her hat, exposing a pale neck. She wore no cosmetics.

She waved at me with two tickets. Good lord! This woman continued to amaze me. First, she tells me she's going to take me as her lover, this in a public place; then she invites me to an assignation; finally, she chooses as the place of assignation a burlesque theater and purchases tickets on her own! Lewd woman or liberated? To my discredit, I was determined to discover which. Or whether she was both.

She again waved the tickets as I approached, treating them as if they were lottery winners. "I have tickets," she said, beaming in self-congratulation.

I was equally quick-witted. "Yes, I see," I said and plucked the tickets from her hand. "Shall we go in? It's almost eight." I cupped her elbow in my hand and moved her toward the entrance. The ornate old edifice, once the pride of the city's theater district, was now faded and worn, a deposed queen unable to stem her slide into seediness.

"What is it that brings us to the Old Howard?" I asked, as we entered the red-carpeted lobby with its dull drapes and lusterless posters of former acts.

She giggled. "Girlfriends of mine are working tonight."

"Oh? And where do you know these ladies from?"

She gave me a smile that said 'I have a sly secret.' With no verbal elaboration, she plunged into the jostling crowd and sought our seats. Main section, thirty rows back. The next hour was something to behold. The orchestra was loud and brassy. A succession of acts ran the gamut from entertaining to clumsily amateurish. Dancers, singers, comedians, jugglers, unicyclists, black-faced minstrel players, and midget tumblers vied for the crowd's adulation. During this parade of uneven talent Eve and I exchanged shrugs, smiles, laughs, nods, and smirks, depending on the quality of the acts. We also touched, patted, or squeezed each other's arms to convey our reactions to the goings-on before us. Several times, she hugged me and pushed her nose into my neck while giggling at the presentations. The raucous acts, enthusiastic orchestra, and exuberant audience discouraged conversation.

However, I took advantage of the intermission to raise the question of Eve's familiarity with Gunther Krael and his activities. "I know the man at the Goldman rally sitting behind you was Krael," I told her. "There's no use denying it. His disguise wasn't all that effective. I know about his role as a labor agitator. What's he doing in Boston?"

She sighed. "He's only been in Boston a few days. Why do you ask?"

"Just curious. He seems to be planning something big."

She shrugged as if that fact shouldn't surprise me. "His commitment is to social justice. He's dedicated to improving conditions for workers," she said.

"He seems to prefer the background rather than the limelight. He stayed in Emma Goldman's shadow at the Workingmen's hall. Bad disguise and all."

She gave me a searing look. "He's interested in results, not publicity."

"Know him well enough to introduce me?"

She squirmed. "Why do you want to—?"

The lights dimmed, the orchestra burst forth with a raucous ditty, and the curtains swung open for the final act. With the band blaring, the stage slowly filled with lovely young women scantily-clad in beads and scarves. What made these young lasses different were the paucity of beads and the skimpiness of their scarves. Billed as "The Caliph's Harem," featuring "twenty-five winsome whites" and "twenty captive creoles," the review consisted of minimal dance steps, the fluttering of scarves, and dramatically heaving bosoms. Or, perhaps it's more accurate to say heaving dramatic bosoms.

"These are the friends you referred to?" I whispered to Eve.

She gave me a smile and a look that said, 'yes and proud of it.' But she said simply, "I know six of them."

"From where?" I asked her.

She giggled. "Four are university students, working their way through. Two are stenographers in university departments. All are members of our Young Women's Labor Movement." I could think of no response and so turned my attention to the gyrating women.

Not five minutes into the act, with the largely male audience at fever pitch, a well-dressed gentleman with two stout policemen in tow, rushed on stage and halted in front of the footlights. Shading his eyes with one hand, he shouted something about city ordinances and ordered the orchestra to cease. A few girls gamely continued to go through their paces, others slowed to a foolish shuffle; still others froze altogether.

I could not hear the man's every word. What I could see was a red-faced gent, waving his arms in a criss-cross fashion at the band and the girls, signaling them to stop. Several men in the front rows stood and made equally explicit gestures at the man and his bookend coppers. When fellows in the upper boxes joined in the verbal assault, the two policemen began to slap their truncheons menacingly against their palms.

"There's going to be trouble," I told Eve, again exhibiting my quick wit.

"Of course, there will be," she agreed. Her eyes were wide and bright in anticipation. No sooner had she made her observation than several in the audience charged the stage. The biggest copper filled his cheeks and huffed on his whistle, sending a shrill scream through the theater, then began to pound on a man crawling up out of the orchestra pit onto the stage. In seconds, the stage was filled with shrieking, near-naked women, rowdy patrons, one very harried city official, and two of Boston's finest. For reasons clear only to themselves, members of the audience began verbally and physically to assault other ticket holders. What with the shouts and curses of the men and the hysterical screams of the near-naked dancers, the place was bedlam.

The copper's second shrill whistle brought results. Both doors behind us burst open and a torrent of blue-clad bulls poured down the aisles. They tumbled over each other like third-act clowns in their rush to support their beleaguered comrades.

Eve bolted out of her seat and seized my arm. "Come on!" she shouted.

I stood and stared at her. "Where?"

She didn't answer. She pulled me along, stumbling past others in the row that were now standing, applauding, or screaming obscenities. Clamping onto my hand, she plunged down the main aisle and up the stairs to the stage. She pushed and shoved and shouted for men to step aside, tugging me in her tow.

"We're going the wrong way!" I shouted, shouldering aside a huge, pale man who gazed around with shocked, confused eyes. He wore only a collar above his waist. His shirt, torn to shreds, hung from his belt, exposing a round white gut and flabby breasts that cried out for beads and scarves.

"We've got to save the women," Eve cried. "They'll be arrested by these Cossacks." She released me and scrambled toward the lead dancer. Clamping her arm, Eve pulled the dancer toward the backstage area, all the time screaming at the other women to follow her.

I grabbed two dancers who appeared petrified by the pandemonium around them and pushed them backstage through the curtain. Eve was standing at the door leading to the alley behind the Old Howard, urging the women to hurry outside. I joined her in time to shove the last two dancers into the alley. The door swung shut behind them.

"Go," I shouted at Eve. "I'll follow you."

I'd hardly shouted those words when a beefy copper brought his billy down on my shoulder and a second drove his shoulder into me, slamming me into Eve, and pinning her against the door with a sickening crunch. Ignoring the pain in my shoulder, I twisted to push the first copper from me so that I could drive a fist into his face.

While I maneuvered to launch the punch, the second bull slammed his truncheon against my ear. Bright lights exploded before my eyes. I had the vague sense of a third policeman swallowing a struggling Eve in his embrace before I crashed to the floor. I heard myself grunting as the solid-toed brogans of the policemen began to pound out a tune on my ribs.

22

By the time we were hauled before the richly carved judicial pulpit behind which a magistrate lounged, the pounding in my head had subsided and my vision had cleared somewhat. I remained puzzled as to how I'd hurt my eye and mouth, but the throbbing of my bloodied lip and the swelling above my eye—and my blurred vision—told me I had. My ear and shoulder pulsed with pain. My right hand also was puffed and my knuckles were skinned and red. It felt like a porcupine had slammed his tail into my mitt. What's more, my ribs ached from the pounding they'd taken after I crumpled to the floor. I shot a fuzzy glance at Eve who was standing to my right.

She stood quietly, hands clasped in front of her, hair badly mussed. A bright red spot blossomed above her left eye and a purple bruise covered her cheek. She ran her tongue over her puffed lips. Still, she appeared undaunted, defiant even, and she kept her eyes locked on the magistrate.

Beyond her, modestly wrapped in an assortment of blankets, tablecloths, and borrowed coats, clustered the Caliphs' Harem. Obviously, our efforts to rescue them from arrest had fallen short.

The magistrate's court was a small, wood-paneled room illuminated by gaslights. Its tables and wooden benches were scarred from generations of hard use, its curtains faded and dusty. Only the impressive pulpit behind which the magistrate sat seemed to have escaped careless use. The room's carpet was as threadbare and thin as a politician's promises. Indeed, the whole room gave off the impression of being worn out and neglected, as did its official personnel.

The court clerk, an ancient man with liver spots sprinkled across a pate with no hair to speak of, read the charges against the women in a bored voice. But there would be no jury trials for them. A cherubic, bald man in a boldly-checkered vest and a suit that looked like he slept in it, stepped forward to plead the women guilty and to pay their fines. The exercise went quickly and smoothly. Clearly, all parties had honed their roles with frequent practice. The magistrate pounded his gavel to lend official approval to the swift transaction.

The clerk then read the charges against me: assaulting an officer, impeding an officer in the pursuit of his duty, abetting an escape, public intoxication, indecent conduct, and riot. I was being charged with everything but lewd winking.

"Your honor," I protested. "That's absurd! I wasn't drunk and I didn't—"

The magistrate's pounding gavel drowned out my protest. I was about to repeat it, and elaborate upon it, when the squat man with the bold vest and badly-rumpled suit stepped in front of me. "Your honor," he said, "If those charges are leveled against my young friend here, he will demand a jury trial. In an hour I will have fifty witnesses willing to testify the charges are bogus. They will, in addition, establish that members of our city police wantonly attacked peaceful citizens, struck terror into the hearts of innocent female bystanders, and caused damage to an ancient and revered building."

He paused to assess the effect of his words on the magistrate. Apparently thinking that he needed more ammunition, he continued. "What's more, your honor, they will testify that not only did the policemen deny"—he gestured toward the women—"these ladies a chance to earn a living, they groped and fondled them in a disgusting and illicit fashion."

The magistrate was a skeletal man with a toupee that wouldn't fool a blind man, and an Adam's apple that lurched up and down when he spoke. He glared at the lawyer for a long moment, apparently weighing the man's threats. "Would your 'client' plead guilty to common assault and accept a fine?" he asked in exasperation. His demeanor made Queen Victoria seem absolutely radiant.

The lawyer stepped forward and put his hand on the edge of the magistrate's desk, as if to establish proprietary claim to the bench. "How much of a fine, your honor?"

"Three dollars."

"Make it two?"

The magistrate rolled his pale, watery eyes. "Two then."

The man looked back at me and arched his eyebrows in question.

I quickly nodded my acceptance.

The magistrate pointed at Eve with his gavel, looking skeptical. "Her, too?"

Eve shook her head. She was not about to cave in to the forces of money and power. Or to their judicial minions. "No, your honor. Never. I stand innocent before you, and I will *not* plead guilty to something I did not do."

The judge cringed as if a giant beetle had flown smack into his forehead. He glared at the clock behind us, his Adam's apple jumping in his throat. "For crying out loud," he muttered. He looked pleadingly at the stub of a lawyer, then at me and held out his hands in a gesture of imploring.

The lawyer also begged Eve with hand and arm gestures. "Please, ma'am? For the sake of expediting matters and limiting the time and cost of proceedings?"

Eve shook her head and folded her arms under her breasts. "This isn't a case of assault or riot. It's class oppression," she insisted.

The wrinkles in the lawyer's forehead grew closer together and a cloud drifted across his eyes. A muscle in his jaw twitched. "Class oppression, ma'am?"

She uncrossed her arms and put her hands on her hips, spreading her feet slightly as if to ensure better balance should a physical confrontation ensue. "Those blue-coated lackies of the rich are determined to keep poor girls from making a living," she scolded the hoary judge. The women grinned and clapped their hands. Some in their enthusiasm hopped in place.

The portly lawyer glanced over at them severely, then spoke to Eve. "Ma'am," he said, "These women, eh, ladies—"

I laid my right hand on her arm. With my left I probed my sore ribs and grimaced. "Please, Eve?"

After a long moment of staring at the judge, apparently considering her options, weighing her convictions against the convenience of quickly escaping this place, and doubtless contemplating my ribs, she shrugged. "Just this once."

The magistrate's Adam's apple bounced, and he slammed his gavel down. "Done. Now get out of here, all of you."

I carefully shook hands with my newly-found attorney friend and offered to pay him. He refused my kindness, clapping me on the shoulder and telling me that, as a Royal Rooter, he'd seen me many a time at the Grounds and it was the least he could do for a fellow Beaneater fan. I did pay both my fine and Eve's—despite her protest—and led her out of the courtroom.

Outside, under the glare of the streetlight Eve seemed to have already forgotten her resentment over capitulating to the system. She was flushed and excited, her eyes blazing with our victory over the forces of tyranny. She stood close, looking up at me, with eyes wide. "Wasn't that marvelous?"

I wasn't quite that excited about having my ear crushed, my eye punched, and my ribs caved in. Social justice came with a high price. "It got a little hairy," I admitted.

My lack of enthusiasm made no impression on her. "And you were so heroic!" she cried. "You stood up to those stooges and matched them punch for punch." Eve tended toward hyperbole.

I touched my eye, felt my reddened ear, and mentally inventoried my ribs. "Well, perhaps not exactly blow for blow."

She giggled, then went up on her tiptoes and kissed me. First quickly. Then more longingly. Finally, deeply. "Those poor working women almost got away from the oppression of the law. Thanks to you," she sighed. "Join our cause."

I tasted her on my lips. "What cause is that?"

"The cause of justice and equity."

"I believe in all those things," I said, lamely.

"Then *join* us. Help us rid the country of exploitation."

My head was throbbing like a steam-driven piston again. My ribs made breathing difficult. I edged back from her. "Look, maybe—" I paused and thought about her invitation. "Would you introduce me to Krael?"

Apparently I had misunderstood the nature of her invitation. She ignored my question. Instead, she pressed forward and I felt her soft breath against my mouth. She kissed me deeply again. "Come home with me, Will," she breathed.

Krael and Eve would have to wait. "I can't, Eve. I feel like I've gone twenty rounds with Jake Kilrain. And lost."

She softly probed my swollen lip with her finger. "I'll take care of you," she whispered. "Shared pain binds the oppressed."

She was breathing rapidly now, her bosom rising and falling as if beckoning me. Even so, I wasn't in the mood to listen to something Eve had memorized from radical pamphlets or heard at union gatherings. Even more than the promise of Eve's eager company tonight, I needed to recuperate. I looked into her soft eyes and muttered words heretofore foreign to my rhetoric. "Not tonight, Eve," I said.

23

By the time I eased myself down the stairs of the Denihur's boardinghouse Saturday morning I had a better grasp of Eve and her world. Last evening's adventure had etched in my mind her beauty, fearlessness, commitment—and naiveté. She obviously felt keenly the inequities of Boston's economic and legal systems, and was not about to stand idly by while citizens were unfairly denied rights or penalized by the law. Authority and convention didn't intimidate her. I admired that. At the same time, I sensed in her the same impetuousness and proclivity for misadventure that I was trying to put behind me.

The more I thought about her and our misadventures the previous night, the more obvious it was to me that I had wasted my time with her. I had discovered nothing about Gunther Krael from her. In fact, the only thing I'd learned was a new way to spend money and to lose a good night's sleep.

When I reached the breakfast room, I'd put thoughts of Eve Seilor and Gunther Krael behind me, and steeled myself to confront my deteriorating relationship with Claire. Sean had insisted we not put this off; that we find out what was going on between Win Hart and the Denihurs. A restless night of endlessly turning over in my mind Soden's proposal to look for the Bradford manuscript did not help. Eventually, though, I convinced myself Sean was right. We had a right to know where we stood.

The usual coterie of boarders was already at the breakfast table. So was Sean. I found a seat next to him and slowly lowered myelf into a chair, grunting with the effort. "Cait and Claire around?" I asked.

If he noticed my awkwardness in sitting, or my many bumps and cuts, he didn't comment on them. He indicated a plate of sausages in front of the others with his fork and spoke softly, "I just got here. Haven't seen either one, but someone's in the kitchen."

"You ready for this?" I asked, watching him fidget with his fork.

He reached out and stabbed a sausage. "As ready as I'll ever be."

The doors of the kitchen swung open and Abby McCorkle swept into the room, her face and neck glistening with perspiration, her plump hands full of steaming plates. Abby was an Irish lady who sometimes helped Cait and Claire with the cleaning and cooking. She set a dish of eggs in front of Sean.

"Where's Cait?" Sean asked, worry in his voice.

Abby stared at him as if to judge whether he had the right to ask her the question. Apparently she decided he had and, moreover, that he deserved an answer. "She and Claire are spending the day at the seashore, Mr. Dennison," she told him.

Sean and I exchanged bewildered looks. Neither of us doubted that the sisters were spending the day with Win Hart. "Just the two of them?" Sean asked slowly, desperate for confirmation.

The look on Abby's face left little doubt that Sean's question told her that she was treading on precarious ground; "I would think so, wouldn't you?" she said, cautiously.

Sean laid his fork and napkin on his plate and stood. "I'm not hungry," he growled, heading for the back door and slamming it behind him with force enough to rattle its windowpanes.

I'd lost my appetite as well. It occurred to me to press Abby for more details of her conversation with Claire this morning, but I thought better of it. It made no sense to put her on the spot. Abby was as loyal to Claire as a Siamese twin. If I wanted to confirm that Hart was spending the day at the beach with Claire, I knew how to do it without asking Abby to break confidences. A quick trip to the Hart gallery would suffice. Going there, I might even discover if the Ella that I'd met at the game was indeed Hart's *cousin*. Ammunition is ammunition. I shoved back my plate and followed Sean out the door. The day was already hot and humid. The heavily-leafed and overarching neighborhood trees created a veritable hot house.

I found Sean out front standing by his bicycle, still looking steamed. He turned toward me and watched me carefully as I moved slowly toward him, as if seeing me for the first time. "Jayzus," he said. "That big guy didn't—?"

"No, it wasn't 'the big guy'," I told him, then proceeded to relate to him my adventures at the Old Howard Theater and, later, at the magistrates' court.

He shook his head as he absorbed the particulars. "Blessed saints! You in any condition to go job hunting? Or to check on stolen property?"

"Oh, yeah. I move slowly, but I move. I can even breathe occasionally without pain. Not often, but sometimes. However, I don't need to go job hunting; I have some money and, besides, Soden gave me a lead on a job. And I'm seeing Honey Fitz tonight in Orchard Beach. Right now, I'm going to revisit the gallery."

He laid a hand on my arm. "Wait a minute, boyo. How in the blessed skirts o' Mary did you get Soden to help you? And when did this happen?"

I gave him a Cheshire cat's grin. "I got Collins' watch back and won my bet with the ol' man. And now I want to go to the gallery."

He frowned. "Don't give me that you-pissed-in-your-drawers grin. How'd you get the watch back? Got my stuff back too, did you?"

That wiped the smirk from my face. "Sean, lad, I haven't gotten any of your items back. I was just lucky that someone gave me Collins' watch. It's a long story that even I don't yet understand. What I *do* know is that I *am* going to visit Hart's gallery in the next hour. You coming?"

A shadow fell across his face. "Why'n hell do you want to stare at paintings while Cait and Claire are froliking at the seashore with a damned shark?"

I pulled him around to face me. "I prefer to act on facts, not emotion. You should try it occasionally. In the first place, we don't know if Cait and Claire are with Hart. In the second place, Win is interested in Claire, not Cait. You have nothing to worry about when it comes to him."

He bounced his bicycle as if to shake its dust loose. "Well, Cait doesn't need to be at the beach with him."

I nodded. "I'm angry with both Claire and Hart. I don't know what's going on, but I can find out at his gallery. That's the unemotional course to pursue, friend."

He gave me a pained expression. "Okay, okay. We're in this together."

He returned his bicycle to the backyard and we hurried to the corner, in so far as I could hurry, where we boarded a trolley. We arrived at Hart's in less than twenty minutes. The registry in the lobby informed us that Hart's office was on the third floor, above the gallery. We stepped into the spanking new Otis elevator and nodded to the colored operator. "Mr. Hart's office, please."

As we stepped out of the elevator on the third floor we faced a lobby where a huge desk was occupied by an aged crone. The woman had to be sixty years old and judging by appearances not one of them had been kind to her. With her white dress, pale skin, and small black eyes, she looked like a fish one might find in an open-market stall. "Yes?" she asked, the sound of reprimand in her voice.

I held my hat piously in front of me. "Beg pardon, Miss. I'm Will Beaman." I motioned toward Sean. "And this is Mr. Sean Dennison. We're here to see Mr. Hart."

She nodded primly and consulted her appointment book with the care of a Talmudic scholar. "I'm afraid that's not possible. You have no appointment." She eyed us disapprovingly.

I chose to ignore the tone of her voice and unfriendly manner. "Is Mr. Hart in? He'd want to see us. We're friends of his," I assured her.

Her mouth puckered ominously. "Mr. Hart is not in."

"When will he be available, Mrs., uh?"

"Miss," she said, her becoming even more pronounced.

"Of course. When will Mr. Hart be in, Miss—?"

"He will be away from the office on business all day."

Tiring of her stone-walling, I leaned forward, hands on her desk. "Do you have an address where we might reach him? It's important." I glanced at Sean who was rolling his eyes heavenward at the woman's truculence.

The harridan was not the least bit intimidated by my size, tone, or encroachment upon her desk. She did straighten up a wee bit and lean back slightly with her back rigid, but her eyes remained defiant. "Mr. Hart cannot be disturbed," she insisted.

As the crone made her statement with the finality of a tax collector, a door swung open behind her and the lady with the beautiful swan neck appeared. Etta. No, Ella. She was dressed more sedately now than when I saw her at the game, but there was no mistaken those velvet brown eyes, auburn hair, and graceful, kissable neck. "Who can't be disturbed, Miss Sizemore?" she asked as she approached us.

Miss Sizemore spun around, looking for all the world like a startled bird. "I was telling these gentlemen that Mr. Hart is not available," she mumbled.

The woman nodded, then laughed gaily and raised her brow in recognition. "Hello again, Mr. Beaman."

While I swelled with the knowledge that she'd remembered me, she was looking hard at my bruised face. She said nothing, however. She finally canted her head toward Sean. "I don't believe that I've met this gentleman."

"My apologies," I said. "This is Mr. Sean Dennison, Ella. Miss—?"

"Watson. Ella Watson."

She *was* his cousin! Of course. The Hart *and Watson* Gallery and Bookstore. I expelled breath I didn't realize I was holding.

"Please, come into my office," she said, and ushered us through the door she had just come out of. She offered us chairs and took one facing us. She was wearing a crimson suit, tight at the waist and bodice. No full shoulders or frills to detract from her voluptuous figure. "Don't mind Miss Sizemore," she said. "She's upset. We had an incident in the alley last night."

"Another attempt against the Remington paintings?" I asked.

She shook her head, setting her curls a jiggling. "We don't even know if we were the target. The police think the men might have been trying to break into the coin shop across the alley."

"Any one hurt?" I asked.

Ella Watson laughed, a wonderful musical laugh. "No. No, and no break-in. Actually Miss Sizemore is always sour and upset at something.

She's been like that forever. And she's very protective of Win. She's been protecting Win's father for three decades. She's now determined to protect Win with equal fervor."

"Protect him from what?" I asked.

"Oh, Win's at the shore today with two young ladies he's met. Miss Sizemore prefers to pretend he's on a business trip." She smiled warmly, her look of amusement seemingly perpetual. " Win does love the ladies." Then, after a pause: "So did his father, as Miss Sizemore well knows."

My mind flashed to the seashore. Sure as shootin' Claire was there with Hart. I knew from being around him and watching him that he was athletic and finely muscled. I could imagine the impression he'd make on Claire in a bathing suit. After all, it was my intent to similarly impress Claire that lay behind *my* asking Claire to the beach.

Ella Watson snapped me back to attention. "Why are you here?" she asked.

Sean leaned forward, his face giving no hint of his facetiousness. "We wish to discuss the merits of Remington's work with him, ma'am."

She smiled broadly. "I'd be happy to discuss Remington's work with you," she told him, accepting his statement at face value. "I'm considered something of an expert on artists of the west. Indeed, if I may be permitted some immodesty, I believe I know more than Win does about western artists and their work."

Sean backtracked quickly. "Our business involves Mr. Hart," he insisted.

She looked at Sean, then at me. After what seemed a long moment, she shook her head and smiled. "I don't believe you are being candid with me, Mr. Dennison." She started to get up, then settled back into her chair. "By any chance, do you know the young women Win is spending the day with?"

"I doubt that very much!" Sean huffed, nonplused by her sharp insight.

I didn't need more time with Ella Watson to know that verbally fencing with her would not be wise or gainful. And even had I not reached that conclusion, she cut off any opportunity that I might have taken to step into a fresh cowpie. "Well, Mr. Dennison, Mr. Beaman," she said, "I will inform Win of your interest in, uh, Remington's work. He'll be delighted."

"Oh, that won't be necessary atall," Sean squeaked. "We'll stop by again."

As we all paused in front of the door before exiting, Ella Watson pointed at my battered face. "It wasn't Win who—?"

"No."

"Good," she said. "That would displease me." Once again, she gave us the benefit of an enigmatic smile. "Perhaps you'll visit our offices again, Mr. Beaman? I would be happy to be of service. And, believe me, the more candid you are with me the more helpful I can be."

As we exited Miss Watson's office and stepped into the elevator, I thought I heard Ella laughing. My ears were red from embarrassment and my scalp prickled. Later, outside on the sidewalk, Sean turned to me. "Well, that was the proverbial turd on the dinner plate. What now?"

"I don't know about you," I told him, "but I'm catching a train. It's a bad time to be leaving the city, I know. I don't doubt Claire and Cait are with Hart. At the moment there's nothing I can do about that. But I'm very interested in what Honey Fitz has in mind for me." I didn't tell Sean that I needed to know what Honey Fitz wanted from me before I could decide what to do about Soden's proposal. I simply told him I was going to the boardinghouse to get my valise, then I would be off to Old Orchard Beach. I jabbed a finger at him for emphasis as I warned him, "You stay away from big guys with sour dispositions."

24

The train got me to Old Orchard Beach just as the sun disappeared below the forest that bordered the town on the west. Old Orchard Beach was just what Sean had described: a collection of shops, inns, cafes, arcades, fruit stands, bazaars, and galleries, sprinkled with lawn tennis courts, skeet shooting platforms, and brightly-colored beach-side dressing tents. It was Labor Day weekend and male visitors strolled leisurely along the streets and beach in white duck pants, white shoes, casual jackets, and a variety of straw boaters and golf caps. The women seemed to vie with each other for the most ostentatious and colorful headwear. Barefooted and scantily-clad children, seemingly unfettered by parental supervision, frolicked and whooped, rolling hoops, playing tag, and flying kites.

As I stepped off the train, I heard my name called. The slim, mustachioed man who'd hailed me hurried up and clasped my free hand. "Mr. Beaman?" He froze and took in my still-swollen eye and puffed lip. "John didn't mention you were a pugilist."

"I'm not; perhaps, if I improve my pugilist skills, I'd have fewer bruises."

He chuckled. "I'm Henry Fitzgerald. John's brother. Here, let me take your valise." I noticed that he used his brother's Christian name rather than calling him "Honey Fitz" as virtually everyone else did. Without waiting for permission, he gripped my suitcase and handed it to a colored porter. He gestured toward the station house. "My carriage is over there."

Henry Fitzgerald checked me into a modest but clean and comfortable hotel. He accompanied me to my room, eyed it with obvious satisfaction, and clapped a hand on my shoulder. "This should serve you nicely. You'll have dinner with us tonight. Eight o'clock at the Old Orchard Beach House." He pointed vaguely out the window. "Go one block toward the sea, then turn north. Casual dress. Until then?" He bestowed a friendly smile on me and departed, leaving me to myself.

I drew a bath and soaked for nearly thirty minutes, trying to heal my body and contemplating the day's events. I read several accounts of Boston's 9-1 Friday victory in local newspapers and learned that Manager Selee was going to let Smiling Jack Stivetts make a rare start against Buck Ewing's Cincinnati Redlegs today. Once a fine pitcher, Stivetts had recently been relegated to occasional starts in the outfield and even more infrequent pitching assignments. I tried to concentrate on the pennant race but my mind kept wandering to other matters. My suspicions about Hart being a ladies man had been confirmed. So had his presence with Claire. For the second time in a week robbers had been sniffing around the Hart and Watson gallery and bookstore. Or the nearby coin shop, whatever. Did those snoopings have anything to do with the recent rash of robberies, including the Bradford manuscript? Or with the mess with Shady Porch, Jimmy Collins and Sean?

I also contemplated this evening. Henry Fitzgerald appeared to be younger than Honey Fitz and every bit as gregarious. For all his friendly demeanor, however, he'd given me no hint of what his brother had in mind for me. Honey Fitz was a political creature first and foremost. If he'd been impressed with my connection to my father's detective agency, or by my success in identifying Germany Long's assailant a month ago, he probably had something he wanted me to investigate. But what?

I had no trouble locating the Old Orchard Beach House. Henry Fitzgerald met me in front of the building at five minutes to eight and ushered me into a small wood-paneled room where a modest table was set for four. "John will be here shortly," he informed me.

As if that were his cue, Honey Fitz strolled into the room accompanied by another look-alike. Ignoring my bruised face, Honey Fitz clamped my hand and shook it vigorously. "Mr. Beaman," he said with great enthusiasm. If my hand had been a water pump, he'd already have filled a five-gallon drum by the time he stopped. For all his enthusiasm there was something of the practiced routine in Honey Fitz's greeting. The man was a street politician and had learned his lessons well. He pointed to the man who resembled him even more faithfully than did young Henry. "You've met Henry," he said. "This is my older brother, James." James shook my hand with much greater restraint than had his politician brother.

Honey Fitz motioned toward the table. "Gentlemen, let's eat."

Ah, a no-nonsense man, I thought. I was wrong. Throughout dinner the three Fitzgeralds kept the conversation on the Beaneaters, the torrid pennant race, and on vacation life in Old Orchard Beach. We also compared notes on Joseph Lee and his new Massachusetts Civic League's projected social reforms, including Sunday recreation. The Fitzgeralds were convinced that if Lee enjoyed any success, it would be among the state's Catholics. Nothing was said about why I'd been asked to sup with them. Each man was affable, gregarious, and a grand raconteur. James was more reserved than Honey Fitz or Henry, more content to observe their behavior and mull over their utterances. And it was James who finally pushed back his plate and held out cigars to each of us in turn. "Shall we get down to business?" he suggested.

Honey Fitz fussed with snipping off the end of his cigar and lighting up. "James is the serious one among the Fitzgerald boys," he grinned. "He's my chief advisor." James leaned forward, arms crossed on the table before him, his cigar stuck between two fingers. He blew a stream of blue smoke toward the ceiling and watched it dissipate. "You're doubtless wondering why we asked you to meet with us. Well, Mr. Beaman, we have a proposal for you."

Despite my eagerness to hear the proposal, I took my time in inhaling my cigar and exhaling a burst of smoke toward where the residue from James'effort still floated near the ceiling. "What proposal is that?" I asked, trying to appear only mildly interested.

"We want you to find the Bradford Manuscript."

My pulse quickened and the blood pounded in my ears. The Bradford Manuscript! It was an epidemic! I stared at Honey Fitz in disbelief.

Honey Fitz ignored my open-mouth, blank stare. He just gave me a tight smile, and nodded.

I got myself under control. "*Everyone* wants the manuscript returned," I blurted, "why are *you* interested in seeing it found?"

James answered for his brother. "It's quite simple, Mr. Beaman. A great deal of political notoriety will accrue to the man who finds it. Your job will be to find it for John."

I spoke the obvious. "So John can realize the political rewards."

"Exactly. As you perhaps have surmised, we have our eyes on the mayor's office. By receiving credit for returning the manuscript, we would guarantee a victory. We want to, uh, dot the I's and cross the T's, so to speak." His liberal use of the royal 'we' did not escape me.

"Fair enough," I said. But why me? Others have better credentials and more experience in these types of things. I know nothing about artifacts or who collects them, or who might steal them." I sounded like an echo from my conversations with Hart and Soden.

Honey Fitz was bobbing his head in agreement and trying to shush me. "First, we're not convinced that this was a simple theft of an historical document by someone interested in collecting it or selling it to a collector," he said. "Secondly, It's you we want. You know how to go about these affairs, you can do it unobtrusively, and you know how to work people. And despite the present condition of your face, I've heard you can take care of yourself." His last observation was accompanied by a wink and a knowing smile.

I managed a weak smile while I sucked on my cigar and weighed what I'd heard, trying to figure out what to tell them. What the Fitzgeralds were proposing was exactly what Soden had suggested. It wouldn't be square to take pay from two men for doing the same job. On the other hand, Soden was offering me a bonus or reward, not regular pay, for finding the manuscript. Could I have the same arrangement with Honey Fitz? If I were lucky enough to find the blessed thing, could Soden and Honey Fitz somehow share credit? "What do you have in mind?" I asked, finally. "If I did accept your proposition, how am I going to pull it off?" I looked around the table at each in turn.

James smiled knowingly. "We have an, uh, understanding with the incumbent mayor. In exchange for our, uh, support on various issues, we have certain offices at our disposal. You're going to receive one of those posts—in the Board of Health."

"We want you to have the access to city personnel that you'll need for your investigation," Honey Fitz chimed in, pressing forward in his eagerness. "You'll have a legitimate reason to talk with anyone in any department, Health, Water, Parks, Sewer, Streets, Transportation, and Weights and Measures. It ought to make efforts to trace the manuscript easier." He sent another plume of smoke toward the ceiling and gazed at me with a self-satisfied smile. "What do you think?"

I couldn't help but grimace. "I think what I know about the Health Department you could put in your eye and still see."

Honey Fitz pounded the table again. Apparently, it was a habit of his when amused. "We'll make you a part-time supervisor," he added.

"You'd pay me a salary for that?"

It was James who nodded and answered. "Yes, and we'll pay you an advance when you start and a bonus once you locate the manuscript and bring it to us."

I sighed in resignation. "Tell me more about this proposal of yours."

The Fitzgeralds were charming and persuasive men. Before the evening was up and the brandy drained, I had promised them my help, taken advance money from them, and been named as an inspector-at-large for Boston's Board of Health. We agreed to talk again Sunday. I didn't know whether I was relieved or disappointed. A week ago I had been summarily fired. Now, on Labor Day, I'd gotten work. I didn't need to go to Soden's son for a job slopping hot tar in the boiling sun. But I wasn't in base ball and that's where I wanted to be. Nonetheless, if I had as much luck in securing the manuscript as I did Jimmy Collins' watch there would be no end to the problems I could put behind me. That is, *if* I could talk Soden and Honey Fitz into sharing the glory of any discovery I might make.

25

I spent Sunday morning enjoying the sea breeze and reviving my battered body. The Fitzgerald brothers remained with their families, and I saw nothing of them. A group of young people invited me to join them in a badminton 'tournament' that helped me pass the time. What with my sore ribs I didn't move around like I wanted to, but among the unathletic and fun-loving vacationers I held my own. Several of the young ladies flirted outrageously with me. All very public and harmless, of course.

After lunch, as planned, I met again with the Fitzgeralds. We went over our understanding once more and probed possible avenues of investigation. They discussed the personnel in various offices who might prove useful. They also informed me of political friends and enemies of theirs, arguing that knowing a man's political affiliations would eliminate potential mine fields. James thrust more bills at me. He called it a welcoming gift for joining the Fitzgerald team.

Buoyed by my diminishing soreness, the fresh wad of bills in my pocket, the promise of steady paychecks, and the prospects of not just one, but two bonuses should I be lucky, I boarded the train at three o'clock. With what seemed like half the visitors to Old Orchard Beach, many exhausted and sunburnt, I slept most of the way to Boston.

Arriving in the city just minutes after five, I flagged a hansom and headed toward the boardinghouse. "What have the Beaneaters been up to?" I asked the aged driver.

"They sneaked by Cincinnati yesterday, 7-6," he grumbled, "An' looked like hell doing it. Stivetts had no curveball and couldn't throw his speed pitch past *me*. Marty Bergen was erratic—as always. He let three balls get by him, but he also threw out two runners and drove in four runs. You never know how that guy's gonna play. But Baltimore keeps winning, too. They may never lose another ball game."

A brisk breeze coming off the ocean chilled my face, and I buttoned my coat to the throat. Having warmed up with his complaints about Stivetts' and Bergen's performances, the driver assaulted me throughout the trip with arguments claiming the superiority of Cincinnati's Bid McPhee over the Beaneaters' second baseman, Bobby Lowe, and the greater power of Cincinnati's Jake Beckley over Boston's Fred Tenney at first base. And then he started describing yesterday's Labor Day parade. He was a man of many words and he held none of them back.

At the boardinghouse I discovered the dining room darkened. I quietly opened the back door and slipped in. I was two steps up the stairwell when a voice froze me.

"Hello, Will."

It was Cait. She was standing by the big coal range, just inside the dimly-lit kitchen to my left, drying a pan with a large white towel. Her large jet-black eyes were soft and sad. Still, she had that pensive elegance and beauty that John Singer Sergeant captures so dramatically in his portraits of females. "Cait! You surprised me," I said. You're working late."

Her smile didn't reach her eyes. "There's always something to do around here," she said. "Did you have a pleasant Labor Day weekend?"

I told her I had, and asked her if she had seen Sean.

She stepped back into the kitchen and exchanged the dry pan for a freshly washed one. "I haven't seen him for several days to talk to," she said in a quiet voice while moving toward me, away from the light. "Sometimes he sketches society events for the Sunday edition. He makes extra money helping out his chums at the Society Desk. He'll probably be late."

"Claire in?"

She seemed suddenly very interested in the pan she was drying, scrubbing frantically at a spot that seemed to displease her. "No."

Well. Well. "I see," I muttered, hoping that my obvious disappointment would provoke her into being more forthright about Claire's whereabouts. It didn't, so I moved toward the stairs. "Goodnight, then, Cait. I'll see Sean tomorrow. Claire, too."

"Will?"

"Yes?" I paused in my ascent.

She retrieved the note from a bulletin board near the calendar and handed it to me with a damp hand. "I almost forgot," she said. "A young boy delivered a note for you." "He said it was from a Miss Seilor. He expected a reply, but I told him you weren't in. I hope it's not bad news."

I considered opening and reading the note but decided against it. Instead, I stuffed it into my coat pocket. "I'm sure it's not bad news. I'll take care of it," I said, and excused myself.

While in my bath, I read Eve's note. It suggested we meet Tuesday and gave me a time and an address that meant nothing to me. I returned to my room from my bath physically refreshed, but more troubled than ever. And not about tomorrow's proposed rendezvous with Eve where I planned to push her harder on Krael and the possibility of me meeting him. It continued to trouble me that Krael might have had something to do with the attacks upon Porch, Collins, and Sean, and with the theft of Sean's sketchbook. It also bothered me that I'd seen Krael at the gallery and, following that, two attempted burglaries had occurred in the alley behind the gallery. And then, of course, there was Tony Onofrio's death. Unearthing Krael might be the first step in carrying out Honey Fitz's scheme and embracing Soden's offer.

While toweling my damp hair, I sat on my bed, more than a little pensive. It was now obvious to me that Win Hart and Claire were spending both days and evenings together. Exactly what that portended I didn't know. She could, of course, merely be showing him the city, doing what any friend would do. Perhaps Hart was simply her source of western lore. It could really be a harmless thing. Romance didn't have to enter it. On the other hand—

To weigh Claire's behavior, I needed time to confirm where she was tonight and who she was with. And what she was doing. In the meantime, I knew I had to stanch any idea of romance Eve had for me. At the same time I needed to convince her to bring me in contact with Gunther Krael. In fairness, I had to deal with her face-to-face.

I left my door ajar, waiting for Sean to come in. I fell asleep at some point after midnight. Sean had not returned by the time I dozed off.

26

Early Monday I met Sean coming out of the water closet. He looked like hell, his face pale and eyes puffy. He winced as if in pain and rubbed his forehead with his fingers, trying to remove a phantom smudge.

"I've seen corpses who looked more sprightly than you do," I told him.

He puffed his cheeks and expelled his breath while continuing to rub his forehead. "I spent hours on the racing track Saturday, then ended up covering two society bashes. Must have sketched every wealthy dowager in Boston *and* their spoiled granddaughters. Yesterday, I sketched in Franklin Park for next week's Sunday supplement."

"You've done as much before—and survived."

He made a face. "I didn't drink my way through those."

"Ah." I rested my hand on his shoulder. "Poor Sod. Cait told me that you two haven't talked for several days. Do you plan on confronting her about Hart this morning? If so, I suggest you postpone it. Considering your condition, you'll have neither the subtlety nor delicacy for the task. And maybe not the strength. Anyway, I was right, wasn't I? Hart is interested in Claire. It wasn't Cait who was with Hart last night; it was Claire. Cait was here when I came in."

He squinted at me, as if suffering new pain, and continued to massage his brow. "Blessed saints! Which of the hundred or so questions you've cast my way do you want me to answer?" He didn't wait for my response. "No, I haven't talked to Cait yet. And yes, I'm going to do so this morning. I've got to find out what's going on. I haven't been able to sit her down and talk to her for three bloody days."

"Can't I convince you not to do this?"

"No, by jayzus."

"Into the valley of death rode the six hundred—" I intoned.

Twenty minutes later, we descended the stairs. By the time we pulled up chairs at the breakfast table, the usual gang was already well into their meal. Bobbed heads and grunts greeted us. The only two chairs available were between two salesmen, including the Fuller Brush drummer with a ponderous sample case. I shoved the valise closer to him with my foot, and sat. Sean slid in beside me and reached for a platter of eggs. Except for a quiet discussion of America's policy toward Spanish rule in Cuba among three boarders at the end of the table, the meal was eaten in silence. Sean shoveled a forkful into his mouth and chewed on eggs as if he hated them.

I tried to divert his attention. "Parson Lewis is pitching today against the Cincinnatis," I told him. "Let's take in the game. My treat. You can do a few sketches of ol' Buck Ewing. Or Dummy Hoy. Tim's readers would love sketches of Hoy." Sean wasn't about to be distracted. He shoveled another fork full of eggs into his mouth.

Cait brought out a fresh pot of coffee. She smiled at us as she passed.

Sean watched her fill cups at the end of the table, asking each boarder his wishes in turn. His gaze followed her as she moved toward him, his eyes narrowing. Sean was not a happy chap and he wasn't hiding that fact. "At least she's here today," he muttered.

I saw the disaster between Cait and Sean looming like a summer squall, and tried desperately to prevent it. Seizing his arm and wrenching him toward me, I managed a half-hearted chuckle. "The Fitzgeralds told me they think Massachusetts Catholics will support the Civic League's reforms," I told him, rushing my words. "Including base ball on Sundays. Do you believe them?"

He shook off my arm, ignored my question, and kept his eyes riveted on Cait.

Cait moved behind him. "Coffee, Sean?" she asked pleasantly, holding the large pot toward his cup.

"You're not spending today with Mr. Hart?" he asked.

I cringed involuntarily. Oh, oh, I thought.

Her eyes widened and her mouth formed a perfect O. The coffeepot remained poised over his cup. "I beg your pardon?" she said icily.

The table went silent. Heads craned toward us, eyes curious. It didn't intimidate the red-headed son of Eire. No, sir.

"You're not spending another day with Mr. Hart?" he asked again, his voice dripping sarcasm.

She set the coffeepot on the table next to his cup. "What are you talking about?"

He twisted to look up at her as she stood behind his left shoulder. "I'm talking about the fact that I've seen more of Abby McCorkle around here than I've seen of you."

Several boarders smiled knowingly. Others smirked and began to drop napkins in plates and shove themselves away from the table. This was like watching a street urchin grab an apple from the bottom of a pyramid of apples in a public market. I put my hand on Sean's wrist, knowing it was already too late. "This isn't the time or place, Sean."

Her eyes still wide, Cait glanced at me. "Time or place for what, Mr. Beaman?" she asked in a frosty voice.

Before I could comment, Sean blurted, "To find out your intentions toward Mr. Hart, Cait. You *and* Claire's." The remaining two boarders crammed the remains of their toast into their mouths, quickly gulped their coffee, pushed back their chairs, and shuffled off, looking back over their shoulders at us as they did so.

Cait paid them no heed. She pointed a menacing finger at Sean. "You wait right here, Sean Dennison." She hurried toward the kitchen, then stopped and looked back. "You, too, Will." She plunged into the kitchen. For several minutes we sat silently, listening to the voices of Claire and Cait rising and falling in the next room.

"You were as subtle as a vinegar douche," I moaned.

"Sure, 'n you'd have been so slick that we'd never have gotten to the heart of the matter."

"Oh, we're going to get to the heart of the matter now, all right," I muttered, glancing at the kitchen door.

When Cait returned, Claire was with her, clutching a dishtowel with which she wiped her hands. Both women were angry, their usual pale faces flushed, their lips thin lines. Irritably, Claire swiped at a curl of hair that had fallen over her eyes. Her other hand continued to clutch the towel, her knuckles white. "What's this all about, Sean?" she asked, spacing her words deliberately.

The fiery Sean didn't back off, I'll give him that. He was like a man retrieving a gold coin from a chamberpot. He had to know he didn't look, feel, or smell good, but he was not about to let go. "I thought we had an understanding, Cait," he said. "But never mind that, I guess. You've spent more time with Winthrop Hart than you have with me this past week." Apparently deciding suddenly that he was too exposed, he pulled me into the controversy. "And the same with you, Claire. You haven't spent time with Will in days."

Cait grabbed the bait first. "What Claire and I do with our time is our business, *Mr.* Dennison," she spat.

Claire was more temperate but equally adamant. "For one thing, Sean, both you and Will have been busy yourself and absent much of the time. Aside from that, we have every right to spend time with Mr. Hart."

"You've seen him virtually every day!" Sean protested in a thinly disguised whine.

I had listened in silence to this point, trying to calm the discussion and get the answers I wanted without embarrassing myself or enflaming the situation. I still hadn't come up with anything when Cait huffed, "Well, Mr. Sean Dennison. Not only have we spent time with Mr. Hart these past few days, but we are going to spend *today* with him as well. So there."

Sean bolted to his feet and flung his napkin down. "Well, that cuts it then, Cait."

I grabbed his elbow. "Sean, sit down." He brushed my hand away and stalked out of the room. Cait burst into tears and raced for the kitchen, slamming the door behind her.

I stood and stared at Claire. She stared back, her eyes hard and flat. "Claire," I said, trying to defuse the tension and to create some bridge to her, "You probably should be with Cait now. You and I can talk later. Calmly and quietly."

She glanced toward the kitchen where the sounds of Cait sobbing could be heard.

"In a minute. Cait and I have spent several days enjoying Mr. Hart's company and showing him the city, Will. Cait has come along on occasion because I asked her to. She has in no way compromised her relationship with Sean. Nor has she done anything to cause him embarrassment or distress."

I tried to break in, but she was in no mood to be interrupted.

"I have spent time with Mr. Hart because he is charming and he is curious about Boston. I am curious about Montana. There is nothing untoward in my behavior toward Mr. Hart. And I do not feel I owe you any explanation or apology."

I knew she was right, but her words wounded me, nonetheless. "Don't you? Don't you indeed? I thought you cared for me."

Her eyes softened. "I do care for you."

Though I should have let it end there, I plunged on. "Apparently not as much as I thought you did." I was starting to sound like Sean.

She shook her head, as if not believing what I'd said. "I do care for you, Will. But we have no formal understanding. And even if we did, my time with Mr. Hart should in no way jeopardize that."

"I believe it does." Jeez, I had to be honest.

My candor didn't impress her. "Well, Mr. Beaman, I have promised Mr. Hart that Cait and I would attend Boston's annual horse show with him at Mechanics Hall today, and we are going to. You will have to be mature enough to accept that fact."

The heat rose in me. "Are you suggesting I'm being immature?" For someone who'd badgered Sean about his shoot-from-the-hip responses, I was making my own mess. And I knew it.

"Today you and Sean are acting like disappointed schoolboys, yes," she said.

I reached for her hand. "I'm sorry, Claire. I didn't want this to happen."

She withdrew her hand and retreated a step. "I will not be told who I can see."

"I wasn't doing that, Claire. Neither was Sean."

"Perhaps not. But now I've got to see to Cait. And we have to finish up here and prepare to meet Mr. Hart. We promised him." She moved swiftly to the kitchen where Cait's crying could still be heard.

Later, after hurrying through my ablutions, I left the boardinghouse. Neither Claire nor Cait was in the breakfast room when I departed. I poked my head into the kitchen in search of them, but it was empty. Sean was nowhere to be seen. So much for us spending an exciting day at the Grounds watching Parson Lewis and the Beaneaters.

I headed for the public library. I wanted to read about everything that happened in the city two days before and two days following the pilfering of the Bradford manuscript. It seemed an intelligent way to start on my assignments from Honey Fitz and Soden. It also seemed wise to do before talking with Eve Seilor. More important, perhaps, it was an effective way to put this morning's unmitigated disaster behind me for a few hours. I had some serious thinking to do on both fronts.

27

The cavernous public library was nearly empty. The occasional conversation or chair scraping against the floor echoed in the high-ceiling rooms. I had a large table to myself. Once I told the librarians that I was interested in reading about the theft of the Bradford manuscript, they couldn't do enough for me. For two hours I pored over the materials urged upon me, scribbling notes, sketching crude maps, and forming a list of questions for which I needed answers. I also concocted a rough chronology of events around the ceremonial site on the day of the heist, and roughed out a location chart of where individuals and groups were known to be when the manuscript went missing.

Taking advantage of the staff's eagerness, I asked them to collect all instances where individuals had been arrested for playing base ball on Sunday in the state. I wanted to know the disposition of these cases. I also requested all information they had on the Civic League. They scurried about while I worked and quickly presented me with a sizable folder.

Satisfied that I'd done all I could in the library, I thanked my helpers and proceeded to the Streets Department to ask the whereabouts of the Superintendent of Streets, Gerald Staley. I was told he was overseeing a work crew near Faneuil Hall, on North Street, just off Congress. The Hall was where, a week before, the ambassador had been scheduled to hand over the Bradford manuscript. I wanted to talk with Staley. I also wanted to reconnoiter the area, to determine for myself access possibilities to the manuscript as well as potential escape routes for those who swiped it

I found Staley easily enough. An obese gentleman in a light, worsted suit, his nose was large enough to permit him to smoke a cigar in a downpour. He was prodding a half dozen men wielding shovels. The men, naked to their waists, stood in a hole nearly to their necks flinging dirt in a steady rhythm out onto piles around the excavation. Other than berating his men, Staley's hardest task seemed to be keeping the flying dirt and dust off his shiny patent leather shoes.

"Mr. Staley?"

He turned rheumy eyes upon me. "Yeah?"

Trying not to stare at his prodigious nose, I showed him my badge identifying me as a Health Inspector. "I'm Will Beaman. Mind answering a few questions for me?"

"What kinda questions?" he asked sourly.

"I was told that you helped supervise the Bradford manuscript ceremony."

He frowned. "So what? Why're you asking about that?" He gestured at my badge. "You're in the Health Department."

I had rehearsed my response to such skeptics. "I have authority to investigate any events or conditions affecting the public health," I told him, assuming my most imperial voice.

It didn't impress Staley. "What the hell does the Bradford manuscript have to do with public health?" he wanted to know, glaring down into the hole. "Come on, Murphy," he bellowed, "Fer crissakes, bend yore goddamn back!"

Staley obviously was in need of some prodding himself. I leaned toward the hole, peered in, and shook my head sadly. "I'm afraid I'm going to have to halt this operation," I informed him.

He glared at me, a combination of anger and puzzlement crossing his face. "Like hell you will. I was told to have this work finished today."

I feigned understanding, but remained insistent. "I fear you're nearing a gas line, Mr. Staley. I'm going to have to suspend operations until I can verify the placement of the pipe."

He looked like I'd told him that worms could fly. "Fer crissakes, there ain't no gas lines down there." Again he leaned over the excavation. "Jesus! Carmody, why don't you just take a goddamm nap? Moooove!"

I did my best imitation of an officious bureaucrat. "Sorry, sir, the possibility exists that you're going to damage a gas line. It could explode. Even if it doesn't, it'll present a hazard in the area. You'll have to cease digging immediately until I can study this."

Staley was fat and rheumy-eyed, but he wasn't stupid. He began to nod his head as if he'd just discovered water ran downhill. "Oookay, son," he growled. "Let's stop with the crap. What kind of questions do you have?"

For the next ten minutes, while Murphy, Carmody, and friends increased the piles of dirt around the excavation, Staley walked through the day of the theft for me. He and his workers had blocked all vehicle traffic for two blocks around Faneuil Hall two hours before the festivities began. Only individuals with invitations were permitted to enter the area around the Hall where a dais and bleachers had been set up. The general public had been kept across the street. He finished and made a dismissive gesture with his hands. "Okay?" Without waiting for my confirmation, he turned his attention to the hole. "Ah, come onnnn, Murphy! Fer crissakes, act like you've seen a goddamn spade before, man."

I didn't let him dismiss me. "One more thing, Mr. Staley," I said.

He waved me off and studied the excavation. "I've told you all I know," he said.

"How clear were the streets?"

He exhaled noisily. "From about a half hour before the ceremony began to five or so minutes after it ended in confusion, the streets were clear." he told me, clearly angry. "No streetcars. No carriages. No pedestrians. Those goddamn streets were clear."

"Any idea how the thieves reached the manuscript, then got away with it?"

"Nope. And I've given it a lot of thought. That it, now?"

It wasn't. "Could anyone have passed himself off as one of your workers to get close to the podium or the dais?" I asked.

His face wrinkled in disbelief. "Absolutely not," he growled. "Goddamn, I was walking around the whole time, checking. There were coppers all around too. I know patrolmen in this neighborhood as well as I know my workers. I didn't see anything—or anyone—suspicious. Now, get the hell out of here and let me finish this job."

Satisfied that I'd gotten from Staley all I could get, I left him to his excavation and walked toward Faneuil Hall. Its bottom floors were still used as a public market; its upper floors for a variety of public affairs. Because it was showing wear, Mayor Quincy recently had requested funds to fireproof and rehabilitate it. Still, it was an impressive edifice. I moved around the Hall checking out the streets and the buildings lining them, finally pausing before the area where the ceremony took place. Nothing. No way that I could see for someone to grab the manuscript and skedaddle.

I strolled around the corner to the side of the building. There I watched as a city worker placed a barrier to warn traffic, then began to direct vehicles and horses around it. A second worker pried open a steel sewer cover and motioned a third fellow to descend.

I approached the man who'd pried up the cover and flashed my Health Department supervisory badge. "How often do you check these sewers?" I asked him.

He didn't have Gerald Staley's suspicion of my badge or authority. But, then, he didn't seem to understand what I'd said, or why I was addressing him, either. Assuming he hadn't heard me I repeated my question, noting all the while that he, like his companions, was short, swarthy, and mustachioed. His eyes swung frantically, first to the man who now sat with his legs dangling into the sewer opening, then to the flagman. The flagman spoke rapid Italian to the man in the hole, handed him the flag, and moved toward us, shaking his head. "Antonio, he no speaka English."

I nodded and repeated my question.

The flagman held up four stubby, calloused fingers. "Four. Eacha year. Sometimes more, iffa dere's a trouble." His companions watched him intently looking for hints of what we were talking about.

"You walk through them?" I asked him. "Examine them carefully?"
He nodded.

"When was the last time you or your crew checked this neighborhood?"

He looked at his friends, as if they understood the question, then shrugged. "Tree mon's?" he ventured.

"That's a long time ago."

"We a suppose to do it two week ago, but . . . no."

That piqued my interest. "The inspection was called off?"

"We tol' to inspect. We inspect. We tol' not to inspect, we no do it."

"Why was the inspection called off?"

The man gave me an exaggerated shrug.

"*Who* called it off?"

Again, the pronounced rolling of his shoulders. I pointed to the sewer opening. "These sewers are connected throughout the downtown area? You can go down into the system here and come up somewhere else?"

"Shore. Easy."

Chewing on this new information, I left the sewer workers to their task and grabbed an electric car for the Grounds. I was prepared, if necessary, to inspect the ball field as part of my *official* duties as an excuse for being there for the game against Buck Ewing's Cincinnati club. But I really needed to find Tim who had invited me to accompany him to Tony Onofrio's funeral. By the time I arrived Haggerty had the diamond raked and preened. Not enough fans showed up to move the turnstiles. Cincinnati proved to be a tough mark, beating Lewis and the Beaneaters, 5-3 to crimp Boston's hopes for the pennant. Old Buck Ewing's lads played tough. Their lefty Ted Breitenstein was almost unhittable, Jake Beckley provided all the punch that the Reds needed, and the fleet Dummy Hoy played terriffic defense.

I hung around while Tim wrote his account of the game and then we left for the funeral. Boston's disappointing loss to Cincinnati put us in a funereal mood long before we reached the cemetery. It turned out to be a small affair and very brief. Probably there were more detectives present than family or fellow workers. After the ceremony I passed on my condolesces to Sean who brooded about the harm we'd brought to his father's friend, and to the family, then excused myself and returned to Faneuil Hall.

At the Hall, I began a building-by-building survey, questioning wholesalers, shopkeepers, artisans, tradesmen, landlords, tenants, and whomever else I came across. I tried to keep my questions general, relevant to matters of health, so as not to provoke undue suspicions. Still, most persons quickly saw through me. Virtually everyone I talked with told me the same thing: they'd been questioned repeatedly by the street patrolmen and by city detectives. Residents told me what they'd told interrogators before me, they had seen nothing that would throw light on how the manuscript was boosted. After a withered and prickly woman who ran a boardinghouse told me in no uncertain terms to leave her alone, I gave up. I was nearly to the stairs when the old crone yelled at me. I turned. "What's that, ma'am?"

"The horse die, did it?" she asked.

"Ma'am?"

"The horse. That collapsed." She seemed exasperated with my ignorance.

I walked back toward her, my interest piqued. She was pale as a grub, her white hair the thinnest cotton. "You saw a horse collapse?"

"Isn't that what I just told you?" she said, her voice ripe with impatience.

"The day of the ceremony for the Bradford manuscript?"

She was clearly irritated by my apparent slowness in grasping the situation. "Yes." For the next half-hour, in excruciating detail, she told me about the unfortunate animal. After almost five years, the classical education I'd received at Harvard was rapidly blurring in my mind, but as I listened to the old lady's tale I remembered enough history to appreciate that the Trojan horse of ancient Troy had spawned many a novel imitation.

28

Tuesday morning, I headed for my meeting with Eve Seilor. My intention was to terminate our relationship, at least any possible romantic relationship. But not before she helped me connect with Gunther Krael. During the ride I played the old woman's story over and over in my mind. According to her, minutes before the Bradford manuscript was to be handed over by the British government to the state of Massachusetts, three men had struggled with an agitated horse. Harnessed to an empty two-passenger chaise, the skittish horse bolted through police lines, tugging the men through the thoroughfare. When the spooked horse neared the celebrity area, additional policemen and bystanders tried to quiet it. Two men eventually led the horse away and the police reset the barriers. At that point the horse collapsed. That in itself was not an unusual sight in Boston. Horses—overworked, ill-treated, or just plain old—died in streets all over the country.

Still, the woman was troubled over the equine's fate. She insisted that three men accompanied the horse across the street during its panic; two led it away from the Hall. It was her description of the men that made my pulse quicken. One, according to her, "was a giant of a man." The second was of medium height "and average looking." The third was "shorter, plug-like, bearded, and darker." I suspected that I'd seen two of them at the Emma Goldman rally, and one of them at the Remington exhibit.

Though my chat with the Italian sewer workers and the old woman had given me leads I wanted to pursue, it was getting late and I needed to end this nonsense with Eve and patch things up with Claire. I was weary of pursuing a double-standard in my relations with these women.

Knowing Eve's exuberance for the rights of workers, and having already witnessed her idea of a tryst at the Old Howard Theater, I should have anticipated what I was riding into. Nonetheless, even the fact that the streets got more and more crowded as I neared my destination failed to alert me. The crowd was so thick by the time I got within a block of my destination with Eve at Chauncy and Bedford that the streetcar slowed to a crawl. Like other impatient riders, I hopped off and made my way on foot.

It was only after I turned the corner onto Chauncy that I heard the faint sounds of a band. I noticed the placards and banners at the same moment. I couldn't see those waving the signs over the heads of the crowd, but it was clear that there was a parade or protest. It was still a block or two away, moving toward me. Hopping onto a shop step, I could make out some of the signs carried by the marchers. "Justice," one said. "A Fair Wage," said another. Several read simply, "Strike."

Those around me became more agitated as the marchers neared. A thin man in a boater and cinnamon mustache clutched my arm. "What bunch is it this time? The shoemakers?" Before I could answer a fellow in front of me said, "Yeah, it's the bloody shoemakers. And probably the glaziers and gas fitters, too."

"Populist bastards," the thin man growled.

I wasn't in the mood to debate the virtues or failings of the union movement; I pushed past them and tried to work my way along the crowded sidewalks toward my meeting place with Eve. Traffic had come to a standstill. Fighting panic, horses pulling a variety of conveyances began to snort and rear. Trolleys were barely crawling. Bicyclists had to dismount and jostle through the melee with the rest. Dogs barked. Children darted among pedestrians and horses, some snatching at women's purses. The cacophony nearly drowned out the band.

A half dozen mounted policemen urged their horses into the crowd. The Bedford-Chauncy intersection seemed to bulge. As I was bumped and shoved, I glimpsed an open space at the mouth of an alley. Frustrated with my lack of progress, I slipped into the alley to catch my breath. Ten yards further into the alley—and in semi shadow—a half dozen men were deep in an animated conversation. One, a fire-plug of a man, was grabbing shoulders and shouting orders.

Gunther Krael! A bare second after I recognized him, he saw me. He jabbed a finger toward me and bellowed something. Several of his henchmen charged. One was a veritable giant.

Resistance never entered my mind. I fled into the crowd. My size saved me. That and strength and athletic agility which permitted me to slip my way through the crowd—bulldozing when necessary—and the apparent reluctance of Krael's goons to mistreat the crowd to the point it might turn on them. As a consequence, I put enough distance between us that they soon left off the chase. I collapsed against a storefront and tried to catch my breath and satisfy myself that the chase had ended.

Someone touched my arm. "Will! You came!"

Eve Seilor was beaming, a placard reading "Support Justice / Support Unionism," resting on her shoulder. She was dressed in a simple black skirt, white, high-necked blouse held by a brooch, and a man's golf cap. She gripped her sign with both hands.

"Came to *what*?" I asked her. "I thought you wanted to see me."

"I *do*," she smiled, "but first things first."

A group of street toughs shoved past us and moved toward the protesters, waving fists and shouting obscenities. Where they moved they left an empty path. Eve tugged my arm. "Come on, let's get closer." She pulled me into the wake left by the thugs.

As we neared the cross streets the parade was entering, coming straight for us, I saw a streetcar pulling away from Mechanics Hall. It approached from the left. Claire and Cait had spent the day at Mechanics Hall with Win Hart, attending the horse show. It flitted through my mind that they could be on that streetcar, being sucked into the fracas.

At that same moment, the two men from the alley who'd pursued me on Krael's orders burst into the street. The larger man grabbed a policeman and hauled him off his horse. The crowd howled and surged toward the fallen officer and his assailant.

"My God!" Eve shouted, excitement in her voice. She tugged me forward.

I groaned. "Oh, Sweet Jesus. Not again."

29

Tradesmen, shopkeepers, shoppers, hecklers, recent attendees from the Horse Show, and street thugs pushed into the protesters and band members, forcing them into the intersection. The strikers' chants became more strident. Policemen, those still astride steeds, pounded the ribs of their mounts with their heels to urge them toward the fallen copper. They blew their whistles and flailed away with their truncheons. I could no longer see the rowdies who'd pulled the policeman from his horse, but hoodlums, quick to take advantage of an opportunity, had pounced on the fallen officer.

By now, the streetcar, carrying passengers from the horse show, had edged into the intersection where it was halted by the teeming mob. Shouting insanely, hooligans began to rock the streetcar, triggering angry protests and hysterical screams from its passengers. The music stopped. Musicians were now using their instruments to defend themselves. Union marchers were resorting to fists and placards to fend off anyone and everyone. Onlookers milled in the intersection, braying at the strikers.

Eve was a battler. Wielding her placard, she pounded on the back of a hoodlum who was trying to kick a fallen man. She struck him so hard and so frequently that her placard shredded and its pole splintered. Unarmed, she drummed on the man with her fists, screeching at him like a fish wife. I pulled her away so that I could get at him.

As I swung her aside, I found myself facing those who were roaring insanely and rocking the streetcar. Their numbers were great enough to bring the trolley's wheels off the tracks each time they rocked the car. Terrified passengers tried to scramble off the besieged vehicle. Others were flung off by the rocking. Male passengers beat on the heads of those swarming the trolley trying to derail it, or tried to help females escape the car. For a second the crowd parted sufficiently for me to glimpse the front of the trolley.

There, Win Hart was kicking out at an assailant and trying to usher Claire and Cait off the encircled car. I froze and held my breath. Claire seemed on the brink of serious injury—or even death. To this point, I'd been half-irritated, half-exhilerated. Rough and tumble never intimidates me; I can take care of myself and the threat of physical pain has never slowed me. However, seeing Claire surrounded by that mob paralyzed me. But only for a split second. I set Eve down. To hell with the thug. Someone else would have to deal with him. "Come on!" I urged Eve, and shouldered my way toward the swaying streetcar.

At that moment, as if in slow motion, I saw three things. The first was Win Hart springing from the trolley still clutching Claire and Cait. The second was the trolley toppling over amid a thunderous clang and sparks and the increased roar of the crowd. Finally, as the car was shoved over by the maddened crowd, I spotted Gunther Krael, just beyond it, thrusting his fist in triumph and scurrying away.

Dogs and horses went mad amidst the sound and fury. Women shrieked. Children wailed. Men cursed. More and more mounted police poured into the cross streets.

"Stay with me," I shouted again at Eve, trying to pull her behind me toward the Denihurs. Someone had set the car on fire and smoke bellowed from it. I was within five yards of it when I felt Eve's hand slip from mine as she was sucked into the crowd.

Virtually at the same time I closed to a few yards of Claire and Cait. I glanced frantically around to locate Eve, and not seeing her, shouted at Claire. "Claire! Here!"

She saw me, gripped Cait by the blouse, and fell against me.

I gathered them in. "Where's Hart?" I shouted.

Claire looked up at me, her eyes wide with terror and confusion. "He was . . . swept away," she said in a tone that said she didn't believe it herself.

"We're going to die," Cait sobbed.

I desperately tried to locate Win or Eve. No luck. "We're not going to die," I assured Cait. "Come on." Trying to shield them under each arm, I began to force my way toward a nearby store. It seemed to take forever. A bald-headed shopkeeper in a green apron and arm cuffs struggled to keep us—or anyone, for that matter—from entering, but my desperation added strength to my imposing size. I crashed through his door, sending the shopkeeper sprawling. I helped him up and shouted, "You have an upstairs apartment?"

He nodded as if dazed.

Rumaging in my pocket, I extracted a bill, and slapped it into his quaking palm. "Where these ladies will be safe?"

He nodded dumbly and pointed toward a staircase at the back of the store.

I helped him pull a counter of goods in front of the door to block it, then, with Claire and Cait, followed him upstairs. He led us to a small living room overlooking the street. We stood there, the four of us, shaken, perspiring, breathing hard, watching the chaos below. Cait was still sobbing but quieter now.

I didn't see Eve in the mass of humanity below us, but I saw Win Hart immediately. He had corralled the riderless policeman's horse and had mounted it. He was now spurring the animal through the crowd toward a cluster of female unionists huddling together like Custer's troops at the Little Big Horn. The man had sand. "You ladies stay here," I told them. "You'll be safe. I'll be back for you."

I thundered down the stairs, hurled aside the counter, and plunged once more into the pandemonium. People were now straining to put distance between themselves and the flaming streetcar. Pungent black smoke belched from the car and hovered in the intersection. I heard the distant sound of fire engines.

By the time I'd muscled my way across the street, two mounted officers had joined Hart. The three of them were trying to position themselves and their steeds between the union members and their attackers. Hart skillfully whirled his horse, kicking out at those around him. He looked like a Remington character on a rambunctuous bronc.

It was pure luck that I saw Eve. At the very instant I spotted her she was knocked off her feet. A half dozen thugs who'd lost interest in attacking unionists and had turned their attention to the women in the crowd, swarmed over her. They groped her, pulling at her skirt and petticoats.

"Hart," I screamed at Win, and grabbed at him. "Hart!"

He whirled his mount and lashed out at me with his boot. "Get the hell . . ." he bellowed, then froze, his eyes wide. "Will?"

I pointed to the roughnecks hovering over Eve. "I need help."

He never hesitated. Taking in the situation immediately, he urged his horse through the crowd, slamming his mount into the bullies standing around Eve and sending them sprawling against a storefront.

I followed in his backwash. When he slammed the thugs, I crashed into those squatting over Eve, my fists and knees pumping. Taken by surprise, the bullies were momentarily stunned. In that instant I seized the young tough straddling Eve and flung him aside. Quickly recovering, he charged me. My right hand punch dropped him like a sack of oats. I could hear his nose crunch and watched in satisfaction as blood sprayed from his flattened proboscis. The gang members stared stupidly at their prostrate chum.

I took advantage of the brief lull to lift Eve from the sidewalk. She seemed to have no weight at all. "Hart!" I bellowed, "Here!"

He read my mind. Even as I shouted to him, he was maneuvering his steed alongside me, its dancing hooves sounding like gunshots on the pavement. I hoisted Eve and helped her sit behind him. It wasn't very lady-like with her having to straddle the horse in her long skirt, but there was no time for propriety. In any case, she wasn't persnickety; she paid no heed to her unladylike position. She began kicking at the toughs.

"Get her out of here," I shouted. "Claire and Cait are safe."

"You're sure they're safe?" he yelled.

Assured that they were, he canted his head toward the thugs. "What about them?"

They wanted no more of us. Several had already slunk away; those who stayed seemed cowed. "I'm okay," I hollered. "Go."

Hart whooped and swirled his hat, cowboy fashion. "You're the boss," he shouted, and clattered away.

I pushed back through the crowd for Claire and Cait. By the time we'd thanked the storeowner, helped him straighten out his store, and checked the condition of the front door, the intersection was virtually deserted, except for policemen. They were everywhere, urging stragglers to move along, helping the injured, arresting lingerers.

A husky red-faced man sat in the middle of the road. His vest was torn open and buttonless. His shirt and tie were ripped. His collar was gone. He gingerly fingered an upper tooth. Blood oozed from over one of his eyes. He smiled as we passed. "A helluva brawl, eh?" he said, shaking his head, "A ring-tailed, shit-kicking, snot-flying brawl."

30

On Wednesday, I rose early. Might as well. I hadn't slept much, what with replaying the events of Tuesday's riot in my mind all night, and fretting over my culpability in Tony Onofrio's death. I had gotten Claire and Cait home by mid-afternoon after the riot. Both were exhausted and happy to be safe. I saw no more of Hart or Eve and I made no effort to search for them. Instead, despite being tired and disheveled, I headed for the Grounds. I knew I should pursue my 'duties' as a health inspector, but I still didn't know where to find Gunther Krael. There seemed no urgency to find him today. Besides, Boston was playing a late game with Cincinnati before St. Louis came to town for a three-game series. Kid Nichols was to pitch, and no serious fan of the Beaneaters or base ball, for that matter, would miss a chance to watch Nichols work.

It was the third inning before I got to the game and Boston had already rung up seven runs. Boston pounded the fourth-place Reds, 10-2, to stay within one game of Baltimore. Nichols was in command the entire game. His speed pitch froze Cincinnati's strikers. When they looked outside, he pitched inside. When they thought he would jam them, he stayed outside. He threw no more than a half-dozen curve balls, preferring to rely on his blazer and pinpoint control.

I turned in early although, as I've said, I got no rest and little sleep.

Now, with the early Wednesday morning sun streaming into my room, I sat at my little table, still in my nightshirt, head throbbing and eyes crusty, I opened a pocket notebook I carry with me. I wanted to make a list of events of the past eleven days, and to make sense of them. It's an old habit of mine from my days at Harvard, this making lists. I can't say that it's always helpful, mind you. My grades proved that. But old habits die slowly. Ninety minutes later my headache was gone and my lists were completed. I turned to the morning edition of the *Globe* to check out the weekend's scores. Baltimore had beaten Pittsburgh and now had seventy-seven wins and thirty-three losses. Boston had two more wins and two more loses than the Orioles. New York had won two games over the weekend but I didn't think they could dislodge either Boston or Baltimore. Boston had eighteen games to play, twelve at the Grounds and three away games each with the Orioles and Giants. By the time I read all the accounts of the games, I'd missed breakfast and the Denihur sisters. And Sean. I'd have to hunt him down today and bring him up to snuff on yesterday's events.

Because the game was several hours away, I washed up, dressed, then visited taverns along the West End, looking for the giant who'd been the muscle in the killing of Shady Porch and the robbery of Sean and Collins. And who, I bet, later pursued me on Chauncy under orders from Krael. He could well be the man who killed Tony Onofrio. I would have been delighted to run into Krael, too. More and more I was convinced that Krael and the big thug I'd dubbed Paul Bunyan in my mind, were connected both to the thefts of Collins' watch and Sean's sketchbook and the Bradford manuscript. And somehow, though I didn't know how, I was sure that those thefts were tied to Krael's aims for the larger labor developments in the city. Unfortunately, I learned nothing about either Paul Bunyan or Krael on my Wednesday search.

Later, as I pushed through the turnstiles at the Grounds, the Beaneaters were taking the field and Fred Klobedanz, the left-handed twirler, was strolling to the box. St. Louis was not a good team. Boston could ill afford to stumble against this crew. Sean was sitting near the St. Louis bench eating peanuts and sketching the wiry and scrappy shortstop, Monte Cross. He didn't greet me. He simply looked up and threw a crumpled, empty peanut bag on the ground. "Thirty seven," he announced.

"Thirty seven?"

"These bags now have thirty-seven peanuts."

"How many did they have?"

"Thirty-five."

"Lordy, lordy," I said, rolling my eyes in mock wonderment. "And still five cents. Progress seems as inevitable as the tide."

Sean looked grouchy and shrugged, as if to say, 'I bring you good news and you scoff at it.'

I let his theatrics pass. "You missed a real donnybrook yesterday, my friend."

"So I heard," he grumbled. "Cait couldn't wait to give everyone at the breakfast table the details. Told us you and Hart were real heroes, you were." He made an obscene sound. "The very thing I wanted to hear about Hart, of course."

I smiled in spite of myself. "But you and Cait are talking again? Civilly?"

"Oh, yeah, sure. I got down to breakfast early this morning and dropped to me knees on the floor before her. Offered to cut out me tongue, I did, and give her half me blood, as but a wee gesture of my sorrow for me poor attitude and insinuations."

"You sweet talking Irish rogue, you."

He shot me a hard look. "What did it get me? She talked for the next half hour about you and Hart and your heroics."

"Hart *was* impressive," I said, shrugging. "It's hard not to admire the bastard. He's all wool and a yard wide."

"Jaysus," Sean muttered, rubbing the back of his neck as if it suddenly ached. "So, what are you doing here, besides watching two teams going different directions?"

His remark drew my eyes to Klobedanz whose tosses weren't exactly popping into Marty Bergen's glove. He gave up three runs but retired Monte Cross on a spectacular grab at shortstop by Germany Long. As the Bostons hustled in to bat, I turned back to Sean. "I think I ran into the giant who mugged you and stole your sketchbook."

That got his full attention. "Where?"

I told him the woman's story of the three men and the horse, and the fact that one of the men had been huge. I told him about my being pursued by the giant at yesterday's riot. Meanwhile, the St. Louis pitcher, hapless Bill Hart, was being tatooed by Boston hitters.

"So," said Sean, putting aside his sketchbook, "assuming that we are talking about the same gent in each case, what does that tell us? That he also killed Shady and Tony?"

A good question, and one I was ready for. "It might tell us that the same people interested in protecting the identity of labor agitators by stealing your sketchbook are determined to provoke violence. And that they are the people who were in the vicinity of the manuscript theft. And maybe in the alley behind Hart's gallery and rare bookstore. And, more, maybe they were on the docks seeing that no one talked about them. And that Gunther Krael is in the middle of the whole mess."

He looked like he'd bitten into a wormy apple. "Krael? How so?"

I told him about seeing Krael in the alley, having him sic his goons on me, and later watching him direct the attack upon the trolley and celebrate its destruction.

Sean's face contorted in surprise. "You told Honey Fitz any of this?" he asked.

Below us, Klobedanz had recovered and was now putting up goose eggs against the punchless Browns, fooling two of them into taking third strikes on roundhouse curves. A good deal of kicking and flailing of arms on the part of the Browns failed to move umpire Tim Hurst.

"Nope," I told Sean, turning back to him, "I've said nothing to Honey Fitz. First, I need to check out the woman's story and take a closer look at the sewers around Faneuil Hall. And I want to talk with Krael—if I can find him."

He snorted. "How you gonna manage that, laddybuck?"

"I'm hoping Eve will help me."

136

Boston put up six runs in the fifth inning. Hart, who'd already given up a home run to Chick Stahl was now raging at Hurst following virtually each pitch. Boston fans jeered him unmercifully.

"What was Eve doing at the riot, anyhow?" Sean wanted to know.

I didn't tell him that she had invited me to the demonstration. I did tell him what I knew about her activities and how, finally, she'd been saved and carried off by Hart.

He brightened. "By the blessed skirts o' Mary, maybe the two of them will find love in Montana! That'd solve one of my problems. One of yours, too."

"Come on, Sean," I said, punching him playfully on the shoulder. "Cait seems more interested in Montana and horses than in Hart. It's Claire who's attracted to him."

For the next several innings, Sean pressed me about the riot and Cait's reactions to it. He interrogated me on her every move, every word. No prosecuting attorney could have covered the ground more thoroughly. He made small sounds deep in his throat and offered pained expressions throughout my narrative.

Boston led 13-4 in the sixth. Klobedanz was not particularly sharp and he was tiring. Selee brought in seldom-used Charles "Piano Legs" Hickman to pitch the late innings and get some work. Collins made a play at third that seemed humanly impossible. Libby's knickers! It was easy to love the game—and to miss it when away from it. Still, I had work to do. "I hate to miss the rest of this game and your sunny disposition," I told Sean as I stood, "but I've got to double check the tale of the horse and see for myself what's in the sewers beneath Faneuil Hall."

I hailed a peanut vendor and purchased a bag. I hadn't had breakfast. Then I went looking for Eve Seilor and Gunther Krael.

31

The city had swallowed Eve, Krael, and Krael's mammoth chum without a trace. Four days of searching netted me not a single lead. I swear I talked to everyone between Washington and Commercial Streets. Afternoons, I checked out haunts frequented by workers along Atlantic. No one owned up to knowing the three or their whereabouts. So busy was I pursuing these elusive figures, I paid only cursory attention to the Beaneaters who won two slugfests against St. Louis, then ran roughshod over an inferior Philadelphia team in a three-game series. Klobedanz followed up his unspectacular win against St. Louis with a marvelous whitewash of Philadelphia on Saturday. Baltimore continued apace, ending the week clinging to their percentage points lead over Boston. There were less than two weeks to play.

By Monday, in desperation at not finding Eve, Krael, or the giant, I again hunted up Street Superintendent, Gerald Staley. I found him and his crew excavating a street two blocks from the Hart and Watson building. Staley's shoes were as shiny as the first time I saw him. His girth, always ample, seemed to have expanded several inches since our last encounter. His nose was as spectacularly monstrous as ever. If one can judge from Staley's hollering, Carmody and Murphy were being their usual balky selves.

Staley greeted me with a sour look. "Still harassing the city's laboring people, are you?" he groaned.

"Health inspectors never rest," I told him with a straight face. "Always vigilant in their quest for a cleaner, healthier city."

"Health inspector, my pimply arse," he scoffed. "You have all the credibility of an apple in a pail of rabbit scat."

Grinning, I waved my badge at him. "This gives me all the credibility I need."

The badge drew a pained expression from him. "Christ almighty," he sighed. "Well, whatta ya want this time?"

I moved closer to him, letting him appreciate my superior height. "You seem belligerent, Mr. Staley. Bad day? Tough job? Belt too tight? Congenital sourness?"

He looked up at me. "I don't like you, Mr. Beaman. You're young, good lookin' and a smart alec. Also, you enjoy pestering people."

I touched his arm in a placating gesture. "Bear with me a moment, my candid friend, and I'll be out of your sight and mind in a flash. Did you see a horse panic and collapse the day the Bradford manuscript was stolen?"

His eyes rolled back in disbelief. "Christ Almighty! See!"

He was right about me. I did enjoy hectoring people like himself. His irritation fueled my inclination to torment him. I spread my hands, rolled my shoulders theatrically, and told him sanctimoniously, "In the pursuit of truth and justice and the advance of civilization, I never rest." Without waiting for his reaction, I added more sternly, "did you see a horse die on that day, or not?"

He put his fists on his hips, all the while chewing furiously at his stogie. "Fer crissakes, I told you everything I know about that day," he stormed. "You wasted my time then, and you're wasting it now. The police are working on the case and they know a damn sight more about these things than you do. Get the hell out of here and let me do my business."

I stepped even closer to him and put an edge on my words. "Mr. Staley. If you refuse to cooperate, I'll have to inform your superiors. They will not be happy with a city employee thwarting a health inspector in pursuit of his official duties."

He didn't back down, I'll give him that. He thrust out his chin and continued to maul his stogie with his big square teeth. "Sonny, you tell my supervisors what you like. I got this job from the mayor who just happens to be my second cousin. I'll be overseeing street excavations long after you're sleepin' under a newspaper behind some grogshop on pokey street."

I pasted an arrogant grin on my face and playfully tapped the end of his unlit cigar with a stiff index finger. "Mr. Staley. My closest friend, who in all likelihood will be the city's *next* mayor, is responsible for *my* having *this* job. He and his friends guaranteed me that anyone standing in my way will soon be shoveling sheepshit barefooted in Nowheresville. If you want your job to last beyond the next election you'd better be more forthcoming." I arched my eyebrows in a 'what're-you-going-to-say-about-that' look.

He flung his cigar in the dirt and stared balefully at the pit his men were digging, as if he'd dismissed me. After a long moment, however, he turned back, took a deep breath, and expelled it. "Yeah, yeah," he muttered, "I did see a horse. Just before the celebration began. It spooked. Dragged a couple of guys. So what? Happens all the time."

"The horse crossed from North Market to Faneuil Hall?"

He nodded. Barely.

I pushed my interrogation. "Men tried to calm the animal. How many?"

He puffed his cheeks as he glared at me, looking like a man with two tennis balls in his mouth. Finally, he released his breath, with a small pneumatic sound. "Couple. Three, I think."

"One a big fellah?"

He scowled. "Yeah. Couldn't think of his name at the time."

"And now?"

He glanced around us, gnawing on this bottom lip. "You didn't get this from me."

His abrupt anxiety made me jumpy and I found myself checking nearby pedestrians for hulking characters. "Okay," I told him.

He stared at me for a long moment before speaking. "Kaiser Steuben. Herman Steuben. Everyone calls him Kaiser. A pugilist. Fights in the North End pits. Saw him fight that colored boy, Joe Walcott once. Tough. Clumsy. A punching bag, but usually stays on his feet. Sharkey, Corbett or Sullivan would kill him. But at the time I was happy to have someone his size helping with the horse."

"Know where I can find him?"

He found his discarded cigar and mashed it with a polished shoe. "I'm a goddamned tour guide now?"

"With your sunny disposition and helpful nature, you'd make a splendid guide."

My wit failed to charm him. He cocked his head, shut one eye and stared at me. "I don't know, and I wouldn't tell you if I did."

I let that pass. "Did you recognize the two helping Steuben with the horse? Tell me who they were and I'll disappear and let you and your workers return to your frenetic pace."

He sighed, his huge body seeming to deflate. "Union guys."

"Know their names?"

"Nah, I don't have nothing to do with union workers." He spun toward the hole. "Holy Mother, Carmody, your goddammed shadow hasn't moved in five minutes!"

"Where do they hang out?"

By now his jaws were twitching as if he had a mouthful of frogs. "Just seen 'em around, that's all I can tell you."

"Think the horse was a diversion? Somehow connected with the theft?"

He banged his fist on his forehead. "Horses die all the time. In winter draymen haul a half dozen of 'em a day out of the streets. We have drayman that's all they do."

"Then, you don't think it was a diversion?"

He stared hard at me. "Hell, I . . . ." He shook his head in confusion and turned to stare down into the pit. "I . . . suppose it could have been," he finally said. "I never thought about it." He twisted angrily toward the pit. "Carmody, lad, you're gonna have to move occasionally, if I'm to keep you on the payroll. You see that now, doncha?"

I handed him one of my cards. "Think about the business with the horse. If anything comes to you, I'd appreciate hearing about it." I winked. "An' I'll put in a good word for you with the next city administration."

He hawked deep in his throat and spat in the dirt at my feet.

32

The proximity of the Hart and Watson gallery and bookstore was too tempting. I couldn't pass up the opportunity to pick Win Hart's brain. I'd been trying to reach him for days without success. Among other things, I hoped he could help me hunt down Eve. After all, he'd ridden off with her like a knight in shining armor during Tuesday's riot. He'd taken her someplace. I gave Gerald Staley a wave and headed for the gallery. Over my shoulder I saw Staley pitch my card and a string of profanity meant for me into the hole.

Hart was in. Miss Sizemore, pale as a cod fillet, ushered me into his office after gracing me with a look suggesting she had a fishhook lodged in her throat. Hart greeted me with a firm handshake and a welcoming smile. Except for the highly-polished western boots he wore, he looked for all the world like a successful banker. Taking my arm, he showed me to a soft leather chair and then took a matching one. I declined the drink he offered. He skipped the libation as well.

"You and the fair damsel escape safely the other day?" I asked.

His laughter boomed. "Oh, yes. And my faithful steed, too. I stopped by the Denihurs' the next day to confirm they were safe and fully recovered from the shock of the riot. Thanks for seeing to that."

"My pleasure," I told him. "I'm sorry I missed you at the roominghouse. I came by today to see how you were, and whether you know where I could find Miss Seilor. I assume you know she was the young lady you carried from the crowd?"

Again the lusty laughter. "What male would fail to inquire Miss Seilor's name? She's one impressive filly."

"I have to talk to her," I told him.

He couldn't hide his surprise. He leaned forward expectantly, his brows furrowing. "Where do you know Eve from?"

Eve, was it? I became even more curious about where he'd spent the previous days. "I saw her first at your gallery," I told him.

He pursed his lips and looked perplexed. "Apparently, I missed her."

Because you were preoccupied with Claire, I wanted to shout. But I didn't. At some point he and I were going to have to confront this thing about Claire head on, but today wasn't the day. I had to locate Eve. "I subsequently saw her at a labor rally where Emma Goldman spoke," I added.

He gave me a questioning look. "What do you two have to talk about? Or, shouldn't I ask?"

I let his question hang in the air. "Do you know where she lives?"

"I know where she lives," he said, grinning broadly and arching his eyebrows slowly. "Do you think it wise to share this information with another male? Even a friend such as yourself?" In mock gravity, he curled his large cowboy hands around the arms of his chair and slowly shook his head. "Out my way, you know, we're coming up on the rutting season. Big ol' bull Elks vying for the cows. Not much sentimentality or generosity among them ol' boys." He picked up a brightly-polished humidor from the small table between us and held it up to me. "Cigar?" His comments and questions were delivered in an exaggerated western accent.

I refused the offer with a wave of my hand. "You have nothing to fear from me as regards Eve," I assured him stiffly.

He threw up his big hands as if shooing flies. "Oh, hell no! Big, handsome fellow like you poses no threat with the ladies." Again, he put a western twang to his words.

I watched and listened to Win Hart, part banker, part art expert, part cowboy, part good ol' boy, part mirror-image of myself. I *think* he was having his way with me. Well, half kidding me, maybe, half probing my feelings for Eve. I *think* that was what was going on. For a fleeting moment I knew how Gerald Staley must have felt putting up with my flippancy. "Look, Win—" I said, trying to get back to the topic of Eve's adddress.

He shushed me by holding his palms outward. "Will. Friend. You tell me you have no interest in the lovely Miss Seilor, I believe you. Clearly, you have strong feelings for Claire Denihur. I've seen that. But Eve's a comely young lady. And you're a good-looking fellow." He leaned forward, elbows on knees, hands dangling limply. "Hard for a fellow like yourself not to be attracted to her."

His comment did nothing to lessen my uncertainty regarding the level of his seriousness. His eyes were bright. From what, I thought? Amusement? Combativeness? Competitiveness? "With all due respect, Win," I said, "I find your observations—"

Again he held his palms toward me in a gesture of peace. "You want her address, Will, I'll give it to you." He gave me an address on Charles Street, on the backside of Beacon Hill where a good many maids and cooks lived who worked in the big homes on Brimmer. He then let a long moment creep by, his legs stretched before him, his hands folded at his belt, his eyes on his boots. When he finally raised his eyes to me, he said, "Eve's an interesting woman, all in all—both more and less than what she seems, I think. It's her potential to be more than what she appears that intrigues me." He sat up suddenly and slapped his knees. "Well, enough of such prattle. Wasn't that a dandy brouhaha Tuesday?"

As much as I would have gained from an elaboration of his assessment of Eve, I let him change the subject. For the next quarter of an hour, we exchanged tales of the riot and our experiences that day, crowing about our feats. He viewed the whole affair as a lark, joking about the bruises he'd collected and modestly suggesting that he'd handed a few out, as well. He thought he and I had done ourselves proud, and made a good team.

We also chatted about the pennant race. His observations made clear that he'd become a serious student of the game and closely read accounts of the games. To my amusement, he spouted team records and player statistics as readily as the most ardent rooter. He admitted to attending two games since joining me for the Chicago game.

Twenty minutes later, we said our goodbyes. As I passed Miss Sizemore's desk on my way out, I gave her my most raffish smile. Based on the look she returned, she was still struggling with the fishhook.

As I stood in the hot sun outside, idly contemplating an ancient pocket almanac in the Hart and Watson display window, I realized I now had a name for Krael's gigantic goon and a possible location for him. I also had Eve's address. I still didn't know where Krael hung out, but I was pretty sure Eve could supply that information. That was the sole purpose of my running her aground. At least that's what I kept telling myself. The previous Thursday the Italian sewer crew had given me a tour of the city's tunnels beneath Dock Square and Faneuil Hall. I was now sure I knew how the theft had been accomplished. What I needed to nail down next was *who* did it—and why. Tomorrow I would start with Eve Seilor.

33

Though Tuesday was another bright, warm day, the breeze was blustery enough to tumble leaves and litter along the pavement. I hailed a coach and directed the driver to Charles Street. We wound our way up Chestnut with its stables and barns redolent of leather, horseflesh, and manure. The street was crowded with horse-drawn conveyances and riders. Many of the riders were quite young. Hacks stood in lines awaiting renters.

I surrendered my coach at Charles and, following Hart's directions, walked past a cluster of dilapidated row houses. Eve's rented room was in a three-story brick rooming house next to an ancient livery. I consulted the registry, then took the stairs to her second-floor room and knocked. Eve's face was bright with surprise when she opened the door. "Will!" she gasped.

"Hello, Eve. May I come in?"

"Oh, let's walk," she suggested, "it's a beautiful day." And so we walked. Mostly in silence. Down Brimmer, past well-manicured homes. Uniformed nannies and their wards crowded the sidewalks. Most of the young lads were dressed like Frances Hodgson Burnett's Little Lord Fauntleroy, long curls bouncing as they frolicked. Still, they weren't so young that they didn't notice Eve. Many a young male eye followed her as she strolled arm-in-arm with me. I was the one who broke the silence. "You weren't hurt Tuesday? I was worried."

"Nothing but a few bruises and broken finger nails," she said, smiling broadly. "Win whisked me out of there very quickly." She shot me a sidelong glance. "With ample help from you, of course. You both were very brave."

Despite myself, I felt my color rise. "It was a dangerous situation," I conceded.

She squeezed my arm, beaming and bobbing her head. "It was. And exciting. Riding through the streets on the horse with all the noise and confusion was the berries. I felt like a princess being rescued by a Bedouin sheik." She guided me along the street, eventually stopping before a graystone apartment and pointing to the third story. "A student friend lets a room here. She's given me a key. We could . . . talk there."

I stared at the third floor, my throat tightening and my lips dry. There, two windows stood open, their curtains fluttering in the breeze. Our stroll hadn't been spontaneous. Eve'd led me here, intentionally, no doubt about it. I was strangely disturbed by my realization that she had manipulated me. Whether disturbed more by the implication of her suggestion or its possible ramification, or my own vulnerability to it, I wasn't sure. Could this be what Win was warning me about? Preparing me for?

I stared at Eve, barely breathing. Her hair, visible under her hat, shone, spun gold in the sunlight. Pale blue eyes, wide and bright, stared directly back at me. Her rose-red lips were parted, displaying white, even teeth. The pulse in her milk-white neck rose and fell. For the moment it was the only movement on Brimmer as far as I was concerned. Perhaps from simple impulse, or maybe from an instinctive desire to forestall disaster, I don't know, but I blurted, "Does Win Hart know about this room?"

She didn't blink. "Yes." She said it defiantly, without embarrassment. "Yes, and I want you to know about it, too." Her eyes sparkled. "I find you very attractive, and I believe you find me so, as well."

I couldn't deny it. "You're a beautiful woman, Eve," I told her in a hoarse voice.

She touched my arm. "Freedom is for those who want it, Will. It exists only for those willing to exercise it. Repressive conventions are challenged everyday."

"You want to spend the day together—up there," I said stupidly, pointing to the rippling curtains.

"Yes."

Without realizing I did it, I quickly checked those around us to see if anyone had heard her. Only after assuring myself that not a single soul had registered Eve's raw proposal, did I turn back to her. I had seriously misjudged her. I had clung to the fiction that she was a classroom radical, more talk than action. Her naked stare in the bright sunshine on a public sidewalk, surrounded by cavorting children, gossiping nannies, and hustling hawkers, blew that assumption all to hell. It occurred to me how ludicrous I must have appeared, standing before this attractive woman, mouth agape, head on a swivel. The little humor that I could squeeze from my antics died quickly. I could lie to Win. I couldn't lie to myself. Eve's proposition stirred my blood.

Gropping for time to think this through, I took her hands in mine. "Spending the day with you would be wonderful," I told her in a hoarse whisper, "I won't deny that. But I have to know something first."

She looked disappointed. "About Win? Please, Will, don't be jealous. It's so . . . bourgeois. Win is a wonderful man, brave and funny."

Involuntarily, my shoulders slumped. I didn't know if I was relieved or embarrassed or jealous. "Actually, I wasn't referring to Hart when I said that I needed to know something," I told her. "I need to find Gunther Krael."

Her smile faded like a dying lamp. "Gunther? Why?"

"Because he did everything he could to accelerate the violence on Chauncy Tuesday. I saw him. He and his confederates. I watched him order the torching of the trolley and I saw him celebrate when it caught fire."

Her face contorted in anger and her eyes narrowed. "Gunther wouldn't do that."

"Know him well, do you?"

She let a long silence crawl by before seizing my arm. "Will, let's go to my friend's room. All kinds of struggles must be waged in today's world." Her voice was almost a whisper.

It would be so easy. So good. So destructive. "I don't think so," I sighed. "Krael is using you and others to provoke violence. I want to talk to him."

She seemed to shrink. "Friends do not betray each other," she said in a soft voice.

"No, they don't. Friends help friends. I'm your friend aren't I?"

She stamped her foot. "I want you as my lover," she said fiercely. "I've made no secret of that." She met my eyes, smiled ruefully. "We're free agents, Will."

Never had I discussed illicit love so openly and frankly with a woman. And never in the stark light of day on a public street. And never had I had a woman proposition me so brazenly. Or couch it in terms of freedom and joy.

"Come," she urged. "We can talk about Gunther later."

I shook my head sadly. "I'm in love with another woman, Eve."

Again, she didn't blink, I'll give her that. "And I'm in love with other men," she replied. "Love can't be confined to a single lover. It defies human nature."

That stopped me cold. Embarrassing though it is, I must confess that this lad who'd jumped into many a woman's bed, who loved women like bees love honey, turned into a craven sluggard. I'd like to think my hesitancy stemmed from my love for Claire and my desire to elevate my standards of conduct. I'd be less than frank, however, if I didn't admit I might have been intimidated by Eve's open-eyed candor about her desires. Whichever the case, I balked.

Silence settled around us like morning fog. And then an idea came to me. I took her hand. "You've introduced me to your world, Eve, or at least you've tried to. Let me show you my mine. Come to a game with me." I teasingly touched her nose. "It's time you see a different kind of working man."

To my surprise she quickly agreed. Largely, I suspect, to take my mind off Krael, and what she knew about him. Fortunately, the Beaneaters were scheduled to play an early game today as part of a double header. We

147

ate a light meal at J.J. Cosgrove's Base Ball Exchange on Tremont, where she pressed me for details about the pennant race. I patiently explained the tight struggle between Boston and Baltimore, with New York trying to make it a three-team race. Her eyes lit up when I told her that she was going to see the New Yorkers today, a team that had been playing exceptionally well of late. We walked the block and a half to the Grounds where, despite a sizeable crowd, we gained seats directly behind home plate, under the pavilion. The ladies were out in force. When we took our seats the teams had finished their warmups and Boston lefty Fred Klobedanz was ready to serve up the first pitch to George Van Haltren.

"How much are the players paid an hour?" Eve asked, gesturing toward the field as Klobedanz 's first pitch was popped up by Van Haltren to Lowe at second.

"Players aren't paid by the hour," I replied. "They're paid by the year."

She drew back and stared at me in disbelief. "Well, how much per year, then?"

Mike Tiernan, the Giants' cocky rightfielder, grounded Klobedanz's third pitch to Tenney at first who beat him to the bag for the second out. The crowd shouted derision at the Giants' weak efforts.

"A player's salary depends on how good he is," I gestured at Hugh Duffy in left field. "That man out there makes more money than most of the other players because he's had a long career and he's performed at a very high level. Also, he's the team captain."

She contemplated Duffy for a long moment. "How much does he make?"

"Perhaps twenty-four hundred dollars. I don't know exactly. Most of the players make fifteen hundred, or less. Some teams pay even less to players than Boston does."

She couldn't suppress her surprise. "My goodness," she gasped. "Twenty-four hundred dollars! That's a lot of money."

Bill Joyce, the Giants' scrappy third sacker, hit a daisy cutter wide of Collins at third. Long darted to his right, snatched the ball, spun, and threw a bullet to Tenney for the out. The crowd went berserk. Several threw their hats into the air. Some tossed coins onto the field. A small coterie of Royal Rooters beat madly on their drums.

"My Lord," Eve gasped. "How much money do they pay *that* young man? He has dash!" I laughed and told her I didn't know, but Germany Long had been a fine player for years and probably made between fifteen hundred and two thousand dollars a year."

"They don't play *all* year do they?" she asked. "They can't play in *winter*!"

"They play from April to October."

Her eyes widened. "And then what? They can get another job? Make even more money?"

I explained that very few players were skilled enough to be professionals, especially at the National League level. That's why they were paid as well as they were. But, I also told her about the grinding travel schedule, second-rate hotels, unpredictable food, and the many personal costs that fell to the player in spring training and after. I mentioned the injuries and told her of the poor treatment received by the great Ned Williamson from the Chicago White Sox when he got hurt on a world tour. I described the abuse teams sometimes suffered from hostile fans on the way to and from ballparks. And I told her that some of the players were convinced that the reserve rule arbitrarily held down salaries, as did collusion among the teams' owners. I explained about the reserve clause and how players like Mike Kelly and John Clarkson could be sold for large sums of money, none of which ended up in their pockets.

She listened intently. When I concluded, she said, "The players should unionize. With unity comes strength, and with strength comes self-determination."

I told her that players weren't strong union men. If they had held any faith in unions before 1889 most did not now. They'd learned some hard lessons after Johnny Ward convinced them to establish their own league and compete against their old bosses in 1890. They'd suffered badly in that year and in the collapse of their league following it. Most had had their salaries cut to the bone. Many lost their jobs. I told her that today's players were still recovering from their efforts to unionize and were chary of proposals to try it again.

Pausing to give her time to digest what I'd said, I then asked her how the men and women she was helping to unionize thought about Sunday base ball.

She needed no time to compose a response. "Sunday's virtually the only day workers and their families have for recreation," she told me, as if I were a slow child. "My people want Sunday base ball. And they want playgrounds open on Sundays so their kids were have something worthwhile to do. Keeping Sundays free of recreation is blind stubbornness, not intelligent policy."

She sat quietly then, back straight, hands steepled under her chin watching the Bostons take their cuts against the Giants' lanky righthander, Jouett Meekin. I decided the time was right to return to our conversation on

149

Brimmer Street. "You do know Gunther Krael well, don't you?" I asked. Fortunately few fans were sitting close to us, and those who were, were busy shouting scurrility at Meekin. There were so few cranks around us that the hawkers of peanuts and lemonade concentrated their efforts elsewhere.

Eve watched the Giants ring up two runs in the second inning before answering. "Yes, I know Gunther well. And I know that he has the interests of working people in his heart. He could work wonders for these ball players, just as he's doing for city workers."

I let her see my skepticism, then said, "Perhaps, but he wanted the violence to escalate during the labor march. Why, I don't know. How will that help workers, whether inside or outside the Grounds? Do you know where can I find him?"

She hesitated ever so briefly. "No."

I didn't believe her. I put a little more distance between us as I turned to look more squarely at her. "A young boy returned Jimmy Collins' watch to me." I told her, speaking quietly, confidentially, then jabbed my finger at Collins who was waiting to hit. "That's Jimmy Collins. You know Collins?"

Although her open-mouth stare told me she knew what I was talking about, she said nothing.

I reached out and took her arm. "Only a few people knew I was looking for Collins' watch. You among them."

She remained silent, so I continued. "Shortly after I mentioned to you at Emma Goldman's speech that I was looking for Collins' watch, I had the watch back. Was that a coincidence?" She remained silent. "I don't think it was a coincidence," I said. "I think you know who took the watch and who assaulted Jimmy Collins and his chums. And I believe you know they were assaulted to destroy Sean's sketches of Krael and others." I leaned toward her and gently using my finger on her chin, turned her face toward me. "I think you reclaimed Collins' watch as a favor to me. And that tells me you know Krael and people like Kaiser Stueben who do his bidding."

"No." Her voice was small and unconvincing.

"I thought you admired truth and candor."

She raised her chin. "I'm telling the truth."

I swept her denials aside. "Steuben and Krael were at Faneuil Hall the day the Bradford manuscript was taken."

She dropped her eyes. "Gunther wouldn't do that," she said, her voice low.

I ignored her protestations. "Whose idea was it for you and Miss Goldman to attend the Remington exhibit?"

She pouted, letting a long moment pass before sighing sullenly, "So what if it was Krael's?"

"Was he considering stealing a Remington painting before deciding on the Bradford manuscript? Or did he check out the rare books and manuscripts, too?"

She looked around quickly, then glared at me as if I'd gone bonkers. "Why would he be interested in *either*?" she asked sharply.

"That's the hundred dollar question, isn't it? That's why I need you to tell me where to find him."

She squeezed her hands together in her lap. "I don't know where he is."

Meekin continued to mow down the Beaneaters, while Klobedanz surrendered two more runs in the third inning. This wasn't looking good for our nine, but I tried to concentrate on Eve. "You know where Krael stays," I said. "You found the watch quick enough." She didn't deny it. "Do you know where the Bradford manuscript is?" I pressed.

She shook her head, her eyes sullen.

I decided to play hard ball. "Tell me where to find Krael and Steuben," I said. "If you don't, I'll take my suspicions to the police and, better, to the city's newspapers. Gunther won't like that—or you being responsible for it."

Knowing Krael's obsession with remaining clandestine, or fearing his wrath, Eve crumpled and ponied up Krael's address, then stood and straightened her skirt. "Take me home," she said in a voice that brooked no contradiction.

We left the park with the Giants up, 4-0. It was no time for a fan to be leaving the Grounds, if you believed your presence would help the boys win. But I couldn't let Eve leave by herself. It was a long silent trolley ride for us back to Eve's apartment.

34

I found Krael's roost easily enough. Even before I approached his room on Milk Street, I recognized Kaiser Steuben. He was squatting on the front steps, shirt open, sleeves rolled to his biceps, suspenders hanging loose. He dwarfed a man who shared the stoop with him. Both men were smoking and jawing in the late afternoon sun, a pail of beer between the feet of each.

Steuben saw me almost as soon as I turned the corner. He watched me approach, a frown creasing his face. The furrows in his broad brow deepened as I neared.

I stopped in front of the stoop. "Mr. Steuben, isn't it?"

My familiarity startled him and for a brief moment his eyes widened. Perhaps he recognized me as the man he'd been ordered to pursue during the march. If so, he quickly caught himself and asked in a bored voice, "Who wants tuh know?"

"I do." I chose not to share my name with him, although I allowed for the fact that he might already know it. I pulled out my pocket watch and pretended to consult it. "Will you inform Mr. Krael that his 4:14 p.m. appointment is here?"

Steuben's eyes narrowed as he tried to decipher my message and gauge its tone. He looked like a bull that had just been slammed in the forehead with a shovel. "He ain't got no 4:14 appointment," he finally muttered, "He ain't got no appointments, period."

He stood up, towering over me. Even without standing on the stoop, he'd tower over me. "An' besides," he added, "Mr. Krael don't live here." The smaller man scuddled backward on his hands and heels, like a crab, as if he anticipated a sudden explosion.

I continued to address Steuben. "Of course he lives here. Tell him the gentleman from the Remington exhibit, Faneuil Hall, and the striker's march is here to see him." That ought to intrigue him, I thought.

Steuben scowled as he wrestled to assimilate what I'd said. His brow was badly scarred and his nose left little doubt he'd taken more than his share of punches. One of his front teeth was missing. He wore his hair short like most club fighters. Having finally digested my comments and decided Krael would want to see me, he grunted, "stay here," and retreated into the building.

For ten minutes I silently shared the stoop with Steuben's chum whose eyes flitted about like a humming bird. He ignored the cigarette that he clutched between two fingers, letting the ash grow like an emerging worm. He made no move toward his pail of beer. He kept his cigarette-free hand stuffed in his pocket, holding fiercely to something that looked very much like a pistol.

Steuben popped his head out the door. "Mr. Krael says tuh come on up." I followed Steuben along a hallway, past the Super's door, then up a flight of creaky stairs covered with threadbare carpet.

Krael met us at his door. "Mr. Beaman." He greeted me cordially, dressed carelessly, his shirtsleeves rolled up and his open collar revealing a mat of thick, black hair. His trousers and shirt were badly rumpled. Though his attire was that of a working man, his dark, bright, piercing eyes, beribboned glasses, and soft, pale hands left no doubt he was an intellectual. He stood in the middle of a small, worn room furnished with decrepit furniture. The room was every bit as plain and unassuming as those of the men and women he professed to lead. A bed was pushed against one wall. Two faded, easy chairs were against a second wall. A small table in the corner covered with books and papers obviously was being used as a desk. A random assortment of dishes and pans was piled in the corner under the table. The breeze had died and the thin curtains hung unmoving before the only window, which was open. The room throbbed with heat. Perspiration shown on Krael's exposed skin and in his beard, and there were dark spots under his arms. "Sorry about the heat," he said, as if he were responsible for it.

I waved off his comment. "You know my name." I said.

He mimicked my wave. "Of course." He knew, as I did, that he didn't have to tell me it was Eve Seilor who'd provided the identification. "What do you want with me?" he asked, quietly, civilly.

"I believe that we have some things in common."

His eyebrows and thick hairline elevated. "Oh? What's that?" He appeared genuinely interested.

"Well," I said, smiling flippantly, "we apparently enjoy the same art. We have an interest in the sewers around Faneuil Hall. We admire Emma Goldman, and like to attend labor marches. We know Eve Seilor. That's five things."

He stared at me through his thick lenses with wide, unblinking eyes. "You're an amusing man, Mr. Beaman. Am I supposed to know what you're talking about?"

I tried to match his unblinking stare. "I think you do."

He exhaled dramatically. "I'm a simple soul, Mr. Beaman, and a plain-speaking man. Think you could tell me point-blank why you're here?" He did not invite me to sit. The three of us stood, Steuben in the doorway behind me, weight on one leg, arms above his head, gripping the small ledge running along the top of the door.

Krael's feigning that he had no idea why I might want to talk to him rankled me.

Playing a hunch, and betting that they would not attack me in Krael's room, I said, "I think you assaulted Jimmy Collins and Sean Dennison. I think you killed Shady Porch. I think you stole Sean's sketchbook because he sketched you. I think you stole the Bradford manuscript." I jerked a thumb at Kaiser Steuben. "And I think your pal here beat Tony Onofrio to death. Plain enough?"

His eyes slid briefly toward Steuben. His voice gave no hint of shock, however. "You're as subtle as a girlee show," he said, looking at me with what I took to be admiration. "Miss Seilor tells me you work for the Boston nine. If that's a fact, you know what I mean when I tell you that you are *way* off base. Isn't that what they say? Way off base? I'm interested in the rights of laboring people, Mr. Beaman. I don't kill people. I work for better working conditions and fair wages. I'm not a collector of historical artifacts. Why on earth would I steal a, what was it? A manuscript?"

If he had not purloined the manuscript, he'd certainly read about it. His attempt to appear entirely ignorant convinced me I'd been right—at least about the manuscript. "I don't know why you filched it," I told him truthfully. "I was hoping that you'd tell me."

He gave me an exaggeratedly nonchalant shrug. "Well, sorry to disappoint you, Mr. Beaman," he said, continuing his civil manner and tone. "How do *you* think I pulled off this miraculous theft?"

"You and Steuben here,"—I jerked a thumb at Steuben behind me—"and another goon used a distressed horse to cross police barriers near Faneuil Hall and reach a sewer opening. You used the sewers to reach the area where the manuscript was being displayed, and probably used them to whisk it away. Some of this is supposition, of course; I'm not sure of all the particulars, but I have eye-witnesses who'll place you and Paul Bunyan here at the scene."

I sensed Steuben move toward me and heard his low growl, "Mr. Krael?"

Even before I could turn, Krael held up his hand for calm, stopping the oncoming Kaiser. "Who are these eyewitness, Mr. Beaman?" he asked, almost gently.

"I'll share that with you at a later time," I told him, trying to match his understated concern. "For now, perhaps you'll tell me why you were so eager to heighten the violence at the labor march."

154

"You *do* make wild accusations!" he laughed, shaking his head as if in apparent disbelief. "Why in the world would I do that? The violence was being directed against my union comrades, for godssakes."

In for a penny, in for a pound, I thought. "I saw you order the breaking of windows, the assaulting of police, and the burning of the trolley."

His face stiffened and his eyes dulled.

There was that low growl behind me again, the animal sound. "Mr. Krael?"

Standing between the two men, my back to Steuben, was uncomfortable and got more uncomfortable with Steuben's growing unhappiness with me. I felt like a hunter between two bears. I stepped back and pivoted so I could see both.

Krael fluttered his hands to shush Steuben, but spoke softly to me, "What is it you want, Mr. Beaman. Bottom line."

"I want you to give back the manuscript. And stop scaling up the violence against innocent people."

"Assuming that I have this manuscript, why should I do what you want?"

"Because your strategies are counter-productive, that's why. The violence you create is turned on those most innocent. You saw what happened. The police took out their anger on the people least responsible for the agitation, pedestrians caught in the crossfire. It's in your interests to calm ethnic and class differences, not inflame them. Stealing an historical manuscript, whatever your motives, will backfire, too. The manuscript is a state and national treasure. If it's discovered that someone involved with the labor movement is culpable, the cause of labor will be set back a hundred years. And Boston will become an even more divided community than it is now."

Krael remained passive as I jawed, his eyes boring into mine. "You're an interesting man, Mr. Beaman," he said finally, smiling and shaking his head as if he couldn't believe what he'd just said, "but misguided, I'm afraid." He signaled to Steuben. "Kaiser, show Mr. Beaman out. Our, uh, *appointment* is over."

Quicker than I expected, Steuben had his hands on me, clapping his huge mitts on my biceps. Instinctively, I thrust my elbows out and up, wrenching his hands off, and twisted to face him, left hand low to protect my body, right hand held high to guard my face. I pulled my chin in and tucked it against my chest, lessons learned early in my boxing days at Harvard. Steuben had a lot more experience roughhouse fighting than I had, but I was prepared to give him a go.

"No, no," shouted Krael, wedging himself between us and exhibiting the first genuine emotion I'd seen from him that day. "Kaiser, *gently* my man. *Gently.* Just *show* Mr. Beaman out. That's a good lad." He lifted his eyebrows at me and offered a fawning smile. "We're not violent people, Mr. Beaman."

I pushed away from him, snarling, "I'll show myself out, thank you."

Krael kept a restraining hand on Steuben. "Fine. I'm sorry that I could not be more helpful, Mr. Beaman. Perhaps we shall meet again."

"You an' me'll meet, mister, you can bet the rent on that," snapped Steuben.

"Shut up, Kaiser," Krael flared. He smiled at me. "Kaiser is, uh, *impetuous.*"

I suppose the dogs down in the North End rat pits could be termed impetuous as well. "Not to worry, Mr. Krael," I smiled. "You were much more helpful than you know." I departed Krael's quarters convinced that he had taken the manuscript, and still possessed it.

35

The next day, now eager to enlist Sean's help in getting my hands on Bradford's manuscript, I headed for McGreevey's. I hadn't seen Sean since Sunday, but I knew that once he heard of my visits to Eve's and Krael's, he'd want to help. It's his nature as a bold son of Erin. In addition to that, the Beaneaters had split the double header with New York yesterday, losing the first game, 8-5, winning the second, 17-0, as Nichols picked up his thirtieth win. I was itching to learn the particulars of what occurred after Eve and I had departed. No harm in killing two birds with a single stone.

I'd barely stepped into the dim light of McGreevey's when Henry Fitzgerald cut me off. "Got a minute?" he asked, tugging at my arm.

I didn't want to offend the man, but I was eager to find Sean. Trying not to be too obvious, I scanned the room for my redheaded sidekick.

"Come on, Mr. Beaman," Henry urged, "It'll just take a minute. John wants a word with you." He put a hand on my elbow and urged me to the far end of the saloon.

There Honey Fitz was leaning against the bar, a boiled egg in his left hand, a beer in his right. He set the drink down and gave me an enthusiastic handshake. "Well, well," he grinned, "how's the new health inspector?"

"You haven't noticed the improvement in the general well-being?" I quipped.

"Oh, hell yes," he snorted, "Everything's salubrious since you've been on the job." He gave his brother a gregarious clap on the back. "Right, Henry?" Apparently Henry thought the question needed no reply. He quaffed his beer in several gulps, grimacing and belching loudly as he plopped down the near-empty glass.

"What'll you have?" Honey Fitz asked me, beckoning the barkeep.

I gave my order and set my straw lid on the bar, dragging my sleeve across my forehead to wipe away the perspiration.

"We haven't talked since the riot on Chauncey," Honey Fitz said, apparently satisfied that sufficient civilities had been exchanged. "Heard about it?"

"I was smack in the middle of it."

His eyes bulged. "Holy Mother!" He set his half-eaten egg on the plate before him and his beer next to it. He yanked a handkerchief from his back pocket and meticulously wiped his hands. "The powers-that-be are upset with the unions. I've been getting hell all week because most of the marchers were from my ward."

"Much of the violence originated with the police," I pointed out.

He shrugged. "Yeah, maybe. But city and state officers believe the police had no recourse. Dozens of policemen and citizens were injured. Some badly. Not to mention a streetcar being destroyed. It cost the city a pretty penny, it did." He picked up his egg and stuck it whole into his mouth.

"The unions weren't blameless," I admitted. "Their organizers attacked the police and private property."

Honey Fitz paled and stopped in mid-chew. "You *saw* that?" he sputtered.

Before I could answer, Henry leaned in. "This business is turning into a political nightmare. People think unions breed violence. They resent immigrant groups who join 'em. They want the police to clamp down. They want immigration stopped. Hell, the American Protective Association is growing by leaps and bounds. Politicians like Henry Cabot Lodge are pushing for a tighter immigration policy. All this cripples our ward."

Honey Fitz swallowed the last of the egg and nodded at his brother's assessment. "Sure as hell, all this squabbling hurts my chances to become mayor," he conceded as he wiped his mouth with his handkerchief. "I've got to calm things down." He gripped my arm, then glanced around to ensure that no one was eavesdropping. "Made any progress on the Bradford manuscript? I'm thinking its return will divert people from the union issue, and be something the whole city can rally around."

Honey Fitz's blunt admission fed my growing confusion about his motives. I couldn't tell whether a returned manuscript appealed to him more as an instrument of political advancement or public tranquility. But, then, did it matter? Perhaps more important, I had to decide whether my primary loyalty regarding the missing manuscript lay with Honey Fitz or Arthur Soden, or with the larger community. It troubled me that Honey Fitz seemed to have more faces than a Gaelic barrister. I was tempted to confess my suspicions that Krael had taken the manuscript and doubtless still had it in his possession. But I hesitated. Until I could figure Honey Fitz out, it made sense to keep my cards close to my vest and so I kept my reply short. "I've made progress," I told him.

The playfulness drained from his features. "What does *that* mean?"

I shrugged non-committally. "Just that. I'm confident I'm getting closer."

"To what?" He made beckoning motions. "Come on, I'm paying you for details."

I shrugged again. "There are no details specific enough to share yet," I said. "Just strong hunches."

That brought a flush to his face. He snatched my wrist, squeezing with the power of a foundry vice. "Tell me. Once I'm mayor, I'll reward my friends, by Christ. Loyal friends." He abruptly released my arm, but kept his eyes locked on mine.

Ignoring the lingering pain in my wrist, I sipped my beer while studying his crimson face. "People who don't know you well might think you just threatened me," I said, my words purposely low and deliberate. "I know you were merely sharing with me your hopes as future mayor." I paused a long moment to permit my facetiousness to sink in. "I'll tell you about the manuscript when I have something reliable to relate. And not a minute before."

He visibly sagged. "Sorry about that, lad. I'm under some pressure an' all. But look, don't go throwing feathers in me face. If found and returned, the manuscript will bring the city's peoples together. It'll bring peace to our streets. It'll—"

I didn't let him finish. "What if your constituents stole the manuscript?"

He squinted at me. "You trying to tell me something?"

I held my hands out, palms up. "Just raising a possibility."

Henry laid a calming hand on his brother's shoulder. "The return of the Bradford manuscript won't change any of this, John. You might think so; I no longer do."

Honey Fitz winced at his brother's observation. "Perhaps not, Henry. But often it's the little things, a gesture here, a token move there, that defuses crises." He took several healthy swallows of his beer. "At least there's room for optimism."

"I'll keep looking for the manuscript," I promised him.

He grunted. "The city council meets this week to discuss procedures to follow the next time there's a protest. They're in a mood to get tough. I've got maybe three days to soften their hearts."

I couldn't conceal my surprise. "Three days!"

He smiled broadly, but there was no warmth in it. "Nobody said life was easy, lad. Test those wonderful hunches of yours—but do it quick." He thumped my sternum with a stiff finger. "Council members aren't the only ones with little patience."

At that moment, from over Honey Fitz's shoulder, I saw Sean beckon me. "Excuse me," I said, "I see Sean. He and I have business."

As I turned toward Sean, Honey Fitz took my elbow, gently this time. "You heard about Jerry Staley?"

I tried to read his expression. "The Superintendent of Streets?"

Honey Fitz nodded. "He was found dead last night. Skull crushed."

Christ! First Shady, then Tony. Now Gerald Staley. Dead. Blood thundered in my head. "How'd it happen?" I groaned.

Now it was Honey Fitz's turn to shrug. "Someone crushed his skull as he returned home from work. Police think it was a robbery."

Robbery? Or something more sinister? Honey Fitz seemed not to be telling me to frighten me, but I couldn't shake off the feeling that Staley's demise was a bad omen. My mind whirling in confusion, I shoved my way through the crowd to Sean. A man's death is always disquieting, but the second killing of a man who's given you information is even more disturbing. I tugged Sean toward an unoccupied table. "Tim around?" I asked.

"Not yet. Give him a few minutes. What've you been up to?"

I picked up an egg and pickle from the free lunch and held up the plate to Sean. "You hear about Staley?" I had earlier told him of my meeting with Staley.

He slumped. "Honey Fitz told me. It's grim news, it is."

I exhaled too loudly. "I suppose it's Dennis O'Dwyer's problem." I didn't find my own observation very convincing.

Sean took an egg and munched on it. "Found Krael yet?" he asked. "Or the big guy who pounded on me?"

Though I knew I'd have to repeat myself to Tim, I decided to share some of my news with Sean. "I did. I found out Krael keeps Steuben and another goon around."

Sean rolled his shoulders. "We've known that since the Goldman lecture."

"I mean real muscle. Don't know about Steuben, but his friend carries a pistol."

Sean shook his head. "Jayzus, Krael thinks he needs that kind of backup? Huh!"

I leaned toward him and whispered, "I think he has the manuscript. In his room."

Sean jerked back and eyed me skeptically. "You're pulling me leg."

"Nope. And I'm going to find out for sure. I'm going to pay him a visit."

Sean's eyes bulged. "You're gonna *burglarize* Krael?" he asked too loudly.

"Not *burglarize*," I protested, shushing him. "I'm going to visit his room in his absence. It's important for lodgers to maintain high health standards. Periodic checks by health authorities ensure that they do."

Sean sat back, arms straight out, hands flat on the table, grinning. "Oh, well, then. I'm slower than a centipede with bunions! I thought you was talking criminal activity."

I matched his mocking tone. "Shame on you."

160

Sean got serious. "Even if Krael stole the damn thing, why keep it in his apartment? How smart is *that*?"

I had to admit his point. "I don't *know* that it's in his room. But he's a straightforward guy—he told me that several times. Probably thinks no one knows where he lives. And thinks he's the last one any one would suspect, so his room is as safe as any place. Especially with Steuben and the other hard-faced bloke to look after it."

Sean looked quickly over his shoulder at the Fitzgerald brothers. "You've told Honey Fitz all this?"

"No."

He flinched. "By the blessed skirts o' Mary, are you daft, man?"

"Maybe."

He shook his head as if he couldn't believe what he was hearing. "Palling around with you is like playing with nitroglycerin. Dicey, but undeniably exciting." He leaned forward, serious now, eyes bright. "I'm going with you, Will. It'll be better with two, sure, when it comes to getting in and out of Krael's room. Besides, if I can get sketches of the manuscript and where it's been held, it'll be a feather in my cap at the *Globe*. By jayzus, they might even give me a raise or bonus, and I can marry Cait."

I knew he was right about two being better than one, but I had to be practical. There was no way I could drag him into actual law breaking. I held out both hands, palms toward him. "You're not going in with me. I could end up in the pokey. Two fellows I brought into this mess have been found dead. Besides, *Cait* would kill *me*—if Claire didn't beat her to it. You'll be my lookout only, and out of harm's way."

He bolted to his feet, tumbling his chair to the floor. "First, boyo, pokey or no, Cait or no, mysterious death or no, I'm going in with you. I'm not going to miss what may be my big chance." His tone and expression left little room for argument. Especially in the crowded tavern where all eyes had swung toward us and Sean's tumbled chair. "Why do you think Krael stole the damn thing?" he asked.

I scooped up his chair, righted it, and urged Sean to sit, all the while attempting to shush him. "I've got a few ideas about that," I whispered, "but, first, let's find out *if* he has it. Sure you want to go in?"

"Absolutely," he said, calmer now. "What about Tim?"

"Tim can't get involved in a crime. He's got a family. He'll be of greater help once we determine if the manuscript is in Krael's possession. In the meantime, if we see Tim we can have him do additional checks on Krael and on Gerald Staley's death."

Sean executed a quick nod. "It's you and me for now, then," he said.

I raised my beer in salute. My curiosity about the Beaneaters' play yesterday and Baltimore's rare loss to Philadelpia evaporated in the face of our current determination. "Well," I said. "Here's to perhaps our last day as free men."

36

The morning broke damp and gray. Fog prowled the city, turning streets into pewter tunnels. Workers, eyes leaden and mouths grim, plodded listlessly toward unappetizing jobs, oblivious to the fog that was thick enough to dampen shirts and coats. Disguising ourselves with caps and scarves to blend in with bicyclists and pedestrians, Sean and I tried to become just two more gray silhouettes on wheels. The bicycles were Sean's idea. He insisted they would provide a quick escape. We rode by Krael's Milk Street apartment house several times before its door swung open.

Kaiser Steuben and his hard-faced friend stepped out on the stoop and surveyed the street. By keeping a beer wagon between them and us, we passed unnoticed. We turned the corner, dismounted, and peeked back. Wagons filled with halves of beef, coal, and lumber were being unloaded, grotesque shapes in the foggy street. Teamsters urged already-tired nags through the obstacle course. Tradesmen wound their way to nearby tanneries, shoe and boot factories, and saddlers. This was the center of leather manufacturing, and the acrid smell of the tanning vats and softer smells of oil and leather punched through the mist. Occasionally, Steuben would say something to his companion.

After ten minutes or so, Steuben opened the door and hollered something into the building. Shortly, Krael joined the men on the stoop where they again studied the street, sucking deeply on their smokes. At last satisfied that all was safe, they joined a clump of workers drifting toward Pearl Street.

Not sure whether Krael and his chums were going to breakfast, on a more extended trek, or merely were taking a quick stroll, we hesitated. Once convinced that they had not simply walked around the block, we moved fast, first paying a young boy at the mouth of the alley behind the apartment to watch our bicycles. We'd spent several hours the previous night going over our plan for getting into and out of Krael's apartment. Now, we'd see how clever we were.

With Sean in tow, I banged on the door in the long hallway with the tarnished brass plate reading "Superintendent." A woman with a sunken mouth and a faded handkerchief tied on her head peeped out, shielding her eyes with a gnarled hand despite the hall's dimness. Believing that forcefulness and intimidation would serve me well, I didn't wait for her to speak. "You're the Super then, ma'am?"

Her squint deepened. "My hubby is and he ain't 'ere," she said, her toothless mouth twitching as if she were separating seeds from a mouthful of watermelon.

I flashed my Health Department badge. "Health Inspection, ma'am. Checking for gas leaks. We'll need you to let us into each room."

She cocked her head, as if to see us better. "Nobody's complained," she whined.

"This is a required inspection. Just routine," I assured her, eager to hurry her along.

She separated more phantom seeds. "Come back when 'ubby's 'ere."

"Sorry, ma'am. All rooms must be examined. We'll start on the second floor." I pulled a mock list from my coat pocket that we'd prepared the previous evening and pretended to study it. I waved the paper in front of her. "Your second floor is scheduled for today. Orders of the City."

She jerked her head back and blinked. "I ain't climbin' them stairs," she mumbled, "Not with these ankles. Can't see good neither."

Sean leaned around me and spoke gently. "You have a common key, mother?"

She frowned. "Suppose you could use it," she muttered, probing with her tongue for an illusory seed in her upper gums. "Mind you knock first."

Two minutes later we let ourselves into Krael's room. My hope was that we could get out long before the woman thought too deeply about our story and behavior. And our lack of uniforms and tools. Or worse, her hubby returned.

Sean pushed past me, moved quickly to the side of the window, and peered out. "Check the room, I'll watch for Krael." He began searching that side of the room, pausing every few seconds to glance outside.

I wasn't sure exactly what I was looking for, or how big it was. Still, I moved quickly, looking for anything book-size, rifling through stacks of papers, peering under the bed and mattress, probing the chairs, checking in the icebox, and behind the clothes in the small closet. Nothing.

"Look in the mattress," whispered Sean. "Just poke it. It's so thin you'll be able to tell if anything's there."

I did, without luck. I then squatted by the table and moved the dishes and pans stacked under it. Nothing.

"Come on, move," Sean muttered, staring out the window.

"It won't take long," I told him. "The place isn't big enough to hide much."

He dropped suddenly to one knee and leaned out. "Well, you better speed it up, laddybuck. Here they come!"

I froze. "Krael?!"

Sean bumped his head loudly against the opened window as he scrambled to his feet and jerked back into the room. "They just turned the corner. Let's get out of here."

I stood and looked helplessly around. My hands started to shake. Sean was at the door. "Come on. It won't take them long." I frantically scanned the room, reviewing where I'd searched.

Sean scampered back to the window, looked out. "Come on, Will. They're already at the tannery across the street."

I tried to calm myself, to steady my hands. I raced to the closet and checked its ceiling for an opening. Nothing.

"Sweet jayzus, Will, they're crossing the street." He came over and seized me by the coat. "Let's go. Steuben'll kill us with his bare hands."

I twisted away from his grasp and sprung the door of the icebox. I tapped it for false walls. Nothing. I heard the sound of the door opening below us.

"Holy Mother!" Sean groaned.

I eased the door closed and turned. As I did, my eye caught the pile of pans in the corner under the table. I'd moved and looked at all of them, had scattered them around, in fact. All except the bottom pan that rested upside down. I scrambled to it, sank to my knees, and turned it over. And there it was. A package wrapped in brown paper and tied with a heavy string. I didn't have time to verify it, but it had to be the manuscript.

There also was no time to leave the place the way we found it. I scooped up the package and scrambled to the door. The heavy sounds of Stueben's footsteps and those of his companions could be heard on the stairs. There was no way we could exit the same way we'd come. I pulled at Sean, gesturing toward the hallway to our right. Trying to move quickly but quietly, we scuttled down the hall and around the corner. And ran smack into a closed door.

I grabbed the door handle and pulled. It didn't budge. Locked? I pulled again. The hall was thick with heat and both of us were sweating heavily now. And not all the perspiration was caused by the temperature. I scooted back past Sean and peeked around the corner, down the long hallway. Steuben was standing in front of the open door to Krael's apartment, staring in. "What the hell!" he bellowed.

Krael pushed past him into the room. "Sonnuvabitch!" he roared.

Sean frantically grabbed the doorknob and jerked it. The door didn't move.

"The common key! Quick!" Sean said in a hoarse whisper.

I shoved it into his hand. He inserted it and twisted. "I locked it," he said, his confusion palpable. He twisted frantically in the other direction.

"What the hell?" He pulled at the door. "It ain't locked!" he rasped. He pulled again on the doorknob.

I heard Krael shout, "Check the backstairs! Quick, now."

In panic, Sean grabbed the doorknob, leveraged a foot against the wall, wrenched and jerked with all his might. The door flung open to reveal back stairs.

"Go, goddammit!" Steuben shouted, his deep voice echoing in the hallway. He was probably yelling at his skinny chum, but we didn't stay around to find out. We thundered down the stairs, out into the alley, and raced for our bicycles. Sean had the coin for the boy handy when we raced up to him and seized our cycles. "For crissakes, Will," he shouted as we pedaled frantically down Pearl, "we've still got the Super's keys. His wife's going to squeal to the Health Department, sure."

I crouched lower on the bike, clutching the package under one arm and the Super's key in one hand, trying desperately to steer with the other. I pedaled as fast as I could, thankful that we were nearing Washington, a direct route out of the district. Still my mind swirled with my last glimpses of Krael and Steuben, and the obvious frenzy that gripped them. "That's the least of our worries," I groaned.

37

That night we stayed in a flophouse on Atlantic near Clinton. It had no luxuries, simply two beds, a table, two chairs, an icebox, and a coal stove, all in a single, cramped room. Its small windows, which looked out onto an alley, were nailed shut. The fog having burned off long ago, the tiny room pulsed from the late afternoon heat. We thought it prudent not to return to our roominghouse. Krael would have little difficulty tracing us there. We assumed Krael would come after me first. After all, I had accused him of stealing the manuscript just two days before. I didn't want to end up like Tony Onofrio or Gerald Staley. For the moment at least, we hoped to lose ourselves among the North Enders and immigrants swarming Atlantic Avenue.

Sean flopped on one of the beds covered by a thin mattress and threadbare blanket. "Okay, laddybuck," he grunted, "we have the manuscript, let's take a look at it."

I put the manuscript on the table and carefully unwrapped it. The vellum-bound volume measured perhaps eleven inches by eight. I pulled up one of the chairs and gestured for Sean to get up and take the other. He did. Someone had written on the flyleaf, dating it March, 1705, indicating that the book descended first to Bradford's eldest son, William, and then to his younger son, Samuel. I slowly thumbed through the folios, counting just over two hundred and seventy leaves. The ink was faded and the script odd. The various handwritings and different colored inks suggested that several persons had edited the manuscript after Bradford had originally penned it. Or, perhaps Bradford himself had revised it countless times over the years.

"So this is what all the excitement is about," Sean sighed. "Jayzus, it looks old."

And fragile. Deciding against further turning of the brittle pages, I redid the wrapping and tied it securely.

"Well, we've seen what all the hullaballoo is about," Sean said with a shrug. "Now what are we going to do with it?"

I knew what we should do with it. We should turn it over to Arthur Soden so he could present it to authorities. That's what he was paying me for. Or to Honey Fitz, who also was paying me. "What do *you* think we should do with it, Sean?" I asked.

His answer didn't surprise me. "Give it to Honey Fitz. That's why he hired you."

Indicating that I understood his position by the look I gave him, I asked, "How're we going to explain how it came into *our* hands? How will he explain *his* possession of it, do you suppose? It *is* stolen goods, after all."

He rose and returned to the bed, stretching out noisily and clasping his hands behind his head. "Oh, Honey Fitz'll come up with something," he laughed. "He's a clever one."

I couldn't help but laugh, too. "He is that. Of course, if I give it to Art Soden and let him take credit for its return, he'll give me five hundred dollars. Or I can let them both have it and double my reward."

Sean bolted upright. "You schemer! You've been studying this whole thing, eh?"

Making patting motions with my hands to quiet him, I told him, "Not really. That's the problem. I really haven't considered the whole picture. The big question is why Krael pilfered it in the first place."

My redheaded friend made an obscene sound and gazed at the ceiling. "This thick-headed Mick can't help you there," he said. "Damned if it makes sense to me."

I told him that I had toyed with the idea that Krael acted in someone else's behalf, but that I had no idea who that might be, or why. If he acted in his own interests he might have wanted to put pressure on city officials by escalating the labor violence, then to use the manuscript to coerce them into negotiating a peace favorable to the unions. I confessed that I didn't understand why he hadn't acted before now, though. Sean made faces and scatched the back of his neck while he listened to my ramblings, then speculated that perhaps Krael had pilfered the manuscript with the idea of returning it and using that gesture to bring honor to himself and other local leaders. He conceded, however, that Krael would have to deflect suspicion that he himself had stolen Bradford's book. And that wouldn't be easy. I let him know I agreed, but suggested that we forget Krael for a moment and concentrate on how to return the manuscript. And on how we could achieve the greatest good by returning it.

Sean rolled his eyes. "Holy Mother, keep it simple, boyo. We're already up to our armpits in pigeon poop having taken the manuscript from Krael. Don't get so clever we end up in jail charged with the original theft. Or, worse, dead." He made another face and spread his hands. "And what do you mean by the greater good? Greater good for who? "

I scooped up the manuscript and suggested that we go eat and think the whole thing through. He agreed, and we found a small eatery crammed among the neighborhood's factories, flophouses, and pawnshops. We spent the entire meal whispering about what we should do with the manuscript now that we had it. We let ourselves idly contemplate what we would like to gain from the return of Bradford's manuscript. Sean thought it would be grand if he could get some credit for its return, and turn that honor into a promotion and raise at the *Globe*. Both, of course, would allow him to propose to Cait. The more I mulled over what I personally wanted from any credit that might come my way for returning the historical manuscrpt, the more I realized I wanted to get back into base ball. Being outside the game that meant so much to me was intolerable. I wanted a steady job and the chance to promote my standing with Claire, but both those paled in comparison to my desire to be part of the Beaneaters. We surprised ourselves, I think, at the simplicity of our aspirations. Our conversation, filled as it was with personal revelations, sparked an idea about how to return Bradford's book. It didn't burst into full flame but, rather, glowed in my mind, awaiting more fuel.

All the while we tossed about our hopes and dreams, I kept my elbow on the prized manuscript. It was nearly dark when we finished our meal and stepped outside to enjoy the parade of people on Atlantic. The sun was down by now and families were outside. Children rolled hoops and careened down the streets on bicycles, dodging steaming piles of manure and yellow pools of urine from the many horses that pulled wares and people along Atlantic. Boys hawked newspapers. Peddlers, vendors, and tinkers rang their bells and called out their vendibles. Ragmen searched out possibles. Dogs bounded about, barking at anything and everything.

I paid a newsboy a nickel and took a newspaper. As I did so, I caught a glimpse of Steuben's hard-faced companion across the street. He was holding a man by the shoulder and jabbing his finger down Atlantic. Two other blunt-featured men stood by, seemingly awaiting orders. When the man's eyes rested on me for a fraction of a second, I seized the newspaper and spun back toward Sean, tugging my hat low. When I reached Sean I pushed him ahead of me. "Let's go. Keep your face away from the street."

Fear registered on his face. "What's going on?"

"I just saw Steuben's pistol man."

He stiffened. "He see you?"

"I don't know. But let's get back to the room."

Safe in our room, I relaxed by studying the base ball scores and standings. Boston had beaten Cy Seymour and the Giants, 9-3, earlier today before ten thousand hysterical fans. Soden fired me for reasons of economy and he's drawing ten thousand fans! Baltimore still stood atop the league with one less win and two fewer losses than Boston. There were now nine games to play. Nichols had thirty wins, Kloby twenty-three, and Lewis, nineteen. But the Orioles were out there waiting, with four rested pitchers, each with seventeen wins, or more. Still, the birds had to play a dangerous

New York team this week and Boston would face a struggling Brooklyn squad.

Before turning in I searched through the few utensils in the kitchen area until I found an ice pick. I pried the windows open. Sean watched me with growing concern, complaining that thugs wandered alleys looking for open windows. I conceded his point, but told him I didn't like the idea of not having an escape route. I was thinking of poor Staley. I reminded him that an ounce of prevention was worth a pound of cure, according to my mother.

Sean snorted, "Me mom tol' me to keep my nose out of where it don't belong, but that hasn't stopped you an' me yet."

38

I'm not sure what woke me. Something out in the hall. Someone trying a door, maybe. Anyway, something vague and unsettling. I eased out of bed and leaned against the door. Someone was in the hall. I could hear muffled voices.

I scrambled to pull on my clothes and glanced at my watch. Three o'clock in the morning. I shook Sean and told him to get dressed.

"Jayzus, what time is it, anyway?" he moaned. I hissed for him to shut up and get dressed, using gestures to alert him to the problem in the hall.

"It's just some drunks," he whispered, but he hurriedly tugged on his clothes.

"Maybe," I told him. "But I'm not taking chances." I tiptoed over to the windows and quietly opened them. I peered out into the alley. Nothing. I returned to the door, put my ear against it. The voices were still muffled, but closer now. Motioning for Sean to pick up the manuscript and move near the windows, I quietly unlocked our door and eased it open a crack. There stood Steuben. Apparently he and his buddy had just checked the door next to us and were moving toward ours. Of course, by cracking the door to see out, I announced my presence. The bulging of Steuben's eyes told me he'd seen me. I slammed the door shut and fumbled to lock it. "Shit."

My profanity told Sean all he needed to know. Clutching the manuscript, he sat on the sill and swung his legs out into the alley. He dropped to the ground. I followed him through the window, contorting my way through the small opening. Even as I pushed off the sill, the door exploded open behind me. Sean and I fled down the alley, cursing our lack of foresight in not keeping our bicycles close by.

What seemed like an eternity later, we cowered behind a stable four blocks away to catch our breath. The horses, spooked by our presence, milled restlessly and noisily in the pen, nickering and blowing nervously. "What now?" Sean wheezed.

I could barely answer him. My lungs seemed desperate for air. "We've got to find a safe place for this manuscript until we decide what to do with it. And we've got to convince Krael and Steuben we don't have it so we won't have to keep looking behind us." Despite still sucking for air, I stood and pulled him to his feet. "Come on, let's take care of the second item first. We aren't all that far from Milk Street. We've got to get to Krael's before Steuben and his hooligans do."

Twenty minutes later, wet from perspiration, I squatted on a Pearl Street stoop in the pre-dawn darkness, around the corner from Krael's darkened room. The smudge of yellow from a nearby street lamp permitted me to improvise a scheme. Using a scrap of the wrapping paper covering the manuscript and Sean's sketching pencil, I scribbled a note: 'The manuscript is safe and in the hands of others. If you wish to pursue the matter, meet me in the right field bleachers of the South End Grounds Saturday, at three o'clock. Will Beaman.' I addressed it to Krael.

Sean stood at the corner, checking for the return of Steuben and his companion. When he signaled the street clear, we raced to the front door and wedged the note under the knocker. Then we headed for the Y.M.C.A. and a few hours sleep. The Y.M.C.A. was Sean's idea; he'd stayed there before and knew that the facility stayed open all hours.

We found our way to two cots in a common room with perhaps two dozen other men. I slept using Bradford's manuscript as a pillow. We slept until volunteers came in at daybreak to take the linen and hose out the room. We didn't eat at the Y.M.C.A. because we had resources and didn't want to take food better given to others. Instead, we ate breakfast at a nearby restaurant, plotting our next step.

"We give the manuscript to Tim," Sean urged, "no one will suspect him."

"Giving Tim the manuscript is giving him the story," I argued. "There'd be too much temptation for him to break it for the *Globe*."

"Don't tell him what it is."

"You know Tim. He's good at putting two and two together. We couldn't keep him in the dark long. When we need publicity or coverage, we'll bring him in."

The excitement slowly drained from Sean's eyes. "Who, then?" he asked.

"Well, we aren't going to involve Claire or Cait," I pointed out, quickly getting the obvious out of the way. "On the other hand, we know two men who have safes."

"Who's that?"

"Winthrop Hart and Arthur Soden."

Sean clutched his head and moaned. "Oh, Sweet Jayzus. Now, there's a choice, between an enema or mercury up the pipe."

Ten minutes of heated argument later, we settled on Win Hart. We thought he was less likely to ask questions. That he was less directly involved. More friendly to us. And more flexible. An hour after deciding on Hart, having found an odd-sized box and old newspapers to repack the manuscript, and having convinced ourselves we weren't followed, we were at Hart's gallery and bookstore. Miss Sizemore, choleric as ever, ushered us into Hart's office. If Ella Watson was around, I didn't see her. Without telling him what it was, we asked Hart if he would keep a package in his safe. To further throw him off as to what it was, Sean did the asking.

Hart rubbed his forehead with his fingers. "How long you want me to keep it?"

"A few days, no more," Sean answered.

He nodded curtly. "We ought to be able to manage that." He took the package. "It'll be secure here. Just tell me when you want it. I'll be around for awhile, but I'm leaving for Montana in a few weeks."

Sean bent forward, face suddenly flushed. "You're going back to Montana?"

It was evident to me that Hart picked up on the hope in Sean's voice. He grinned. "Probably. I'm still concerned about Ella succeeding with the business. I don't want to leave her with all the work. She, of course, insists that she's capable of running the gallery *and* the bookstore. She has big plans and sees me as something of a ball-and-chain. I understand her ambition, but selling fine art and rare books is a tough business. I'm not sure she fully appreciates that."

Later, on the sidewalk in front of the gallery, Sean shook his head and expressed my own feelings, grousing, "I wish I could dislike that man. He's got sand."

Sean headed for the *Globe* offices on Washington. I spent the rest of the afternoon, first hanging around the police station trying to learn more about Staley's death and, later, trying to find out how the Beaneaters fared with the New York Giants in the fourth game of their series.

When I stepped off the streetcar late Friday, heading for the boardinghouse, the sun was an orange ball, low in the sky. Elongated purple shadows crept out from buildings along Dudley. The light had the warm, thick glow of a late summer evening. The air was still and heavy with insects. With hands, parasols and other weapons, pedestrians swiped at the bothersome flying objects. Though I tried to keep my eyes peeled for anyone stalking me, I was so busy warding off the bothersome flying bugs with my newspaper that I didn't see Eve. That is, until she moved out of the shadows. With her prim skirt and blouse and gold-rim glasses, she looked more like a university student than a labor agitator. But that she was agitated was clear. Her face was pinched and she was chewing nervously on her bottom lip.

"Waiting for me?" I asked unnecessarily. I already knew the answer.

She bobbed her head, but said nothing.

"Something's wrong?"

She nervously gazed up and down the streets. "Can we go someplace to talk?"

I took her by the arm. "Come on, we can get a cup of tea or coffee."

She gave no hint about what was on her mind until we were seated, had ordered, and the waiter brought our coffees. When he'd departed, she spoke softly. "Gunther came to see me this morning."

I sipped my coffee and said nothing.

"He told me the Bradford manuscript had come into his possession."

I'm sure she saw the surprise register on my face. "He tell you how?" I asked.

"Apparently it wasn't stolen at all; someone picked up the box it was in and stored it with signs and bunting for the ceremony. Workers stumbled across it when they were straightening out the storage area."

"Why give it to Krael?" I pressed.

She stared dully at her coffee, cradling it with both hands. "He wants to return it to the city"

I nodded. "He could easily do that."

"He wants to exchange it for concessions from the city. He believes that having a union leader return the manuscript, labor will gain popularity in the city."

"Why hasn't he done so?" I asked, letting my cynicism seep into the question.

She kept her eyes on her coffee. "He says you stole it from him."

I could feel the sudden acceleration of my heart, but I kept my voice steady. "And you're here to ask me, what? Whether I stole it?"

Her eyes rose and met mine. "I'm here to ask you to return the manuscript to Gunther so that he can help the workers."

"By blackmailing the city?"

She looked horrified. "Blackmail? It would be an *exchange*. Part of a *compromise*. That's what negotiations are all about."

"And you think Krael just luckily stumbled upon the manuscript?"

"One of the workers at Faneuil Hall told him about it. Then gave it to him."

"And he said I stole it?"

She fished a piece of torn brown paper from her purse and held it up. I recognized it immediately. It was the note Sean and I had left for Krael. "You did steal it, didn't you?" she asked.

Though I was surprised that she had the note, I didn't blink. "That note simply tells him the manuscript is in safe keeping and he should not hound us about it. It also invites him to discuss the matter like a gentleman."

Her eyes locked on mine. "Win thinks Gunther's plan makes sense."

My throat went dry. Why in the world had she brought Hart into this? To give myself a moment to think, I studiously swiped at insects around our table. Finally, I asked her, "You've talked to Hart about this? Why?"

"I wanted someone to talk to I could trust before I came to you."

"You don't trust me?"

"I did. Once. I thought you sympathized with the down-trodden. Now Gunther says you're in the pay of the money interests."

I didn't try to contradict her. "Have you told Krael that you've talked to Win?"

She dropped her eyes. "No."

"Because you don't trust him to know that Hart is aware of the manuscript?"

She stared hard at me. "I'm not sure why I haven't mentioned it to him."

I nodded my understanding of her dilemma. "You've made the wise choice in not telling him. Hart's health might depend on your silence. Is Krael going to accept my invitation to talk about the manuscript Saturday?"

She fiddled with her napkin. "He didn't say."

I leaned forward and covered her hands with mine. "Join us at the game. Come with Krael. We'll talk about the manuscript and how it got into his hands. And whether or not it should be returned to him."

She shrank from my touch and gathered up her purse. She stood. She hadn't touched her coffee except to slide the cup around in front of her. "I'll think about it," she said, "but, please, return the manuscript to Gunther. Working class people need all the leverage they can get." She departed the restaurant without looking back.

41

Fifteen minutes later I stepped into the Denihurs' breakfast room. The lamps were not lit and the room was cool and dim. At the table sat Claire, Cait, Sean, and Win Hart, silent and solemn, drinking coffee. They turned to me with expectant looks. I acknowledged them with a wave of my newspaper.

Hart rose and approached me, appearing unusually grim. "I was waiting for you," he said. "We need to talk." The three at the table continued to stare at me, their coffee unattended, no hint of what was on their minds. Hart grasped my arm and maneuvered me back toward the door. "We really do need to talk. Alone. Now," he said quietly.

We sat on a bench at the rear of the yard. Neither of us spoke; we just sat there and listened to the birds and the hum of insects. Early fireflies skimmed along the grass, their glow diminished by the dusk light. I figured that if Hart sought me out, he could set the agenda and its schedule. But I had a pretty good idea what was on his mind.

He finally spoke. "Eve came to see me. Says you stole the Bradford manuscript."

I chose not to make it easy for him. I thought I might as well find out exactly what Eve had told him. "Stole it from—?"

"Gunther Krael."

"You know Krael?"

"Only what she's told me."

"How do you suppose he came to have possession of the manuscript?"

"Eve says a worker at Faneuil Hall discovered it and gave it to him."

"Fortuitous," I said, letting my doubt hang in the word.

"Apparently the worker thought Krael would use it in the interests of Labor."

"Again, fortuitous, don't you think?"

He swept hair from his eyes with his fingers. "It makes sense, I suppose. Unionism is against the wall. By returning the manuscript Krael can curry public favor and perhaps gain concessions in negotiations with management."

"You support that strategem?"

He gave me a barely perceptible nod. "It seems just."

"And you believe I have the manuscript?"

He made a noise, as if in pain. "Eve showed me the note you wrote Krael."

"You're here to confirm I stole it and to plead with me to return it to Krael?"

"No."

The man constantly surprised me. From his questions and comments I'd assumed he was going to beg me to return the manuscript and help Krael. "No?" I asked. "What, then?"

He laid a finger on my arm. "My aim is narrower," he said. "If it's the manuscript that you and Sean placed in my safe, I want you to remove it. Having possession of it is a crime, I presume, and I want no part of a criminal action. I can't afford to have our business involved in a police matter. For Ella's sake mostly, but also for mine. And for my late father's reputation."

He had a point. I'd thoughtlessly implicated him by putting the manuscript in his safe. And Ella, who would have the long-term responsibility for the business. I had no right to do that. I stood and put a hand on his shoulder. "Have you spoken to Claire or Cait about this?"

"No. Nor Sean. I figured it was between you and me."

"Good. I'll come with you now and retrieve the package."

"Then what?"

"Then I'll have to think about what to do next. I'll have to think about its moral dimension. I will say this, Krael's scheme opens a real can of worms."

Hart's brows knit. "How so?"

"If it's acceptable to return the manuscript to help one cause," I pointed out, "isn't it equally acceptable to orchestrate its return to help others?"

"You have a lot to think about," he sighed. "Let's go get your 'package.'"

42

It took us thirty minutes to reach Hart's office. Miss Sizemore
was gone by the time we arrived, and the doors were locked. Hart let us in
with his own key. The rooms were cool. The cozy wood-paneled walls and
rich leather furniture reminded me of my Harvard past. Hart opened the safe
and handed me the package. As we again passed through the reception area
he motioned for me to sit. "Why steal the manuscript from Krael?" he
wanted to know. "Why not just let the police retrieve it once you located it?"

Settling in a large leather chair, the package in my lap, I smiled at
him. "Well, for the record, I have not admitted this *is* the manuscript, or that
I took this package from Krael. As an innocent bystander you should keep
that in mind. It will be your best legal defense, if you ever need one. But to
answer your question: Krael has no right to the manuscript. It's not his, and
he may well have killed to cover up its theft. I'm not convinced it's his right
to use it as a part of his political agenda. It should be returned to the proper
authorities."

"I did note the ommissions in your confession," Hart replied without
smiling, "You were very selective in what you told me—or didn't tell me.
And I know nothing about any killings related to Krael. Having said that,
can I be of any help to you?"

"Thank you, but no. I have to tie up some loose ends and then
figure out what to do." I didn't elaborate on what those loose ends were, or
what I had to figure out. Hell, I'm not sure I knew what all I needed to
consider. And I wondered if I needed to know more about his inclinations
before making up my own mind on what to do. Hart's reticence played
heavily on my mind; I was not accustomed to him acting as dour as a Danish
bachelor. "You've made it clear you do not want this package in your
business safe," I said. "Does the same hold true for you, personally?"

He sat in one of the large easy chairs and pulled it closer to mine so
that our knees almost touched. "Well, I agree that the manuscript should be
returned to whoever has custody of historical documents. It belongs to the
public. There's no question that it must be returned, and quickly. The
question is, can it be returned in a way to achieve other important goals.
Krael says yes, working conditions and wages for the city's large working
class can be bettered by having him return the manuscript in the name of
organized labor." He edged forward. "I think he's right. Workers in this city
often live and work in dreadful conditions."

"An interesting argument, cousin."

Hart and I swiveled our heads toward the voice. It was Ella Watson, standing in the doorway to her office. How long she'd been there I had no idea.

Hart bounded to his feet. "Ella! I assumed you'd left with Miss Sizemore. Mr. Beaman and I were exchanging opinions on——."

She finished the sentence for him, saying, "Whether blackmail is legitimate so long as the cause is just."

He threw up his hands and snorted. "That's not what we were arguing *at all.*"

She moved into the room. "Of course it was. Your point to Mr. Beaman was that if this Mr. Krael could use the manuscript to bribe authorities into making concessions to his demands, he should do so. That *was* your point, wasn't it?"

I chimed in. "Miss Watson, his position wasn't *quite* as cynical as you suggest."

She gave us her best smile. "Nonsense. It boils down to bribery, doesn't it? Gunther Krael will give the manuscript to officials if they give him what he wants in return. It's of only secondary importance that workers might profit from his scheme. The primary object is to strengthen unionism and Krael's control over it." She leaned on Miss Sizemore's desk. "I'm not criticizing your argument; I agree with it. However, I believe that you two and Krael are naïve if you think his returning the manuscript will translate into advances for workers. Krael might gain some goodwill, but that's all. Frankly, dear cousin, you'd be smarter to return it yourself and earn goodwill and publicity for our establishment. That would mean more sales. You've said you wanted to leave me in a secure position when you return to Montana. That'd be one way to do it."

Hart sagged in his chair. "Aw, for crissakes, Ella—"

She ignored him, pointing to his office and speaking to me. "You can keep your 'package' in our safe, Mr. Beaman, I have no reservations with your doing so."

"You don't?" Hart sputtered, his surprise obvious.

"Not at all," she said. "As long as you return it to the people of Massachusetts."

"We're getting ahead of ourselves," I interjected. "First, if this *is* the manuscript, it is in *my* possession, not yours or Kraels. Secondly, I was contracted to find the manuscript and to give it to my employers. Whether or not Krael's plan makes economic or moral sense, or whether it's in your interests to return it, my obligation, I suppose, is to consult with my employers. I'll take you up on your offer of the safe until Saturday. Both of you are welcome to meet with Sean and me when we talk with Krael at the game tomorrow. Three o'clock. Right field bleachers. It should be an interesting exchange, and I'd like you there. I suppose in a legal sense anyone in attendance is abetting in the commission of a crime, but I doubt that anyone there will bring charges or offer testimony against the others—for attending a sporting contest."

I handed the package back to Hart. "You give me your word you'll keep this until I call for it?—and keep the secret to yourself?" Both nodded their willingness to do so.

I thanked them for providing the safe, said good-bye, and hurried out into the night in search of Honey Fitz. I still had not eaten an hour later when I found him in McGreevey's surrounded by Royal Rooters. They were loudly lamenting today's split with the Bridegrooms and the Orioles split with the Giants. Brooklyn had scored twelve runs off the usually reliable Nichols in the first game and won, 22-0, but Lewis had salvaged the second game, 9-1. The virtual tie continued, with seven games to go.

I caught Honey Fitz's eye and hailed him. While he was disengaging from the boisterous chorus of complainers, I grabbed a hard-boiled egg from a plate on the bar and sank my teeth into it.

"What's up, lad?" Honey Fitz greeted me. "News?"

While still chewing, I told him the manuscript was in my possession.

His eyes got big and his jaw went slack. "Jesus Christ, lad, where is it then?"

I swallowed the bite of egg and put the remainder down. "It's safe—in a safe."

His cheeks were cherry red. "*Whose? Where?*"

I showed him my palms to calm him. "I need to know something. If I turn the manuscript over to you, what are you going to do with it?"

"I told you," he sputtered. "There's nothing mysterious or complicated about this. I want credit. I want the votes it'll bring. I've never lied to you about that."

I nodded my understanding. "How're you going to return it to authorities."

"How?" he blustered. "With as much fanfare as I can. Public ceremony. Newspaper coverage. Bells and whistles. The works." He clamped my wrist. "I paid you for the manuscript. I provided you a lucrative job. A man keeps his word, son. The manuscript has already been gone, what, nineteen, twenty days? We've got to move, while the public remembers what the damned thing is."

I pried his hand off. "I have a lot of loose ends to pull together," I said. "It's not as simple as you may think it is. Tell you what, come to the right field bleachers before tomorrow's game. Three o'clock. We'll settle this thing."

He scowled. "What do you mean, "we'll settle this thing? Who's *we*? You 'settle the thing' by giving me what I've paid you for. What're you—"

I didn't hear him out. I left my half-eaten egg on the bar plate and walked away. I shouted at him over my shoulder. "Be there or it'll all be decided without you."

I headed for Arthur Soden's office to deliver the same message.

43

Though it was not yet eight o'clock in the morning, the deck of the excursion steamer, *Gray Dove*, was crowded with Saturday revelers heading for Nantasket Beach. The wharf was teeming with additional sun-drenched carousers waiting to board. Men were wearing their summer whites. The women uniformly wore white blouses. What little variety in color existed came from the women's light-colored skirts, wide hats, and parasols. Salt clusters blowing from the sea, gulls soaring overhead, and the steamer's flags snapping in the breeze, added to the blizzard of white.

Sean and I scooped up the baskets with our food and swimming suits and ushered Claire and Cait toward the *Gray Dove*. I'd suggested this get-away for the four of us, viewing it as an opportunity for Sean and me to fine-tune our strategy for returning Bradford's work and, at the same time, mend fences with Claire and Cait, in part by seeking their advice. If our excursion took us out of the easy reach of Krael and his thugs, and out of touch with Arthur Soden and Honey Fitz, so much the better. Jeez, it might be our last adventure if authorities were not impressed with our plans to return the manuscript.

The cruise went smoothly and a half-hour after we debarked at Nantasket we were in the water. The narrow spit of sand was alive with color and activity. White sporting clothes had given way to colorful bathing suits. Resplendent-colored tents were spaced along the peninsula among multi-colored umbrellas. Red, orange, blue, and yellow sand pails and beach balls littered the bright sand. But it wasn't the colors alone that caught my attention. Never had I seen so many bare female legs, arms and necks. It was a gawker's Eden.

Even so, it was difficult keeping my eyes from Claire. She wore a round-necked, short-sleeved suit with pants that tied at the knees. Ruffles at the bosom and hips failed to disguise her curves. She bounced and laughed and splashed me with water, then ducked and squealed and swam away. Only to be caught and dunked by me. Soon tired from our gamboling, we settled in on blankets to enjoy the sun. I rented an umbrella to protect us from burning. We were all too pale to stay out in the sun long, even the morning sun.

Later, after several frolics in the sea, dry and rested, we opened the picnic baskets that Claire and Cait had prepared, and ate. Fried chicken, potato salad, pickles, celery, and bottles of Hires Root Beer. Though the ice that the bottles and salad had been packed in had long since melted, the bottles remained chilled and the salad fresh.

Following our picnic, Sean and Cait lay in the shade of the umbrella and began to talk in low, intimate tones. Clouds gathered in the south. The wind picked up, causing umbrellas and tents to tremble and pop.

I asked Claire if she would walk with me. For days now, even as I plotted the return of the Bradford manuscript, I worried about excluding her from my scheming. After all, whose opinion of me meant more than hers? And, if she felt about me as I hoped she did, who was connected with my fate more closely than she was? If I couldn't trust her, whom could I trust? Besides, I would have no future with her if my ploy for the manuscript—and who must profit from its return—repelled her. We strolled for almost a mile in the warm sand enjoying the exuberance around us before I broached the subject of the manuscript. "Have you read about the theft of William Bradford's history of Plymouth?" I asked her.

She looked over at me, a frown upon her face. "Of course. For two weeks that's all the city's newspapers talked about."

I nodded at her observation. "Well, I haven't been entirely honest with you. Mr. Soden has promised to pay me a substantial sum if I find the manuscript. What's more, Honey Fitz Fitzgerald is also going to pay me if I locate it."

She squinted at me, holding up one hand to shade her eyes. "I don't understand. Why are Mr. Soden and Mr. Fitzgerald paying *you* to find Bradford's book? Don't you mean they're offering a public reward for *whomever* finds Bradford's work?"

I took her hand and urged her to walk with me. "It's a bit complicated. Both Mr. Soden and Mr. Fitzgerald want me to find the manuscript so that I can give it to them and they can return it and gain the credit. Mr. Soden believes it will bring him more business. Mr. Fitzgerald is convinced that it will help him become mayor. Others want the manuscript to make money, or gain fame, or pry concessions from authorities, or whatever."

She peered incredulously at me. "Do you think you *can* find it?"

"I *have* found it," I answered, squeezing her hand. "*That's* my dilemma. Now I need to figure out what's the right thing to do with it. I know it has to be returned to the people of Massachusetts, but I'm not sure how to do it. If I return it myself I'll probably get a lot of attention, but I'll have broken my word to Mr. Soden and Mr. Fitzgerald and I'll have sacrificed their friendship, the money they promised me, and my job. I'll also anger other people who don't like to be crossed."

She puffed her cheeks and blew out her breath. "My goodness. How in heaven's name did *you* get the manuscript?"

I met her eyes. She might as well know the truth. "I took it from men who originally stole it. I'm not proud of that, but I felt I had to get it away from them."

Her frown deepened. "And these men are the ones who might hurt you?"

"Umm."

She said nothing for several minutes as we passed among frolicking children and sunbathing adults. Away from the sea, a base ball game was underway pitting a group of youngsters against adults. "Are you looking to do what's morally right, or the smartest thing for you?" she asked finally.

Digging my toes in the sand, I idly kicked up a spray. "I just want to do the right thing—for everyone, if I can. The manuscript has got to be returned; there's no question about that. But, how it's returned might bring even a greater good."

Her face registered deepening confusion. "Meaning what?"

It took a while, but I explained the whole mess to her, including what I thought was Gunther Krael'scheme. The fact is, the more I explained, the more convoluted the whole thing sounded to me, something that would baffle even Arthur Conan Doyle. I didn't tell her about Tony Onofrio or Gerald Staley—or Kaiser Steuben's threats against me. To her credit, Claire listened intently, silently, face expressionless, only occasionally nodding at specific details. When I finished, she peered at me and asked in some exasperation, "Why in the world did you get involved in all this?"

I told her the truth. That I'd gotten involved because I wanted the money it promised. And, mostly, that I wanted to impress her.

She gripped my hand to halt me. "It's important to you to impress me?"

"You must know it is," I mumbled, nervously wetting my lips.

"Even if it means bringing trouble upon yourself? Perhaps from the law?"

Her comment made me squirm even though I'd thought about the legal repercussions. "You think the law will care who returns it, or how it's returned?" I asked.

She considered my question for a long moment. "It's been, what, three weeks since the manuscript was first stolen? I would think the commonwealth is more interested in getting the manuscript back than in punishing who took it."

"What about using the manuscript to help the cause of others?" I asked.

"You have to give it back. And not to impress me. If people give you credit and reward you for doing it, that's their business. I suppose if you want to let others return it, there's nothing wrong with that. The question seems to be who is going to gain credit for returning it. That, and when and where are you going to do this."

"Next Sunday, if all goes according to my plan. At the Grounds, during the game with Cincinnati. I'm going to try to persuade Soden to reschedule the Saturday doublebill so that the teams play one on Sunday. That will allow workers' families to attend."

"You can't schedule a game for Sunday!" she cried. "There are laws against Sunday sporting contests, particularly commercial ones."

"We'll see." I told her my scheme for Honey Fitz's role, and Krael's. I told her my plans to get the word to the laboring community and city dignitaries. I told her that I thought it all depended on the 'conference' I'd called for later this afternoon.

She frowned. "Why return the manuscript at a game? Seems an odd choice."

"I suppose it is, but Soden thought that a famous American manuscript might as well be returned at a contest considered 'the great American game' or 'the national pastime.' And I agree. Base ball brings all types of people together. It's a great leveler in our community. Anyone can play who has the ability. And anyone can watch and enjoy it. Besides, it's a great opportunity to demonstrate to Soden that I understand promotions. Will you be my guest at the game? Sean is going to bring Cait."

"The police are not going to like your plan," she warned. "Nor are city officials."

I ran my fingers through my hair and stretched. "Probably not. However, I'm hoping that the police won't put a stop to the game until they figure out what's going to happen regarding the manuscript. And that they'll not arrest everyone in sight if the manuscript is returned. They might not want to put a damper on the occasion."

She giggled and tossed her curls. " It should be quite a show. The return of the manuscript *and* base ball on the Sabbath. Of course, I'll be your guest."

I took her arm. As I did, I glanced up. The clouds had thickened and darkened ominously toward the north. The wind also was blowing in bolder gusts, tumbling empty sand pails and forcing strollers and the two of us to lean into the blasts.

44

The *Gray Dove* had us back in Boston by 1:30 p.m. The storm now hung ominously over a gray, cold city. Sean and I took the women to the rooming house, dropped off our shore togs, and jumped a trolley for the South End Grounds. We were thankful for the opportunity to change clothes. Coats were everywhere at the ballpark. Some fans bundled in greatcoats and scarves and sported winter hats. The chilly wind whipped the park flags, producing a stacato sound like Civil War musketry. Outside the gate horses stood, their rumps to the wintery blasts.

I pitied the Boston and Brooklyn players who were trying to limber up in the blustery gusts, their uniforms bellowing and flapping. The Bridegrooms' big first baseman, Candy LaChance, his face clenched, looked like he'd rather be anywhere but in the Grounds. Brooklyn's hurler for today's contest, the lanky lefthander, Harley Payne, was cursing with every warmup pitch.

The spot Sean and I had chosen for our gathering was the top of the right field bleachers, usually thinly occupied except in games featuring the hated Orioles or Spiders.

It didn't take long for our band to gather. I thought Eve might join Krael, and she did. I'd invited—or rather, coerced—Honey Fitz and Soden to come and they, too, showed up on time, albeit grudgingly and in foul moods. Win Hart and Ella Watson also showed up. It was Steuben I feared. I hoped that the public place and the many avenues of escape it presented would protect us. I didn't want to end up like Tony Onofrio or Gerald Staley. Sean and I got there early to stake out the area, and to ensure privacy. If Krael had brought Steuben or other goons to the game with him, they did not enter together. John Haggerty was watching the turnstiles, keeping his eyes peeled for Steuben.

We gathered as a group in the bleachers like day laborers hunching on a cold street corner waiting to be tabbed for work. Sean stood with his shoulders hunched and his hands thrust deep into his pockets. "Sweet jayzus," he mumbled to Win Hart, "you like this weather, do you? President McKinley is visiting our fair city today and he's probably freezing his arse." Hart nodded and folded his arms tighter about him.

Honey Fitz glared at Soden. "What the hell're *you* doing here?" he demanded, half angry, half puzzled, at his friend's presence.

Soden flushed scarlet. "I could ask you the same thing," he snapped.

Honey Fitz made a strangled noise, but said nothing.

"Let's take care of what's *currently* on our plate, shall we?" Soden snarled, and scowled at me. "Well?"

I glanced around. No stranger sat within thirty feet of us. So far, so good. "I'll get things going," I assured him and I motioned for our group to gather around. I kept introductions brief. Even with the exchange of names there were more bewildered frowns than one would see introducing a Hottentot to a Methodist women's group. The civilities were barely completed when Honey Fitz again demanded to know what the hell was going on.

Standing in front of the seated and chilled congregation, I kept it brief. "I was paid to locate and return a stolen object," I said. "My employers want the object returned to its rightful owners. They are frank about wanting credit for its return. I now have the object. Do any of you have problems with me complying with my employers' wishes?"

Below us, Brooklyn's Fielder Jones, Mike Griffin, and Billy Shindle all fell quickly before the speedy shoots of Boston's Happy Jack Stivetts.

But our group was paying scant attention to the game on the field. Both Soden and Fitzgerald crossed their arms across their chests and glared belligerantly at the others, each assuming, I presume, that he was the object of my comments. Krael nonchalantly laced his fingers in front of his knees and directed his comments at me. "If we're thinking about the same object," he drawled. "The item you mention was not stolen originally. It was mislaid, then mistakenly stored with other items. Once discovered, it was put into an individual's possession for safekeeping with the understanding that he would return it to its owners. It became a stolen item only after it was taken from him. The commission of that offense negates any contract you might have. That's what a law court would say, sir. The object should be returned for its original purpose." He shot me an icy, satisfied smile.

I nodded to indicate I'd absorbed his points, but I refused to back down. "Mr. Krael," I replied. "There are witnesses who will swear that the person from whose room the object was taken was guilty of the original theft at Faneuil Hall. Moreover, the police currently are investigating the deaths of two men and the beating of several others whose only mistake may have been talking about the original theft of the item in question."

Krael turned crimson. Eve blanched and looked quizzically at him. Win Hart, Honey Fitz, Ella Watson, and Arthur Soden became suddenly restless, clearly uncomfortable in not being able to follow my cryptic comments.

Taking advantage of the sudden silence, Win Hart spoke up. "The issue of how the object left Faneuil Hall is irrelevant to us. The police might be interested, but I assume everyone here agrees the object should be returned *post haste*. That's what we should be talking about, who's to return it—and how."

On the field, Harley Payne unleashed a wild pitch. It followed singles by Hamilton, Tenney, and Duffy and led to the second run of the inning for the Beaneaters.

Krael, his normal color returned, nodded gravely at Hart. "Mr. Hart is right," he said. "And I'll be candid with you; I want to return it and gain credit for doing so. Not for me personally, mind you. Such credit will serve me well when I negotiate with employers and city officials. If I'm viewed as a hero of sort, they won't be able to stone-wall me when I seek to improve living and working conditions for toiling people."

Honey Fitz lurched forward, suddenly animated. "I not only want the object in question returned to benefit the state, but I contracted with Mr. Beaman to find it. I'm the only one here who was willing to put up good money to facilitate its return." He jerked his thumb at me. "I have a verbal contract with him."

Soden stirred and sneered, "You aren't the only one who paid Mr. Beaman to find the item. I also did. If you're suggesting whomever paid for the item should be able to return it and gain credit, then I should be included." He glowered at me and spat, "Or are we going to hold an auction? Is *that* why we're all here?"

By now Boston had tallied another five runs in the second inning, thumping a clearly angry and ineffective Harley Payne. The wind nearly blew him out of the box as he glared in at batters.

I noticed that no one in our little assemblage had yet identified the item as the Bradford manuscript, or acknowledged culpability for having stolen property in their possession. Or being in possession of information about a crime. Me included. Eve continued the ruse. "More people will benefit if Mr. Krael returns the item," she argued.

"Miss Seilor has a point," Hart insisted. "We agree that whoever returns the item will become something of a hero. What Mr. Krael seems to be arguing is that rather than have one man celebrated for the act, the act ought to lead to the betterment of many." He rolled his shoulders. "Seems firm moral ground to me."

Honey Fitz pushed to his feet. "I think not. The truth is, many of the individuals he claims to want to help are constituents of mine. I have worked tirelessly to better their lives. The more power and influence I have, the more likely I can improve conditions for them. Besides, I reach more people than he ever could." He spread his feet and planted his fists on his hips. "If it's the moral ground you're interested in, I hold it."

Payne retired the Beaneaters in the fourth inning, but not before they'd scored another four runs. Few in our group even wasted a glance on the game that now clearly was won. Soden struggled to his feet and straightened the creases in his trousers as Payne walked slowly to the bench to the derisive applause and stomping of the crowd.

Soden glared at me. "Enough of this self-pleading. You have a plan. Let's hear it." I should have known Soden would cut to the chase.

"We agree that the item in question must be returned," I replied, looking at Sean, then at Ella. Neither had spoken. "Agreed?" Both nodded. "Then," I continued, "all we need to resolve today is when, where, and how it is to be returned. I can't think of a better site than here at the Grounds. During a ball game." I addressed Soden. "That's where you come in, and that's where you get a return for your money."

"Or get arrested," Soden mumbled.

The crowd roared as Boston's Billy Hamilton hit Jack Dunn's first pitch for a single. We all turned from Soden and gaped as Hamilton took a wide turn at first and sped for second. The crowd groaned as he suddenly put on the brakes and returned to first. I turned back to look at each of our group in turn. "I don't care who gets credit for the item's return. I'm prepared to see that all of you share in the glory of its return."

"Or the culpability?" Soden chimed in, with a wan smile.

"That goes with the territory," I conceded. "Anyone have any problem with that?" I didn't wait for answer. "I'm also eager to see the item returned during a game. During a brief ceremony for that purpose. Any one have problems with *that*?" Again, I did not wait for an answer. "I want the game on a Sunday so working men and their families can attend. I want ticket prices cut in half." I stared at Soden. "That'll take some courage. But Cincinnati is in town next weekend and, like the St. Louis and Louisville lads, Cincinnati players aren't as finicky about Sunday base ball as some of our locals are. I think they'll agree to play one of the scheduled double-header Saturday games on Sunday. But Mr. Soden here will have to stick his neck out to reschedule it. And Mr. Fitzgerald will have to support him against powerful resistance."

I paused and waited. No one spoke; they simply stared at me, eyes squinting as they pondered my scheme. Several flicked their eyes to the diamond as Jim Sullivan replaced Stivetts who was clutching his back and grimacing. I tried to regain their attention. "It seems straightforward enough. The citizens of Massachusetts get the Bradford manuscript back. Messrs. Soden, Fitzgerald, and Krael share in the credit and do with their newfound notoriety what they will—help themselves or help others, whatever. The workingmen get a game at a time and price convenient for them. Mr. Soden makes money."

Ella Watson finally broke her silence. "And what about the crimes committed?" she asked.

"If anyone has committed crimes to this point, or commits crimes after today, we leave it to the police to sort out—and we leave it to the consciences of the guilty parties," I said, and clapped my hands sharply. "Curtain—and applause." Despite my effort at humor, my comments were met with stony silence, leaving me feeling like a man who'd just stepped into a chamberpot. My listeners were as subdued as Presbyterians at a free-love lecture. The crowd acccentuated our silence with its own. The clouds had lowered and darkened. The brisk wind had even more bite than earlier. Umpire Tom Lynch periodically studied the sky, his face contorted with concern.

I broke the hush. "You comfortable with this, Sean?"

He offered a lop-sided grin. "It's the best idea I've heard since tootsie rolls."

"What about you, Win?"

Hart stood and brushed off his trousers and tugged at them until they settled over his western boots. "I have no problem with it if Ella doesn't." He looked at her. She smiled and shook her head in approval.

"Mr. Soden? Mr. Fitzgerald?" I queried.

Both shrugged.

"Mr. Krael?"

He rose slowly, frowning deeply. "It seems I have no choice." He stepped close to me and laid a hand on my shoulder. "You've cheated me," he whispered icily. "And you'll regret it."

Eve stared silently and glumly at her feet.

I saw no purpose in acknowledging Krael's threat. I clapped my hands and spoke to everyone. "It's settled, then. We have one week. The Beaneaters leave in two days for games in Baltimore and New York and won't be back until Saturday. I'll be in touch with each of you. We'll aim for next Sunday."

"Where's the, ah, *item*?" asked Krael. "And who will be responsible for getting it to the game?"

I told him to trust me, that I would take care of it.

As our little band broke up and moved out of the bleachers, Boston added another run in their fifth inning, ballooning the score to 12-0. Payne and Stivetts were long gone.

Win Hart watched our assemblage disperse, then pulled me aside and lowered his voice. "You can continue to keep the package in our safe. Anyone else know it's there?"

Lynch suddenly waved the game over, pointing to the nearly black sky. The telegraph board showed that Baltimore had lost to the Giants. Players and managers accepted the umpire's decision without a murmur. The crowd's groan was tepid. Most were happy to be heading for shelter and warmth.

Hart had posed an interesting question. One for which I had no answer. "I don't know if anyone knows you have the manuscript," I told him. "But someone may have wondered why 'n hell you and Ella were here."

He grinned. "Well, Will, you sure enough got the cows arunning. Out west, we learn quickly enough that sometimes once you get 'em moving, all you can do is get out of their way and see where they go. And hope they go where you want 'em to."

45

The following Sunday the South End Grounds was clogged with men, coats draped over their arms, collars tugged loose, and sleeves rolled up. Female fans shrank from the flaming ball in the sky, pointing their parasols at it. Barefooted young boys in knickers romped among the crowd. The pavilion and bleachers had filled up early, and cranks were now pouring onto the outfield and down the base lines. The Royal Rooters, some clutching musical instruments, had gathered in force behind first base. Fans unable to get into the Grounds took up posts on the roofs of flats along Columbus. The more adventurous youths shinnied up electric poles and construction scaffolding along Berlin Street. Policemen were everywhere. Plainsclothes cops doubtless were milling through the crowd inside the Grounds, and outside.

The festive Sunday crowd buzzed with the sounds of Yiddish, Italian, German, and Irish brogues as well as English. Clearly our week of promoting this Sabbath Day clash between Buck Ewing's Cincinnati Reds and the Beaneaters had paid off. While the Boston nine was away from the city taking three games from the Giants in New York and two from the Orioles in Baltimore, which moved them precariously atop the League standings, Sean and I had been filling the city with posters and printsheets advertising today's game. We paid street urchins a penny for every fifty sheets they passed out. Tim Murnane had crammed his daily *Globe* columns with positive comments about the upcoming contest. Jacob Morse of the *Herald* and ball writers from the other dailies, shocked by the prospect of a Sunday game, lambasted it in their columns. Editors began to put comments about the game on their front pages, speculating on how the Boston police should respond. There seemed little disagreement on *whether* they should respond.

Arthur Soden missed the entire bruhaha, opting to remain out of contact with League personnel at his retreat in New Hampshire's White Mountains. In an unusual move, co-owners J.B. Billings and William Conant accompanied the team on the road but, so far as I could tell, remained inaccessible to newspapermen. Even when the Beaneaters took the second game from the Orioles to cling narrowly to the League lead, Billings and Conant managed to elude the press. John Haggerty, too, had disappeared.

How the Cincinnati club handled the week's growing storm I don't know, but from the first they seemed unruffled by the idea of a Sunday contest. Even perfunctory threats from the League and the Boston police failed to intimidate them. The Reds' Tommy Corcoran, Dummy Hoy, and Bid McPhee were former American Association players, a league known as the "beer and whiskey league" and filled with teams not bashful about playing on the Sabbath. Fans in St. Louis, Cincinnati, and Louisville, many of them Germans, thought there was nothing inappropriate about playing Sabbath ball, and were accustomed to it.

Besides overseeing the distribution of posters and broadsides celebrating the upcoming contest, I spent the week going over the details of the proposed program with those in our little conspiracy. I refused to tell anyone where the manuscript was, even though Krael, Fitzgerald, and Soden pressed me hard for that detail. I waited until Friday's evening editions of the city's newspapers to release the news about the Bradford manuscript being returned at the game. I wanted to give city fathers as little time as possible to frustrate our plan, and the police as little time as possible to figure out how best to stop the game without facing a riotous multitude. I also wanted to use the possibility of the manuscript's return to keep the police from acting too quickly to stop the contest. I'm sure there were many tense conferences among authorities on Saturday after the Beaneaters returned from Baltimore, but the game was uneventful, Boston beating Cincinnati. A win today would ensure the Boston nine the pennant.

"Today's could be a record crowd," I said to an antsy Soden who, with me, was lounging near the Cincinnati bench watching the Cincinnati players stretch. Directly in front of us Ted Breitenstein, the Reds' stocky lefthander, was lobbing pitches to his catcher, the lantern-jawed Heinie Peitz.

I was killing time, waiting for Claire who, with Cait, was coming to the game with Sean. I expected them any minute and had exacted a promise from John Haggerty to save six seats. I also was waiting for Ella Watson and Win Hart who were bringing the manuscript from their safe. They had promised to pass along the manuscript to me in the sixth inning. We thought it wise for Hart to keep the manuscript until then, as the police would surely watch me closely and arrest me the minute they thought I had the prize in my possession. They didn't know Win Hart from Adam. I was to pass the manuscript on to Gunther Krael, Honey Fitz Fitzgerald, and Arthur Soden just before the beginning of the seventh inning. They would in turn hand it to Mayor Josiah Quincy and Governor Roger Walcott during a ceremony before the Beaneaters batted in the bottom of the seventh. That is, if all went well.

"Have you seen either Mayor Quincy or Governor Walcott?" I asked Soden.

He bit his lip and watched Breitenstein snap a curve into Peitz's glove. "They're here. Along with a plalanx of policemen."

"There won't be any arrests for playing on Sunday until Quincy and Walcott get the manuscript," I suggested. "We're safe, at least for the moment." I was betting that the transferrence of the document would so delight officials and the general public that the police would overlook one Sunday game and how the manuscript had turned up.

Soden surveyed the overflow crowd. "If it's not a record, it'll be close to it," he conceded, a hint of a smile on his usually taciturn face.

"Don't forget who organized it," I reminded him. "And who's attending."

"Duly noted," he replied. "We all set for the seventh inning?"

"Yessir. Quincy and Walcott will go out to the pitcher's box. You, Honey Fitz, and Krael will join them there and hand it over. Everyone has promised to keep his comments brief. John Haggerty will provide a megaphone, but no one will be able to hear much with all the noise."

He chewed on his cheek and peered at the press section. "The press is here in force."

"A third of today's crowd may be newspaper writers," I laughed. "Another third, policemen."

"Where's the manuscript now?"

"It'll be here," I assured him. "Everyone is going to get what they want if things go as planned."

Soden used his cigar to point over my shoulder. "There's your Mr. Hart."

I turned to see Hart shouldering his way toward me, face grim. His rough behavior with the crowd left little doubt something was amiss. I was sure that the police had their eyes on me and I didn't want to draw their attention to Hart. However, I had little choice, what with Hart's charging at me.

"What's wrong?" I asked, when he finally neared me. Suddenly aware of his empty hands, I added hastily in a harsh whisper, "Where's the manuscript?"

He didn't bother with preliminaries. "It's gone," he said, his face white, "someone snatched the damn thing."

46

I clutched my head. "*Snatched* it? *Again*? For God's sake, *who*?"

He splayed his hands. "Dunno. I took it out of the safe and put it on Miss Sizemore's desk to pick up on my way out. When Ella and I were ready to go it was gone. Ella saw no one. Neither did I."

Soden sidled up behind Hart. "What's wrong?" he asked in a hoarse whisper.

We ignored him. "Where's Ella now?" I asked Hart.

"Here somewhere," he said, eying the crowd. "We split up to find you."

"Which way did she—?" Sonuvabitch! Suddenly, it wasn't Ella I wanted to find. I frantically looked around for Gunther Krael. If anyone was capable of queering the deal, it was Krael. "Have you seen Krael?" I asked.

Hart's face told me he'd reached the same thought at the same time. "No, but we'd better find the bastard. Fast." He started toward third base. "You take the first base line, I'll check the third base crowd. If you see Ella, hang on to her." He hustled off without looking back.

By the time I'd wedged myself through the crowd along the first base players' bench, careful to skirt two policemen, I was near panic. My shirt was soaked and sweat ran in rivelets down my back. Klobedanz had retired the first two Cincinnati batters. Krael was nowhere in sight. I pushed through the throng, looking for him. He was not among those standing or milling around first base. I swung up over the rail and began to elbow my way through the stands. Both Breitenstein and Klobedanz were working quickly and the game was scoreless and already in the third inning by the time I'd worked my way to the end of the rightfield bleachers. Still no Krael. I'd removed my hat and jacket by then. I felt—and probably looked—liked I'd stood under a hose.

Eventually satisfied that Krael was not in the stands, I jumped back onto the field of play and made my way through the mass of spectators packed against the rightfield fence. My alarm increased with each yard. Progress through the densely-packed crowd was not easy. Coppers urged the fans back against the fence to give the outfielders optimum room, squeezing us like sardines and provoking protests and obscenities. Obviously, the bulls' orders were to let the game go on until they heard differently, or until the manuscript was exchanged.

Even above the din of the crowd, the sounds of the Royal Rooters' singing could be heard. Spectators not busy cursing the police sang raucously along with them. Shouldering through the noisy mass while searching out a single face, all the time keeping a wary eye peeled for batted balls, was taxing. I'd hardly gotten beyond the Sleeper's Eye Cigars sign on the rightfield fence when Jimmy Collins rolled out to end the third inning. If I didn't find Krael soon, he'd return the manuscript himself, leaving me at the mercy of Honey Fitz and Soden.

Just as Germany Long grounded into a force out to end the fourth inning I spotted Kaiser Steuben. He was in the corner where the left field fence met the bleachers, his huge frame towering above other heads, a derby perched on his thick head. I expelled breath I seemed to have been holding for ten minutes. Where Steuben was, surely Krael was nearby. I might just save my job—and my reputation, after all. I was nearing Steuben through the crowd when I ran smack into Krael. Despite my surprise, I had the presence of mind to seize him by the arm and jerk him around.

"What the hell?" he grunted, "what're you *doing*?"

Moving quickly for a big man, Steuben lurched forward and wedged himself between Krael and me. "Back off, ya bastard," he flared.

I tried to shove him out of my way, never taking my eyes off Krael.

"Where's the manuscript, you rat?" I growled.

Krael's eyes widened and his jaw dropped. "What do you mean where's the manuscript," he barked. "*You* have it. *Don't* you?" He grabbed me. "*Don't you?*"

I wilted, my sopping collar now an icy band around my neck. I didn't even bother to remove his hands. "You don't have the manuscript?" I groaned.

His faced reddened. "Why would *I* have the damn thing? You told all of us that *you* would bring it to the game." He peered toward the infield. "It's already the fifth inning," he said, anxiety in his voice.

Wait a minute. A thought struck me. "Where's Eve?"

Krael continued to scan the pavilion area. "She's here. Somewhere." He suddenly jerked around to face me. "You don't think *she*'s up to something? Forget it." He made a dismissive gesture.

I thought of Eve's pale blue eyes sparkling at the thought of revolutionary acts. Her enthusiam for audacious behavior. Her delight in tweaking the noses of those in power. "Are you so sure of her?"

"She's not going to double cross us," Krael insisted.

"How do you *know* that?"

He met my eyes and shared a grim smile. "Because, dear boy, she and I discussed the possibility of double-dealing. We concluded it would not be in our interests, or that of our cause to do so. We agreed on this. She wouldn't stab *me* in the back."

"Well, *who* then?"

He licked his lips. "What about that *Hart*? What's *his* role in all this?"

"He reliable," I assured him. I hoped to God he was.

"What about your buddy, Honey Fitz?" snapped Kaiser Steuben.

The blood pounded behind my eyes. Had I miscalculated Honey Fitz's capacity for chicanery? Had I under-estimated his intent to make political capital out of the manuscript? I squeezed Krael's wrist. "Have you seen Honey Fitz?"

Steuben pushed us apart. "No we haven't," he snarled, "but if *you* don't have the manuscript, *he'd* damned well better have it."

"Kaiser's right," Krael said, gritting his teeth and looking around Steuben. "And if he has it, he'd better still be prepared to share the glory of returning it, damn his soul."

I panned the third base stands, my desperation soaring. "*If* he's here," I told them, "he's somewhere between where we are and the pavilion. Let's go." Using Steuben as a battering ram, we clambered over the rail into the stands and began our search for Honey Fitz. Boston was batting in the last of the fifth, the game still scoreless.

So preoccupied was I in finding who'd purloined the manuscript I'd given no thought to Claire. As I tried to remain in the wake produced by Steuben's broad frame and Krael's active elbows, my mind shifted to her. She was probably waiting in the pavilion area, wondering why I'd forsaken her. Hopefully, John Haggerty had made good on his promise to reserve seats for her and Cait, and Sean had explained my absence. I could only hope I'd have an opportunity to apologize to her.

The Royal Rooters burst into song again to rally the Bostons. Even over the crowd noise and the Rooters' song, I could hear the distinctive high-pitched yelp of rooter "Hi Hi" Dixon, urging the Boston players on.

"Will!"

I twisted toward the cry and found myself staring at Sean Dennison shouldering through the confusion toward me.

I lunged forward to halt Krael, but he and Steuben continued mauling the crowd aside and plowing toward the Pavilion area. Conceding my inability to stop them, I turned toward Sean. "Where are the women?" I shouted.

He pointed to the pavilion. "They're okay. And saving two seats for us—if we ever get there to use them. What're you *doing*? You look like someone flushed through a knothole with a fire hose."

I knew I looked a mess. My clothes were clammy and heavy, and they clung to me like soaked burlap. My hair lay flat against my skull. My eyes burned from sweat and I could taste salt on my lips. "Have you seen

Honey Fitz?" I shouted above the uproar as Bobby Lowe doubled, driving in Chick Stahl with a Boston run.

"Yeah. Why?"

I pulled Sean close. "Where is he? I think he's taken the manuscript and is planning to pull a fast one on us."

Sean's eyes looked like saucers. "Oh, jayzus." He jerked a thumb toward the pavilion. "He's standing in the last row. Will, the ceremony is just two innings away."

I tugged at his sleeve. "Come on. We've got to find him."

We found Honey Fitz where Sean said he would be. Unfortunately, by the time we reached him, Boston's rally had fizzled. The Beaneaters were jogging out into the field to take up their defensive positions and to start the sixth inning, clinging to a one run lead. We didn't have much time to reclaim and return the manuscript as scheduled.

"Where've you *been*?" Honey Fitz asked hotly, exasperation in his voice.

My frazzled state eroded the deference I generally exhibited toward him. "Where's the manuscript?" I demanded. "We've got an inning to keep our promises."

His look told me I might as well be speaking Egyptian. "Where's the manuscript?" I shouted into his face.

His mouth hung open. The usually glib politician was speechless.

"You don't have the manuscript." I sighed, my hopes deflating like a ruptured hot-air balloon.

He found his voice. "No, I don't," he sputtered, his stunned bewilderment turning his normally jolly face into a gargoyle. "You have it, don't you? Will? *Don't* you?"

I slumped. "I'm afraid not."

Sean gripped the brim of his hat with both hands. "Oh, sweet Jayzus," he moaned.

"What about Krael?" Honey Fitz suddenly shouted. "If anyone has copped the damned thing, it's that union bastard." He started down the aisle.

I clutched his arm. "Krael doesn't have it. He's as steamed as you are."

"Well, then *who*?" Honey Fitz spat. "*Soden*?"

"What about Eve Seilor?" put in Sean. "She's capable of this."

I expelled my breath. "Maybe. I don't know." I glanced at the diamond below us where Cincinnati's Jake Beckley went down feebly before Klobedanz's slants for the first out. "I do know we have just minutes to find out who has it. If we can't, I know about ten thousand spectators, a dozen politicians, and a whole gaggle of coppers who're going to be after our hides."

"Christ, I'm ruined," Honey Fitz complained. He pronounced it 'rooned.'

"By the blessed skirts of the Virgin," Sean sighed, sagging against a rail. "Maybe we'll get lucky and the game'll go into extra innings and we can locate the manuscript for a ceremony *after* the game. *That* might save our bums."

Honey Fitz ignored Sean's forlorn hope, looking at me with sad puppy-eyes. "What about Mr. Hart? Is *he* trustworthy?"

"I'd stake my life on him," I told him. "He's incapable of deviousness." And then an idea came to me.

47

We approached the Boston bench just as Cincinnati's Dummy Hoy flied lazily to centerfielder Billy Hamilton for the second out. The mayor and governor were huddled around Soden and to judge by their expressions they were still unaware of the manuscript's absence. Mayor Quincy clutched the megaphone Haggerty had provided, a politician's smile pasted on his cherubic face. Doubtless he was mentally polishing his upcoming speech. Obviously nervous, Soden kept looking at Hart, Ella, Krael, and Steuben who milled around the other end of the bench. The players and Manager Frank Selee ignored both groups, just as they paid no heed to the crowd stretching down both lines.

Several policemen stood just behind the players, their heads swiveling between the mayor's party and Hart's. Gray-jawed bruisers in tight suits loitered behind the mayor, obviously plainsclothes cops. Sean, Honey Fitz, and I headed for Hart's contingent. The men, clearly agitated, hunkered together like cattle against a storm. Ella Watson, slightly apart, seemed mesmerized by their antics.

"Honey Fitz doesn't have it," I told them in a half-whisper. "And he insists he doesn't know who does."

Krael seized my forearm in a steel-like grip and leaned toward me so that no one would overhear us. "Who knew where the manuscript was besides you?" he menaced. He was sore to the core.

At that moment Hart shuffled forward and addressed Krael. "I know what's bothering you. Miss Watson and I both knew where it was," he said, "along with Mr. Beaman." He paused. "Of course, after our meeting last week it wouldn't take Thomas Edison to figure out we had it."

The sudden roar of the crowd swung our attention toward the field where Hugh Duffy had run down a fly ball by the Reds' Claude Richey for the final out in the top of the sixth. The shouts and cheers were accompanied by a stamping of feet and waving of caps and scorecards as the multitude collectively sensed that their favorites were a mere three innings from wrapping up the pennant. The Beaneater players seemed to recognize the same thing; they hustled off the field and swarmed around their bench, playfully punching each other, growling encouragement to each other, and offering gestures and words of glee to manager Frank Selee, who remained his stoic self.

None of this made an impression on Krael, whose face was livid as he shoved toward Honey Fitz and stabbed a finger at him. "No one had more to gain from cribbing it than *you*."

The bright crimson flush that spread over Honey Fitz's face was a match for Krael's own scarlet grimace. "This is intolerable!" he sputttered. "You insolent puppy, I'll—" He froze, his eyes darting over Krael's shoulder. "Great Caesar! The mayor and governor—"

The two magistrates, trailed by a hesitant Soden, were moving toward us, a half dozen policemen in tow. The sexes reacted very differently to the approaching dignitaries. We men clustered even closer together, facing the oncoming danger herd-like. On the other hand, Ella Watson backed away from the group as if to gain better perspective of the killing ground that was to be. On the diamond, Herman Long rolled out to the Reds' glue-fingered second baseman, Bid McPhee, for the first out in the bottom of the sixth.

The oblivious and unsuspecting mayor remained jovial. "All set to go, are we?" he puffed, glancing at the field as Hugh Duffy popped weakly to the Reds' third sacker, Charley Irwin, who made a diving catch that wrung a deep groan from the crowd.

There was much foot shuffling. Mine included. "All set," someone mumbled. As if eager to hasten and deepen our predicament, Bobby Lowe ended the inning by swinging at Breitenstein's first pitch and managed only a pathetic pop up to catcher Heinie Peitz.

Seemingly unmindful to our stunned looks and verbal gropings, the governor flashed his teeth. "Let's move out to the pitcher's box then," he said. "This should be splendid." He gazed around the Grounds, as if counting the house. "Let's do it." He turned from us then, canted his head, and motioned for the coppers to follow him. My gut tightened and I found myself holding my breath. Seemingly taking its cue from me, the crowd quieted.

A police officer, clearly in charge, separated himself from his half-dozen colleagues and approached me. "Are we ready? My men and I will accompany you to the center of the infield. Who has the manuscript?" All eyes swung to me. A long silence followed. Several of the men began staring at their hands.

"Miss Watson has it," I said, impulsively pointing to the large purse she clutched to her chest. All eyes now swung toward her. No one spoke. Ella stared at me, confused.

The officer nodded slowly, looking curiously at Ella. Then he curtly bobbed his head to the governor and mayor. "Okay, then. Let's go."

Soden, pale as an unbaked muffin, cupped the mayor's arm and led him and the governor unsteadily out onto the playing field. He looked back at me, a quizzical look on his face. Honey Fitz awoke as if he'd stepped on a live electric wire and hustled out to catch up with the governor. The policeman held out his arm for Ella and the two of them moved in behind the others, themselves trailed by the remaining uniformed and plainclothes cops. It took a minute for Krael to get into motion but he finally half-jogged up to the small group now gathered at the pitcher's box. Players from both teams milled around their benches, eager for the presentation. The crowd was silent in anticipation.

Hart watched Ella being escorted by the big policeman, but he spoke to me under his breath. "Why in tarnation did you say that Ella—"

I shrugged. "I had to say something. Buy time to think. She was the only one among us with a means of hiding it." I was sure my career was just minutes away from being ruined. My chance of regaining my position with Soden's Beaneaters was about as likely as John Rockefeller subsidizing his competitors. Even so, a thought had been tickling the back of my mind since my impulsive and desperate claim that Ella Watson held the manuscript. It still crawled around there. Actually, it had begun when I'd assured Honey Fitz that Win Hart was reliable. I believed he was. But what of his cousin? She had access to the manuscript. She recognized the value to her business of gaining credit for the manuscript's return. She was a strong personality. But was she duplicitous enough to carry out a betrayal of that magnitude?

By the time I snapped out of my reverie, Ella Watson was standing among the coterie of dignitaries and policemen huddled near the pitcher'slab. The mayor handed the megaphone to Soden who seemed confused by the gesture.

I suddenly realized Sean was tugging frantically at my sleeve, his pencil and sketchbook clutched in the other. "For the love of Christ, what're we gonna do, Will?"

48

I didn't know what we were going to do. But I wasn't going down without a fight. I scooped up an extra base from behind the bench and wrapped it tightly in my coat, hurriedly tucking in the sleeves and collar to make it look less like a coat and more like a package. "I'm going out there," I panted, pointing to the gathering on the mound, "I've got an idea. Maybe it'll buy us time if the mayor and governor play along."

"Aw, by all that's holy," moaned Sean, a sheen of sweat covering his face. "It'll never work, boyo. Let's just skedattle."

Hart stepped forward. "No. You go on, podnah. You just might pull it off."

John Haggerty and Tim Murnane had sidled up next to us. I had earlier alerted both of them about our plans for the ceremony, thinking that Tim could later write a story favorable to us. "Lordy, what a day and what a story," he muttered in seeming disbelief.

Ignoring them, I stepped across the first base line clutching the base wrapped in my coat. The contingent in the middle of the infield was staring expectantly at Arthur Soden who stood ashened, staring at the ground, the megaphone hanging at his side. I was maybe two steps out in the infield when Governor Wolcott reached over and took the megaphone from Soden's limp hand. I stopped in my tracks. Looking back toward home plate I studied the crowd for a long minute before I saw Claire. She was sitting next to Cait, eyes wide and mouth a small 0. She was leaning forward as if she thought I was going to whisper to her. I also glimpsed Steuben now standing behind the wire next to Eve Seilor. He was watching the group in the infield. Eve's eyes were on me, an expectant look on her face.

Conscious of movement near me, I looked over my right shoulder, expecting to find that Haggery or Tim had stepped to halt me. It wasn't either of them. Policemen were gathering along the first base line, some idly pounding their truncheons into their palms. I looked toward third base where policemen were preparing to move on to the field, waiting restlessly, as if for a signal. There seemed little doubt that the magistrates expected the arrests to begin as soon as the manuscript changed hands.

As I hesitated on the infield grass, the governor began introducing the mayor, Honey Fitz, Arthur Soden, Gunther Krael, and Ella Watson. He did it quickly and without fanfare. The few in the Grounds who heard the megaphone-amplified names responded with scattered and equally perfunctory applause. The governor then offered a brief summary of the manuscript's history and its importance to the people of the Commonwealth.

Sensing the crowd's growing impatience, he announced that the time had come for the presentation to state authorities of the long-lost manuscript. He pivoted gracefully to hand the megaphone to Ella Watson.

Ella, pale and gnawing on her lip and fumbling with her purse, accepted the megaphone without enthusiasm. The mayor and governor beamed in support. Soden, Honey Fitz, and Krael, grim-faced, their mouths but thin lines, nervously eyed the blue-clad coppers surrounding them.

Ella Watson took a half step forward, slowly put the megaphone to her mouth, and began to speak.

"Distinguished and honorable magistrates and Ladies and gentlemen," she said in a voice that barely carried beyond the lacquered megaphone she gripped in her shaking hand, "it is a great moment in the history of our Commonwealth." She dropped her head, cleared her throat, and then spoke more forcefully into the megaphone. "It is not often that an individual can repay his or her government for the many blessings it has bestowed," she told the crowd.

At her words the governor and mayor seemed to swell and their smiles expanded. They vigorously nodded their heads and looked to the others in the small gathering on the pitcher's slab for approval. But Soden and Honey Fitz remained frozen, looks of stunned bewilderment pasted on their faces. Krael also looked lost, but angry as well, as if his predicament was both under-standable and inexplicable.

I wasn't any more impressive than Soden or Krael. I remained planted firmly in place a few steps out on the infield grass, obsolete at this point, stupidly waiting to see what would transpire in front of me. I hugged my *faux*—and now useless—package to my chest. The crowd dropped once more into near silence.

As if suddenly determined to end the affair, Ella tipped up the megaphone and put it to her mouth. "The Hart and Watson gallery and bookstore, of which I am principal proprietor, has obtained William Bradford's history for the sole purpose of returning it to its rightful owners, the people of Massachusetts," she shouted, "and it is my pleasure to turn this treasure over to the peoples' representatives." She dropped the megaphone at her feet, wrestled the manuscript from her purse, and handed it to the beaming governor. The crowd went nuts. Boston and Cincinnati players twirled bats and waved their caps. I stood there in the South End Grounds, my mouth agape. The policemen stood as stone, truncheons suddenly dangling uselessly at their sides.

Two hours later, after Klobedanz had defeated Cincinnati, 3-1, and ensured that the Beaneaters would win the pennant, the city's late newspaper editions were out. A half-dozen newspapers, including the *Globe* and *Herald*, were scattered about our table at The Liberty Tree Restaurant. In a mind-boggling gesture of generosity, Soden had invited everyone involved in the ceremony and their guests to join him at the fancy eatery to celebrate the day's successes. Unfortunately, not everyone viewed the day a success and most had not accepted his rare graciousness. Honey Fitz had begged off, as had the mayor and governor. The magistrates of course were eager to meet the press and bask in the reflected glory of the returned manuscript. Krael also was absent; he preferred to spend his evening with local labor organizers, perhaps agonizing over what might have been and, doubtless, plotting revenge. So far as I knew, Soden's invitation had not included Kaiser Steuben. Not surprisingly, Ella Watson had passed on the dinner invitation, as well. She claimed that following her presentation of the manuscript several gentlemen had expressed interest in investing in her gallery and bookstore. Presumably, she was now busy courting potential partners.

But Win Hart was at The Liberty Tree. And Tim Murnane, his column already written and published. And John Haggerty. Claire, too, and Cait. Sean, of course. To my amazement, so was Eve Seilor. The nine of us had been poring over the late-edition newspapers, comparing the coverage of the day's events. The collective euphoria among Boston's editors over the return of the Bradford manuscript far overshadowed the few squawks about the Beaneaters playing on Sunday, although local ministers remained harsh in their outrage. The fact that the police and magistrates had permitted the game to be completed, even after the return of the manuscript, seemed to them a stab in the heart. Most fumed that the game never should have been allowed to start, let alone be completed. They seemed incensed that the police had chosen a peaceful and euphoric ending—the return of a national treasure and the Beaneaters' victory—over the certainty of riot and bloodshed.

I tilted back in my chair and caught Hart's eye. "Well, Win, if you had any doubts about Ella's ability to take care of herself and the business, her actions today certainly put them to rest, didn't they?" I teased him.

He snorted good-naturedly and shook his head. "She pulled off a lollapalooza, didn't she?"

Sean grinned. "She outsmarted almost everyone. How by the blessed saints did *you* know she had the manuscript, Will?"

I couldn't hold back my laughter. "Sean," I chuckled, "I didn't have a clue that she possessed the manuscript until she pulled it from her purse. I said she had it earlier because she was the only one of us who had an easy place to hide it. But I really was just stalling for time when I pointed to her."

"Still," said Eve, beaming, "It *was* a daring thing she did, returning the manuscript, taking the credit herself, and publicizing her business. She was wonderful!"

I turned to Eve. "Pretty selfish and exploitive by your standards, wasn't she?"

Her curls fluttered as she vigorously shook her head. "Results are what count," she said and graced Soden with a radiant smile. "Mr. Soden's players won today and are on their way to a pennant. Working families had an opportunity to watch them do it. And at a fair price. The manuscript was returned to the people of Massachusetts. Who could complain?"

Sean made a show of being shocked. "Well, ma'am, I suspect your Mr. Krael could—and is."

"He can't be *too* unhappy." I protested. "Workers saw him with dignitaries in a ceremony returning the manuscript. They'll believe that he was among those responsible for its return."

"He'll have to live with the consequences of his actions," Eve replied, suddenly the severe schoolmarm. "Kaiser admitted to me that he helped Gunther steal the manuscript and provoke violence at the Chauncy Street rally." I asked her if Steuben also confessed to having Sean beaten and robbed. She nodded primly. "He said he did it to ensure that Sean's sketches wouldn't be published. Mr. Collins and Mr. Porch just happened to be there. Mr. Porch wasn't suppose to drown. Kaiser's a simple fellow. He does what he's told."

"Why did they leave us barefooted?" Sean asked, furrowing his brows dramatically to emphasize his confusion.

She waggled her curls. "Gunther is the thinker. He conceived of the idea to leave false leads. Give the police something odd to think about."

"Steuben was arrested at the game," Soden chimed in. "Detective O'Dwyer is probably interrogating him as we speak."

"O'Dwyer knows his business," I mused. "Krael's in deep trouble. O'Dwyer will use Steuben to tie Krael to the deaths of Shady Porch, Tony Onofrio, and Gerald Staley—if there is a tie to the last two."

Eve looked pained. "I now think there is. I've been more than a little naïve about Gunther. He kept me in the dark just as he did Emma Goldman."

I couldn't contain my surprise. "Goldman knew nothing of Krael's plans?"

"Absolutely not," Eve insisted.

Sean passed over that. "And then there's Honey Fitz," he noted.

"Politicians are resilient," I asssured him. "Honey Fitz will survive. His constituents saw him among those returning the manuscript. They'll probably figure he should be credited. Besides, Tim here is going to write about him this week, mentioning his role in negotiating the manuscript's return. Ol' Honey Fitz'll bounce back. And he'll forgive us, especially now that the Beaneaters have won the pennant."

Tim looked behind me to Soden. "You didn't get all you wanted," he observed.

Soden tossed his napkin on his plate. "Maybe, but it was a great crowd and a grand win. Mr. Beaman here kept most of his promises. He spun the turnstiles in grand fashion today."

Hart smiled and added, "And you didn't get arrested; that's a plus."

Soden actually smiled, and I could imagine him doing the sums in his head, calculating the columns on the balance sheet. "That's true, Mr. Hart," he said. "But the mayor told me in no uncertain terms that there would be no repeat performances. Boston's not ready for Sunday ball." He sucked at his cigar and blew a stream of smoke toward the ceiling. "I wasn't arrested for dabbling in the Bradford mess, either. For that, I thank my lucky stars, too."

"Well, my goodness," I said, turning to Eve to tease her, "There's hardly anything left for a young revolutionary to accomplish."

She didn't skip a beat, tossing her napkin in her plate in imitation of Soden. "That's why I'm going to Montana," she giggled.

I arched my eyebrows at Hart as the rest erupted in oohs and ahhhs. "It's true?"

His face flushed. "It's true. There's lots of room for a woman like Eve in Montana." He shrugged. "And it's clear Ella doesn't need me here."

Sean rifled through the piles of newspapers on our table, pulled out the *Globe*, and held it up. "I managed to get over my shock at Miss Watson's antics long enough to get some sketches," he crowed, "*which* I sold to the *Globe*." He basked in our grins and proferred congratulations. "They're going to help finance our wedding," he added, squeezing Cait's hand.

Claire swept out of her chair beside me and hugged her sister. She also gave Sean an enthusiastic squeeze and a buss upon the cheek.

His face bright with embarrassment, Sean plunged on. "With Boston playing the Orioles for the Temple Cup, we're going to Baltimore for our honeymoon."

After the burst of applause and congratulations had tapered off, Soden gripped my forearm. "Mr. Beaman, I don't know what your matrimonial plans are," he said, "but if marriage is in your plans you can certainly afford it. You found the manuscript. And I think I can find a bonus for you after today's performance. You'll have steady work with this organization. You're a resourceful young man and we need to be resourceful enough to find the cash to keep you."

Tim and John Haggerty stared at Soden, jaws slack. It was Tim who finally spoke. "I thought I'd see a triple play before I ever heard you——." He didn't finish as the laughter exploded among us.

Claire reached under the table and took my hand, her eyes sparkling. "Baltimore is a wonderful city," she said. "And it would be grand to watch the Temple Cup games there."

"I could arrange that," I said, and gave her a wink.

Tim showed his teeth and playfully cuffed Haggerty on the shoulder. "Sure 'n I think you and I are going to be attending a double-header, darlin'," he said.

HISTORICAL NOTE:

The historical record is clear. The year 1897 proved to be a successful one for Arthur Soden and his partners. Manager Frank Selee and the Boston Beaneaters won the National League pennant and met the Baltimore Orioles in the Temple Cup Series. T. H. Murnane covered the season and playoff series for the *Boston Globe* and *The Sporting News*. Murnane reported on Jimmy Collins' gold watch, a gift of his Buffalo supporters. He also kept the public apprised of groundskeeper John Haggerty's efforts in behalf of Boston's orphans, and the help in that attempt Haggerty received from Michael T. "Nuf Ced" McGreevey and his Royal Rooter patrons. The British government returned the William Bradford manuscript to the Commonwealth of Massachusetts in the summer of 1897. Emma Goldman lectured at Workingmen's Hall that same summer, and Frederic Remington exhibited his paintings in Boston. Labor discontent, obvious in 1897, continued to plague Boston and its environs for decades. Newspaper advertisements make clear that the Old Howard Theater offered a wide variety of burlesque acts, Mechanics Hall horse shows, and the *Gray Dove* ran shuttles of sun worshippers to Nantasket Beach. John "Honey Fitz" Fitzgerald, grandfather of John F. Kennedy, preferred to vacation at Old Orchard Beach, Maine, often with his brothers Henry and James and their families. Alas, Honey Fitz had to put his mayoral hopes on hold for several years, but he did achieve them. In the meantime, Bostonians did not permit the playing of baseball on the Sabbath, and continued to prohibit it until 1929. Joseph Lee founded his Massachusetts Civic League in 1897 to study Boston's social problems. His League believed that permitting play and sports on Sunday, including base ball, would, among other things, reduce weekend idleness and criminality.

Books by G.S. Rowe

6023 Pocol Drive,
Clifton, Virginia 20124
Tel: (703) 830-5862
email: chrisandtom@erols.com
www.pocolpress.com

From the Will Beaman Baseball Mystery Series

Best Bet in Beantown, 200 pp., $17.95. The year is 1897. The place: Boston, Mass. Star short stop Herman Long has just been beaten and left for dead, alone and in the locker room of the Boston Beaneaters National League base ball team. But, whodunit and why? It's up to ne'er-do-well Will Beaman, who stumbles across Long while trying desperately to secure a front office position with the ball club, to solve the case. Filled with romance, numerous red herrings, exciting game reportage, and shady characters, *Best Bet in Beantown* dives deeply into the sordid world of 19th century base ball. ISBN: 1-929763-14-X.

Squeeze Play in Beantown, 2004, 215 pp., $17.95. In this rollicking fiction set in 1897, Will Beaman is in the employ of the Boston Beaneaters base ball team. Unfortunately, he loses his job and nearly his life trying to solve the murder of one of the Boston players and the assault on star third baseman Jimmy Collins. Beaman becomes mixed up in romance and Boston's Labor strife, while trying to solve the mystery of a stolen historical manuscript. Sequel to *Best Bet in Beantown*. ISBN: 1-929763-05-0.

TO ORDER: Make check or money order payable to Pocol Press. Add $2.00 shipping per book. Priority Mail $4.00 per book. Foreign orders extra. Please see our website for other titles. Book stores and organizational discounts.

Early Dreams by David Nemec - A reprint of the classic narrative featuring Earl "Ducker" Draves, a fictional yet all-too-real young player who recounts the remarkable 1884 base ball season and his whirlwind rookie campaign in Cincinnati. Crammed with insightful comments on base ball's pioneers, box scores, and Draves' surprising reactions to the drinking, gambling, and whoring activities that were central to early base ball. *Early Dreams* manages to cover nearly every nuance of the era, including evolving game strategy, financial squabbles, and racism--all against a backdrop of the rough-and-tumble milieu of the 19th century brand of ball. Nemec's book draws favorable comparisons to Ring Lardner's *You Know Me Al*. Cover illustration by Todd Mueller. 200 pages, $17.95, ISBN: 1-929763-04-2.

MISFITS! Baseball's Worst Ever Team by J. Thomas Hetrick - The tragicomic story of the 1899 Cleveland Spiders, baseball's futility leaders and winners of only 20 out of 154 games that season. Meet some of the most colorful men ever to wear a major league uniform. Follow their unfortunate train-travel odyssey through the National League and straight into obscurity. Marvel at the real desperation of a team forced to turn a cigar store clerk into a starting pitcher. Anecdotes galore. Illustrations, appendices, sordid statistics, bibliography, and index. "Exhaustively detailed." (Cleveland Plain Dealer). 200 pages, $17.95, ISBN 1-929763-00-X.

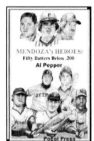

Mendoza's Heroes: Fifty Batters Below .200 by Al Pepper - Baseball's honor rolls are filled with legendary deeds of batting prowess. Throughout history, crowds have risen to cheer the majestic trajectory of a white sphere "crushed" by the likes of Babe Ruth, Willie Mays, and Barry Bonds. But, what about the players who repeatedly produced little more than squibbers to third base, infield pop-ups, or ego-bruising strikeouts? What could possibly be their values to a baseball club? Plenty. Al Pepper reveals the unique, offbeat, and remarkable stories of fifty of these men in *Mendoza's Heroes*. Using eye-opening statistics, interviews with players, and anecdotal biographies, Pepper also presents these players in context of their time. In effect, the book serves as an unabashed tour of baseball history as well. Foreword by ex-big leaguer Mike Stenhouse. Artwork by Jon Gordon. "The superstars get all the ink, but the slap-hitter, the third-string catcher, that's where the fun is. And Al Pepper has done a good job mining the ranks of the unimpressive for interesting nuggets and storylines." (Josh Prager). 250 pages, $17.95, ISBN 1-929763-11-5.